MEOW IS FOR MURDER

MEOW IS FOR MURDER

LINDA O. JOHNSTON

WHEELER
CHIVERS

This Large Print edition is published by Wheeler Publishing, Waterville, Maine, USA and by BBC Audiobooks Ltd, Bath, England.
Wheeler Publishing is an imprint of Thomson Gale, a part of The Thomson Corporation.
Wheeler is a trademark and used herein under license.
A Kendra Ballantyne, Pet-Sitter Mystery.

The text of this Large Print edition is unabridged.
Other aspects of the book may vary from the original edition.
Set in 16 pt. Plantin.

LIBRARY OF CONGRESS CATALOGING-IN-PUBLICATION DATA

Johnston, Linda O.
  Meow is for murder / by Linda O. Johnston.
    p. cm.
  ISBN-13: 978-1-59722-545-8 (softcover : alk. paper)
  ISBN-10: 1-59722-545-2 (softcover : alk. paper)
  1. Stalkers — Fiction. 2. Large type books. I. Title.
PS3610.O387M46 2007
813'.6—dc22   2007011039

BRITISH LIBRARY CATALOGUING-IN-PUBLICATION DATA AVAILABLE

Published in 2007 in the U.S. by arrangement with The Berkley Publishing Group, a member of Penguin Group (USA) Inc.
Published in 2007 in the U.K. by arrangement with the author.

U.K. Hardcover: 978 1 405 64186 9 (Chivers Large Print)
U.K. Softcover: 978 1 405 64187 6 (Camden Large Print)

Printed in the United States of America on permanent paper
10 9 8 7 6 5 4 3 2 1

In loving memory of Linda's father-in-law, Robert Johnston, a true cat lover. And with love to Linda's mother-in-law, Evelyn Johnston, and gratitude for everything, including her encouragement of Linda's writing. Linda again want to thank them both, especially for Fred. And since Kendra thinks he's an okay guy, she'll second the thought.

And then there's Linda's wonderful agent, Paige Wheeler, now with Folio Literary Management, LLC, and her excellent new editor at Berkley, Katie Day. And —

Well, this is getting too long, so even though Kendra likes 'em all, she's going to cut it off now.

— Kendra Ballantyne/Linda O. Johnston

CHAPTER ONE

Standing on the porch facing the bland front door of the standard beige San Fernando Valley cottage, I felt my heartbeat accelerate into an anxious drumroll.

An ugly sense of apprehension deterred me from ringing the bell.

Hell, what did I have to worry about? In my current semivocation as pet-sitter, I'd strode up to plenty of strange homes to visit the occupants — humans and their closest friends of all creature persuasions.

But this was different. Although I'd been invited, it wasn't as a pet-sitter, or even as an attorney, which was how I spent the rest of my working time. (My complementary sets of business cards? *Kendra Ballantyne, Attorney at Law, partner at the firm of Yurick & Associates.* And *Kendra Ballantyne, Managing Member, Critter TLC, LLC.*)

Okay. Enough hesitation. After all, I was a litigator, and a legal one at that — I'd stuck

7

the prior glitch in my career way behind me. Shy and retiring? Not me. Not hardly.

Time to commence the upcoming confrontation.

Although court might have been a cinch in comparison.

I strode to where the doorbell awaited, ready to peal the inside chimes that could foretell my impending fate. The death knell to a perfectly fine potential relationship? Absolutely not — at least, not if I had my way.

The lilac leash strap in my left hand wiggled as, on the ground beside me, my dear and delightful sidekick, Lexie, a tricolor Cavalier King Charles spaniel, stood from where she'd been seated, and whined. At times, like now, she seemed to read my mind. "My sentiments exactly," I told her.

Only, she wasn't staring at the closed front door as I was, but off to the left side of the porch, toward the hedge of thick green pittosporum bordering it.

Recognizing how much I appreciated the distraction as a reason not to immediately reach out and ring that fateful doorbell, I said to her, "What is it, girl?"

She stood at attention, her lovely long black ears set forward. Once more, an uneasy whine escaped her mouth. And then those ears rolled back into a canine sign of warning, even as she began to bark.

"Hush, Lexie," I said, but the usually obedient pup wasn't listening. Instead, she lunged forward so fast that her leash nearly yanked from my grip. "No," I commanded, again to no avail. She barked even more, making me cringe inside. I didn't want to wake this apparently somnolent neighborhood from this day's afternoon siesta.

Even more, facing this home's irritating occupant while dealing with a disobedient pup wasn't in my best interests.

I was about to issue a louder command to Lexie when I finally observed what her keener senses had signaled to her minutes before, spurring her to such uncharacteristic insubordination.

Two cats slowly emerged from beneath the pittosporum branches. To my untrained eye — since I'd always considered canines my best friends and only lately had begun to appreciate the assorted cats who were now my clients — the pair resembled miniature leopards: golden, with dark spots and stripes adorning their fuzzy coats.

"Oh, hello," I said, though I doubt they heard me over Lexie's insistent barks. Interesting that they stood their ground despite the lunging dog issuing oodles of ominous warnings.

Stood their ground? Heck, they issued their own warnings in exchange. Both golden backs arched, their ears turned like alert antennae, and their fur stood on end. They stalked slowly toward Lexie, hissing angrily.

"Stay back," I insisted, as I bent in the tailored black blouse and dressy gray slacks I'd donned earlier for my day at the law office — and with my upcoming meeting in mind. A becoming outfit that fit both professions. One that confirmed I meant business.

The cats didn't appear impressed.

I scooped Lexie into my arms just in time. One feline leapt forward, swiping a claw at the portion of the porch where my pup had just stood.

"Hey," I yelped, jumping back. I didn't need cat scratches to tear my pants . . . or the vulnerable skin of my leg beneath. Even more, I didn't need for Lexie to become the victim of two ferocious felines. I hugged my pup close as the cats stood their ground, snarling and spitting.

Not the kinds of cats to expand my increasing appreciation of the species.

"Stay away," I hissed back.

At that moment the front door opened, and Amanda Hubbard stepped out.

The woman was as beautiful as ever, which made me want to hiss even more. And spit. Her blond hair was piled on top of her head in a nonchalant style that suggested she'd spent hours fussing over it. Her prominent cheekbones underscored gray, flashing eyes, and her lips were pursed in a prim, pink pout.

Then there were her legs, long and lean beneath straight-legged jeans. Beneath her too-tight T-shirt, her apparently flawless boobs seemed to offer themselves to any male grip around.

Do I sound catty? Well, meow. Translation: maybe so. I had admitted, even to myself, that I had a spot of jealousy inside. For good reason.

I wasn't a total loser in the looks department, but I knew my blue eyes, plain nose, and no-longer-highlighted brown hair weren't the stuff that inspired even a mediocre modeling career. Not that I was aware just what Amanda did to earn a living these days, though she'd been in real-estate sales once. Maybe she still was — assuming she did anything. But the point was that her looks could have earned her a career under lights. Mine were okay for pet-sitting and court appearances, but were absolutely ordinary.

"Hello, Kendra," she said, glaring at Lexie in my arms. "I didn't say you could bring your dog." The scornful way she said "dog" did anything but endear her to me.

"You didn't say I couldn't, either." Even if she had, it wouldn't necessarily have made a difference. Take orders from Amanda Hubbard? I'd rather catch a cute and squealing field mouse in my bare hands and feed it, kicking and screaming, to my ball python client, Pythagoras.

"My cats aren't dog friendly." She waved her hand, with its long, red nails, toward the two mini-leopards who hadn't shifted an inch on the porch.

"Not particularly people friendly, either," I remarked.

"That," Amanda said, with a grin so snide that it almost uglified her face, "depends on the person." But then, as if she'd thrown a switch behind her own expression to lighten it, she tossed her shoulders in a shrug and sent a smile my way that seemed almost genuine. "Anyway, I'd love for you to come in, but Cherise and Carnie won't be pleased if your dog visits, too."

Not that her cats should have had any say in what I chose to do, but I didn't want my sweet Lexie subjected to Cherise and Carnie any further. "I'll put Lexie in my car." I sent

12

a final glower in the pusses' direction before turning my back and heading down the walkway away from Amanda's house.

Lexie trembled in my arms, whether from fear or from eagerness to square off against the felines I didn't know. "It's okay, girl," I said as we reached my almost-ten-year-old silver BMW, parked on the street nearby. "I didn't intend to stay more than a few minutes anyway. You're an excellent excuse for me to hear what Amanda wants, then depart pronto. I can't leave you alone in an empty car for long, can I?"

She looked at me with her huge brown eyes and licked my chin, as if to say she understood. Maybe she did, in her Cavalier way.

I'd parked the Beamer beneath a eucalyptus tree. That, combined with the air's early February coolness, kept my car from getting too warm inside. Even so, I slid into the driver's seat and turned the key in the ignition enough to use the controls to roll the windows down a crack, to allow airflow.

"See you soon," I told Lexie as I left. "I promise." Poor pup. I had to push her back inside when she tried to slip out the driver's door behind me.

Then, resolutely, I started back up the

walk toward where Amanda Hubbard waited.

I'd come there only out of curiosity arising from her unanticipated invitation.

What did she really want with me?

Amanda was still standing inside the front door as I strode back from the street. I felt her eyes, as chilly a silver as a northern sea in an ice storm, staring every step of my way. I readied my own internal offenses for our upcoming catfight.

"Come in, Kendra," she said as I reached the porch. Once again, she seemed to stick a smile on her face just for me. And didn't I feel honored by it?

"Thanks," I said with an equally false friendly expression.

I followed her from a small tiled entryway down an airy hall, well lit by two small crystal chandeliers with a skylight in between. The illumination emphasized the artwork lining the walls: watercolors and oil paintings of seascapes. Lovely stuff. Their similar styles were punctuated by several different artists' signatures in the pictures' corners.

Not that I was enough of an art aficionado to know for certain, but I guessed the paintings were originals and likely worth some big bucks if sold at auction, whether live or on eBay.

I found myself slowing to stare. And admire.

Amanda had to have a hefty income these days to afford all this. Either that, or she'd really taken her ex-husband, Jeff Hubbard — my lover for the last few luscious months — for an expensive ride during their divorce, and expended it on artwork.

Seeing Amanda stopped in a doorway, I halted, too.

"Patience," she commanded me.

"Pardon?" I asked in confusion. I thought I'd been acting with utter etiquette so far — not an easy task since I despised my hostess's guts.

"All of the artwork is by the patients at the doctors' office where I work," she said.

Oh . . . *that* kind of patients. Not that I felt fully enlightened. "I didn't realize you worked in a doctors' office," I said. "Weren't you in real estate?"

"Sure, when I met Jeff. I did okay with it, but I found it boring. He understood. While we were together he told me to go back to school, the sweet man. Now, I'm a medical assistant. I work for a group of doctors who specialize in heart problems."

Which didn't exactly explain how Jeff and

she had failed in their own affair of the heart. But I didn't want to inquire about that, so instead I asked, "How does the practice happen to have such talented artists as patients?"

"One of my doctors is well-known for his interest in acquiring paintings from up-and-coming artists. If they or their families need heart care, they flock to him. And they show their appreciation for their excellent treatment and care by selling their stuff to the doctors and staff like me at reduced prices."

"Very nice," I said.

"And before you ask, yes, Leon Lucero is one of the artists and patients. Once Jeff and I broke up, I decided to enjoy life. Date a lot of men and see what happened. Well, I was stupid enough to go out with Leon, and he decided he owned me."

I hadn't asked about Leon. But the conversation would have turned to Amanda's stalker sometime during this get-together, so the seeming non sequitur didn't surprise me.

As if blaming me for Leon's latching on to her, she turned her back and marched through the nearest door. I followed, to find myself in a small but attractive living room also decorated with several seascapes on the walls.

I had to assume Amanda loved the water. Otherwise, talented newcomers or not, I doubted she could live among such wet-looking surroundings for long without screaming.

"So what's up with Leon's latest failure to comply with your temporary restraining order?" I asked sans preamble. That was, indirectly, the reason I was here.

See, several months ago, Amanda had used Leon as her excuse to reenter Jeff's life, begging him for help to convince her unwanted admirer to stay away from her. Jeff had upgraded her home security system and assisted in obtaining a temporary restraining order against Leon.

As if a dedicated stalker ever obeyed a flimsy piece of paper, no matter how massive the weight of courts and law enforcement might be behind it.

"It's a long story," Amanda said with a sibilant sigh, motioning me toward a sleek Scandinavian sofa of bright red cushions on a polished pine frame. I sat obediently — the only act of obedience I intended during this uncomfortable meeting — while she lowered herself as gracefully as a model might onto a matching loveseat.

Almost as if she'd called them, her cats, who hadn't made an appearance since my entrance into the house, padded single file from the hallway and, as gracefully as their mistress, leapt up onto her loveseat and took their places at the opposite sides of its back-rest. Interesting how they apparently stuck together. Another couple of my cat clients did the same, but most of the felines I'd seen stayed solitary, even in households with multiple cat members.

"Hi, darlings," Amanda crooned. Both purred in response, which made me smile despite my irritation at their treatment of Lexie. "They're Bengal cats. Aren't they beautiful? Cherise is the larger one."

Although her inquiry was rhetorical, I nevertheless agreed. Bengal cats? I knew cats sometimes came in breeds as dogs did, but I'd met few in my pet-sitting situations.

Still stroking the kitties, Amanda went on to explain her earlier answer. "My TRO forbids Leon from getting within a hundred feet of my house, or within thirty feet of my person. But it's my doctors' office where he shows up most, and the TRO doesn't cover that."

"Really? Why not ask your lawyer to get the TRO amended?"

She shook her head, and her blond hair bobbed prettily — darn her. "I don't dare. My doctors would be horrified."

"But surely your employers are even more horrified about having a stalker around harassing one of their staff."

"You don't understand," she said. "Leon is claiming lots of cardiac issues — chest pains, palpitations, you name it. Anything to supposedly justify visits to my office. My doctors give him a clean bill of health, but for fear of liability if something's wrong that they haven't found, they let him make further appointments. I try to take those days off, but he always manages to postpone or need further tests . . . In fact, Leon's the main reason I asked you here."

Leon was her excuse to summon me? Yeah, right. Well, whatever her real reason, it was about time that she bared her claws. And that I unsheathed mine.

Still . . . "You need to stop using your stalker as an excuse to keep in contact with Jeff," I asserted pointedly, abandoning all pretext of politeness, at least for this significant moment.

Leon might be the lead-in, but I was sure Amanda had asked me here to engage in a showdown at the Not-So-Okay Corral, a final fight over the currently out-of-town subject of our rivalry. No sense skirting the subject any longer. The litigator in me was ready to take my ten paces and draw.

Amanda just blinked, as if amazed at my effrontery — especially after our somewhat civil conversation. "Tea?" She gestured to a blue ceramic pot and matching cups I'd barely noticed on the low-slung pine table between us. Her skills at subject-changing were stupefying.

"Please," I responded. Drinking would supply me with a superior use of my hands than keeping them balled into fists. Or aiming an imaginary six-shooter.

Amanda started speaking again a minute later as I sipped apple-spiced tea. "I hadn't exactly planned things that way, of course, but I admit that, initially, there was some good in Leon's terrifying me."

"So my suspicions that you hired Leon to stalk you aren't true?"

"I never thought of it," she said with a sigh. "And if I had, I'd have hired someone I could control rather than that scary son of a bitch who won't leave me alone."

"I guess," I admitted.

Damn. The woman was sounding . . . well, human. I liked it better when she showed fangs as fiercely as any wild feline. That way, I could insult her back with impunity.

"Anyway" — I glanced at my watch — "I don't like leaving Lexie in the car. And I need to leave soon anyway. Oh, and by the way, I know you've already blown off the other P.I. Jeff referred you to, to help you deal with Leon."

A few weeks back, Jeff had called us both to his home and essentially handed Amanda her walking papers. Made his choice — me over her — perfectly clear.

That was when he'd given Amanda the name of another investigator to call.

"He wasn't nearly as helpful as Jeff." She shook her head briskly, just as she'd shaken off the advice.

"As if you gave him a chance."

"How would you know?"

"He told Jeff," I replied.

"And Jeff told you?"

I nodded, although, in fact, I was telling a bit of a fib. I'd obtained the info from Jeff's security company's best computer geek, Althea, with whom I'd become buddies. Apparently that P.I. pal of Jeff's had called to vent about the bitch client Jeff had sent his way and Althea's ears had born the brunt of it.

Bengal cats by her side notwithstanding, I'd no intention of further pussyfooting around. "Why don't you just tell me why you asked me here?" I said. *Stop with the niceness that I don't trust any more than I would if a genuine leopard offered to lick my hand.* Was she about to insist that *I* slide out of Jeff's life forevermore so she could slither back in unimpeded, never mind what the man in question wanted?

"I need your help." She sounded as if that admission almost made her upchuck.

My turn to blink. If she thought I would step in and help her get Jeff back, she was certifiably insane. And what other assistance could she imagine I'd give? Did she need legal help?

I didn't represent people I resented.

"Like I said, it's all about Leon," she continued, her gray eyes downcast and sad. What, no more snide smiles? I almost preferred them to her semblance of genuine emotion. "The guy won't give up. I've even had to change my unlisted phone number again. I won't ask your legal advice since I already have a lawyer." And a good thing, too. "But the truth is, I'm scared."

"And you think I can help you how?"

"Honestly? I don't know. But I saw how you helped Jeff when he was accused of murder. I've gathered from him that you're a really nice person."

My lover held conversations about how great I am with his ex who wanted him back?

I felt a trace of warm fuzzies tickling my

insides . . .

Only I couldn't believe it. And even if it were true, and Amanda had stomached Jeff's compliments of me, what was the benefit to her of revealing it to me?

Amanda took a long sip of spiced tea, staring over her cup with those same sad eyes. "You have to know I'm at wit's end for me to even think of turning to you, Kendra. But I am. Jeff's done a good job of trying to keep Leon away, but even he hasn't succeeded. From all I've heard about you, you think outside the box. Maybe you can come up with something to help me get Leon out of my life once and for all."

"Even if I wanted to help you, Amanda —"

"But you don't. I understand. But . . . well, I'm scared enough that I'm leaving town for a couple of weeks. And to give you an idea how hard that is for me, last time I left, when I visited my parents, Cherise and Carnie were so upset at being boarded with their vet that they didn't eat. They even lost some of their pretty coats. But this time I'm flying someplace else, and I can't easily take them with me. I love these cats" — Who happened to hear they were the topic of discussion and snuggled up more with their mistress — "and even so I have to go for a while, since Leon's been around my office nearly every day. I've taken a leave of absence, but I can't be gone too long — I can't afford it. And I'm going to be so worried about Carnie and Cherise."

I looked at the cats in question. They might have been ridiculously rude to sweet Lexie, but they clearly loved Amanda. Not eat? Suffer since their mama had to leave town?

"Have you ever considered leaving your cats here at home?" I asked her. "Maybe they'd do better in a familiar environment."

"Maybe," she acknowledged. "But who'd come in to make sure they were all right?" The somberness of her face suddenly brightened. "You're a pet-sitter. Would you . . . ?"

I suddenly straightened in shock and alarm, recognizing at last where all this was heading. My mouth immediately moved to protest, but Amanda spoke again first.

"No, forget it. Bad idea."

She was absolutely correct. Kowtow to Amanda as a client? Heck, no! "You're right," I agreed. "It'd never work. Hire someone else."

"But I'm leaving first thing tomorrow."

Unfortunately, I'd not yet developed reciprocal relationships with other pet-sitters, or I might otherwise have handed Amanda a referral. That way, I could pat myself on the back for helping someone I hated because it was an emergency. I had a sometime assistant, of course, but using her services would still result in my responsibility for Amanda's cats.

"Sorry," I said. "Even if I could find another sitter, it couldn't be that fast."

"What an awful choice," Amanda said with a sigh. "I can leave them at their vet's. It's familiar and I trust the people, but I know my babies won't eat there, or probably any other place I'd board them away from home. Or, I can ask you to care for them despite hating me." Once again she sighed, then said, "Well, I know things'll be bad for them at the vet's. Please, Kendra. Take care of my kitties for me."

"Forget it. No way will I become your pet-sitter." Or do anything else to help this witch who wouldn't leave my lover alone.

"I'm begging you, Kendra. I'll be so worried about them otherwise."

"You'd trust me to take care of them?" I asked incredulously.

"I know you love animals."

"No," I said, standing.

"You don't love animals?"

"Of course I do, but no way will I watch

25

your cats."

"All right, then," Amanda said, sounding choked. Which caused me to look straight into her face. Her eyes were wet. Tears? Maybe — the crocodile kind. "Good thing Jeff isn't speaking to me, or I'd have to tell him that you're willing to let some poor cats suffer just because you hate me."

Which meant she'd find a way to communicate this wretched and somewhat true thought to him. Would he care?

I'd care.

Well, hell. So what if the woman was more than manipulative, and I wasn't exactly the patsy type? The cats' well-being hung in the balance, not Amanda's. Even if they were hers. And they'd given poor Lexie such a lousy time.

But they *were* kind of cute. And the fact that they didn't have acceptable manners was hardly a surprise since they belonged to a bitch like Amanda.

Was I really considering this?

I knew exactly what Amanda was doing: daring me.

Manipulating me.

If I said no, she'd have something else to sling in my face — that I was a coward. Boy, would she gloat. To me. To Jeff.

If I said yes, she'd feel she had me in her

26

chic pants pocket.

Ah, hell. I was a lot of things, but a wimp wasn't one of them. I looked again at Amanda. Tears streamed down her cheeks. No way was the witch as upset as she appeared. But no matter what I thought about her, the cats' health and welfare could genuinely be at stake.

"Okay, Amanda," I finally said, facing her with a frosty smile. "I'll do it — at triple my usual rate." I quoted the cost, which was outrageous-sounding, even to me.

"What!" she shouted. "No way."

"Yes way," I countered. "Take it or leave it."

I finally left her house a while later, keys and contract in hand. I'd made it clear that this was a one-time honor. Next trip, suffering cats or not, she'd have to make other arrangements.

She had agreed to my inflated rate.

Which left me with the biggest question of all: Why had Amanda *really* wanted to hire me?

CHAPTER TWO

As I strode from Amanda's, I had a driving desire to dump my troubles on my best human friend in the world: Darryl Nestler, owner of the Doggy Indulgence Day Resort on Ventura Boulevard in Studio City. But when I glanced at my watch, I found it was after five and realized how poor my timing would be if I drove to Darryl's. He'd be smack in the middle of saying daily adieus to the canines in his charge.

Instead, I imposed my ranting and raving about Amanda's manipulation, money or not, on Lexie. "I should call her and say my schedule's way too full after all." I grabbed for my purse and the cell inside, then stopped. "But what about the poor cats? I know you don't like them, Lex. I should listen to you and dump the whole dumb idea. Only . . . what would Jeff think if I finked out after agreeing? Do I care what he thinks? He's becoming too much trouble

28

anyway."

I took a right turn too quickly. Lexie slid from her post guarding the dashboard, which made me feel even more guilty. "Sorry," I said. "And as much as I hate to spoil your fun, one of these days I'll have to stick you into a doggy seat belt, for safety's sake."

Her doleful expression suggested she understood. But she turned her back, hopped her furry little bod back up onto the shotgun seat, and again stared out the window — this time sitting instead of perched upright on her paws. I supposed that, if she spoke English, she'd have told me she'd sit still like a good dog should if only I forbore from restraining her.

Although we were sleeping at Jeff and Odin's that night, I aimed our route toward home. I needed a change of clothes.

I also needed to sound out Rachel Preesinger, daughter of Russ, who rented my house. Russ initially moved in as a subtenant, but since my prior lessees were now clearly committed to not returning, I'd recently agreed to lease the place directly to him. More important at this moment, Rachel was my assistant pet-sitter at Critter TLC, LLC, and I needed info about her availability to tend to some nasty cats.

Had I truly allowed myself to be manipulated for hidden reasons I hadn't yet unearthed?

Oh, yeah.

Maybe I was wrong and could take all Amanda said at face value — ignoring how much I despised everything about her, including her face.

On the other hand, maybe she truly had been desperate and hiring me as a pet-sitter had bounced into her brain out of the blue, just because I was there.

I wished I could believe anything that witch did. But when it came right down to it, I was committed to caring for her cats.

And why did all my concerns really matter, when the good thing was that the witch herself wouldn't be anywhere near her kitty coven?

"What do you think, Lexie?" I stopped the Beamer on the winding street where our home resided and pushed the button to unfurl our unfriendly wrought-iron security gate.

Unfriendly, that is, to people we didn't want inside. With Jeff's assistance, I'd enhanced our security system substantially after the murder in the main house some months ago. And fortunately, the Preesingers weren't the partying kind like my original tenants — who'd been accused of that very murder.

Lexie didn't respond to my obscure inquiry, but instead edged over till her front paws rested on the leg I needed available to control the brake and gas pedal. I pushed her gently away.

"No opinion whether I should ask Rachel to handle Amanda's nasty cats?" I pulled the Beamer into the driveway and halted in its habitual parking place outside the garage. Due to my reversals in fortune awhile back, after I was accused of an awful ethics violation, I'd been forced to resign from the major law firm where I'd been a well-paid junior partner. As a result, I'd had to file for bankruptcy, since I suddenly was living way beyond my means instead of simply abutting their envelope. I'd only been able to retain fee title to the fantastic, huge home I'd fallen in love with by renting it out to pay its mortgage.

The whole matter had been mortifying, but I'd managed to muddle through it. I now had my law license back and was a junior partner at the Yurick firm, which was much more laid-back and gave me lots of latitude about which cases I handled. My boss and senior partner Borden Yurick had made it clear I could continue my enjoyable pet-sitting avocation if I wished. His only stipulation was that I'd need to assist on some cases he brought in. Since most involved interesting issues, I had been pleased to accept his offer.

Of course, our way of practicing law also meant money didn't pour into my pockets as it once did. Ergo, I still had to rent out that big, beloved house. Lexie and I resided in a small but comfy flat over the garage. Our tenants leased the right to park inside. Hence, my Beamer's special spot outside.

"We're here," I informed Lexie unnecessarily. She was ricocheting from one car window to another, eager to visit her digs. "But you never answered my question. Do you think I should take care of Amanda's cats myself? I mean, I have insurance now, in case they injure Rachel. Of course I'd warn her about how they acted toward you. They didn't actually attack me except when I held you, and Rachel's a really nice person, so they're unlikely to dislike her at first sight. I'd pay extra, and —"

That was when Beggar, the beautiful Irish setter belonging to Russ and Rachel, bounded out of the big house toward us. The security gate had closed once the Beamer was beyond it, so I had no worries about Beggar's safety. Lexie's, either, although the Beamer might be in peril of acquiring claw marks on both sides if the pups attempted to dig their ways through to one another.

"Okay, forget it," I told Lexie. "Go have some fun." I opened the car door and she leapt out. In moments, she and Beggar were romping enthusiastically around the side yard.

The setter's presence meant Rachel was home. Russ, a Hollywood location scout, was off on one of his many missions to find the finest settings — this time, for an upcoming adventure starring one of the industry's biggest box-office draws.

I slipped out of the Beamer and locked it. That's when I noticed that Rachel had exited the house and was racing down the walkway toward me.

She was officially an adult at age nineteen, but her waiflike appearance, including big brown eyes and the short and shaggy style of her brunette hair, made her appear much younger. Her enthusiastic attitude toward life lent her an enchanting youthful exuberance, too.

Her parents were divorced, and she'd followed her dad here to Hollywood, sure that he'd taken on his new career solely to ensure her a future in film roles.

"Kendra, hi!" she called as she ran. "Wait till you hear." She slid to a stop in front of me. "That audition I told you about? The one where that friend of the grip on the last film Dad worked on thought I would have a chance at landing a speaking role? Well, it's tomorrow. I'm so excited!"

This last comment was unnecessary, given her little leaps in the air.

Despite Lexie's lack of an answer to me earlier, I'd already realized that my success in trying to talk myself into having Rachel handle Amanda's cats was waning. Even so, I had to ask, "How early does it start? And any idea how long it'll last?"

Only then did it dawn on my young assistant that I might not completely share her exuberance. Her big smile segued into a larger frown of dismay. "I have to be there at 6 a.m. And if they like me, I'll need to hang around. Kendra, I'm sorry, but the pet-sitting stuff I'm doing right now . . . can you handle it tomorrow? The only thing that should be a problem is the midday stuff, right? And right now, that's only Widget."

Widget was a highly energetic terrier mix who lived in the northern Valley. I'd walked him midday myself until I got my law license back. For a while, I'd had to tell his owner I couldn't care for him during the

34

day — until I'd hired Rachel. Then, I'd turned him over to her.

Rachel had attended auditions before. She'd even achieved a teensy role in a play once. I wished her well in her acting ambitions. But if she ever landed a role of substance, or one that required filming out of town . . . well, without Rachel's services, I wasn't sure what I'd do.

But I'd think of something. Who was I to pop a pin into Rachel's big, beautiful balloon of anticipation? Besides, our arrangements with her as my assistant were always based on her availability, allowing her to follow her acting dream.

And if I'd any actual ideas of turning Amanda's cats over to Rachel, even just for tomorrow, they'd long since slunk away.

"Break a leg, Rachel," I said with a genuine smile, which felt good after all the false ones I'd flung at Amanda earlier.

"What, not all the bones in my body, like you told me before?"

"I never said all of them. But however many it takes."

"Thanks, Kendra. You're the best. And if I land the role —"

"*When* you land it," I interjected insistently.

"*When* I land it," she amended, her grin-

ning face glowing, "I promise to find someone to help with Widget and the rest."

"Of course, but we'll worry about it then."
Of course, I'd worry about it now.

Fretting was half of my function.

And I was already doing a damned fine
job of it.

Later, at Jeff's, I'd showered and was just
settling Lexie, Odin, and me into bed —
the dogs' on the floor, mine a comfy mat-
tress — when the owner of the house himself
made his nightly call.

"Hi, Kendra," Jeff Hubbard said in his
sexy masculine voice. "You in bed yet?"

"Getting there," I replied, smiling seduc-
tively despite how I sat stretching my legs
with only his long-distance presence to turn
me on. "You?"

"Yeah. Just got under the covers in my
hotel room, which immediately made me
think of you. It's chilly here in Chicago, and
I forgot my pajamas."

"You're nude?" I shivered at the fire that
flamed through me at the picture that
flashed into my mind. That beautiful hard
body of Jeff Hubbard in the flesh.

A situation I'd appreciatively encountered
numerous times before. And hoped to in in-
numerable episodes ahead.

Except — the conflagration inside me suddenly shifted to ice as my mind reeled in an alternate direction. My earlier whereabouts that day with Amanda.

Hearing my own tone change to somewhere between remote and rancid, I said, "I visited with Amanda today. She's leaving town tomorrow and wanted to hire me to care for her cats." I waited for Jeff's reaction.

He stayed silent as I counted the seconds. Five. Six. Seven . . . "I assume you told her no," he finally said.

"No, I agreed to do it. Otherwise, her cats could starve. She signed my contract. Promised to pay lots more than my standard kitty rate. I just have to check on them, change their litter boxes, make sure they have water and food . . ." Okay, so I babbled a bit. I needed for him to break in and say . . . well, something to make me feel a whole bunch better about the entire uncomfortable situation.

"Where is she going?" he asked.

"Up north, I think." Although my image of her goal as San Francisco resulted from her offhand mention of a bay during our negotiation. Or some other body of water. The woman was obsessed with seascapes, so maybe it was an ocean. "Since I have her cell phone number, I'll always be able to reach her," I said.

"Well, it's your pet-sitting business." His flat tone failed to improve my state of mind.

"Sure is," I continued icily. "Her cats didn't make a good first impression, but I didn't want anything bad to happen to them. And if I left Amanda in the lurch, she might think I was still concerned something's going on between you and her."

"You know there's nothing between us. Not now."

"Poor thing seems really scared about her stalker, Jeff." Or she put on a perfect act. "I wouldn't be surprised if she contacts you again soon, since she didn't feel she could rely on the P.I. you recommended." Okay, I was fishing. Would he snap up the bait and admit enough sympathy for his ex that I'd know our relationship was doomed? Or had he been serious when he'd chosen me?

"If she does, I'll give her another referral," Jeff said. "So what are you wearing?"

That sudden change of subject reminded me of our earlier conversation . . . and how turned on I had been. Which was exactly what Jeff intended, I was sure.

"Guess," I responded, my voice sinking to a sexy whisper. "But think black lace. If anything at all." I glanced down at my long gray T-shirt with the boob-level Cavalier picture. What Jeff didn't know would only entice him further. And might convince him to keep on avoiding Amanda. I hoped.

Only after I'd hung up the phone did the doubts descend again. Okay, I admit I'm the suspicious sort. But I know how miserable my taste in men has been. Could Jeff really resist playing hero if his beautiful ex insisted she still needed a champion?

He seemed to think he could. Yet I couldn't help wondering whether Jeff Hubbard was a better actor than star-wannabe Rachel.

I'd an amazingly active agenda the next day — including Amanda's cats.

So there I was, with all my pet-sitting clients waiting for my visits, thanks to Rachel's unavailability. That included spending my lunchtime walking Widget, the wild terrier.

Which was why I'd dropped Lexie at Darryl's doggy daycare resort first thing, so she wouldn't feel deserted while I devoted attention to others' pets.

In between, I spent my office hours drafting a complaint for one of Borden Yurick's senior-citizen clients. That particular age range was his specialty, both in cases and in hiring other attorneys for the firm. I was the sole exception.

I took off a little early that afternoon. All went well with my pet visits, despite their multiplication. I couldn't help but wonder, with Rachel's skipping out, good reason or not, whether or not I should start seeking a second assistant. A whole staff of wannabe actors who needed to toil for sustenance between roles? Very L.A. Maybe I'd be better off with people who dedicated all attention to their real employment — working for me.

I intentionally left my evening visit to Amanda's until last. I wasn't there yet when I received a call from her on my cell phone. My phone still played the Bon Jovi song "It's My Life." I loved the tune, but this time "It's My Life" almost made me sling the phone across my Beamer, once I saw the caller ID. Now that I'd had time for further reflection, the song suggested to me that I'd compromised too completely by being conned into Amanda's assignment.

"Hello, Amanda," I answered neutrally.

"Have you visited Cherise and Carnie yet?"

"Sure. They were fine this morning."

"I mean now. This afternoon."

"Not yet," I said through teeth gritted so hard they could have cracked. "They aren't my only clients, you know."

"But I'm paying you good money. What if they're not eating, like at the vet's? Kendra, you promised to take good care of them, and I'm holding you to that."

Hell. As I'd feared, now that I was in Amanda's employ, she clearly wasn't about to allow me to forget it. Was that why she'd manipulated me into this — so she could have the pleasure of pushing me around pursuant to our contract?

"I'm treating them just fine, Amanda. I'll see them soon." I withheld my wrath with amazing effort.

"And be sure to call me from my house," she insisted, inspiring an urge in me to cast my phone not only across the Beamer, but to smash it under the wheels. "I want to be sure they're all right."

"Fine," I asserted irritably. Why injure my phone, when it was the caller I wanted to cudgel? Not only that, I'd an urge to leave her cats till midnight — no, 4 a.m. — to provide me with an excuse to call her really late. But the poor felines weren't responsible for my dislike of their infuriating owner.

Well, heck. After hanging up, I decided to vary my intended route and get that visit out of the way. Fast.

Still sitting in my Beamer, I made a note

about my just-completed visit in the log I'd begun when I made my pet-sitting business official as a limited liability company, complete with instructions and contracts for my clients.

Then, I headed inside Amanda's.

At first, when I disarmed the security system Jeff had installed, opened the door, and stepped into Amanda's painting-lined corridor, there was no sign of her cats. Great. Other feline clients occasionally played kitty tricks by staging false — but thankfully temporary — disappearances. These two, too?

But then I heard a meow chorus and chased it to the kitchen. There the two leopardlike cats both sat. "Hi, girls. Have you missed me since this morning?" I spoke cheerfully, attempting to read their inscrutable feline faces.

Then Cherise, the larger of the two, ducked beneath the kitchen table and immediately emerged again with an inert mouse carcass dangling from her mouth. She deposited her largesse on the floor.

"For me?" I gushed falsely. "You shouldn't have. Really."

I couldn't help shivering more than just a smidgen. It wasn't as if I'd had no contact with mice since I'd started pet-sitting. I'd had to feed my client Py, the python, dead and defrosted ones, after all.

And, of course, I knew that cats were naturally predatory and proud of it. I'd even heard that they often showed off by presenting their prey to the people they like most. Maybe such gifts arrived often for Amanda from her feline friends.

That didn't mean I had to enjoy dealing with deceased rodents.

I completed my more typical pet-sitting tasks. Then, as gracefully as possible with my nose wrinkled and eyes almost closed, I gingerly lifted their gift in shaky hands clad in rubber gloves from beneath Amanda's sink . . . and tossed the poor rodent, and gloves, into a plastic bag for disposal in the garbage outside. Only then did I start breathing again.

As promised, I called Amanda — using her own kitchen phone instead of my cell. Why expend my own purchased minutes? "Everything here is fine," I assured her, then told her about how I'd been regaled by a rodent gift.

"Really?" Her voice didn't effervesce with enthusiasm but sounded on the chill side. "They've never done that before."

My grin was its nastiest. Why not? This unwelcome client couldn't see it. "Maybe it was special thanks for the care I've been giving them in your absence. Cats do that, you know. And we've gotten along famously."

A split second of silence. Then, "You know, I'm sure, that my cats are special. Smart. Most likely, showing you their kill was a warning. The poor dears undoubtedly consider you an interloper."

Yeah, right. She was reaching.

Even so, I couldn't completely discount what she said. Not that I'd ever met true attack cats, but these guys did look like little leopards. I wouldn't turn my back while caring for them.

"Give me a call tomorrow after you've seen to them again, Kendra," Amanda said into my ear. No please. No thank you.

No surprise.

Still, my grin didn't waver.

Until I got outside and saw my Beamer blocked in the driveway by a white Chevy sedan parked crossways along it on the street. It was a smaller model, but I couldn't maneuver out around it.

I scanned the street for the owner, ready to ask for the car's removal politely, at least at first.

I heard a sound off to my side, where some ficus trees stood. Only then did I notice the large man striding toward me. He wore a muscle shirt, tight jeans, and an ugly grimace as he approached.

"Who are you?" he demanded. "What are you doing in Amanda's house? Where is she?" He stopped only inches from me and glared down with light brown eyes filled with frenzy and fury.

As his hands reached toward me, I realized who this crazed man had to be.

Amanda Hubbard's stalker.

CHAPTER THREE

I ducked smoothly to avoid his grasp and darted away, one hand sliding into my large purse. I groped inside until I felt my small cell phone, which I clasped as if it was a lifeline.

Maybe it was.

"Well, hi, Leon," I chirped amicably to the man as he changed course and continued to approach. "You are Leon Lucero, aren't you? Amanda has told me so much about you." Yeah, like you're a fruitcake who might just like to slice and dice her. Or maybe merely make her your sex slave.

"Yeah, I'm Leon. Who are you?"

How to play this? Well, we were outside on a residential street. Although I failed to see any friendly neighbors, I figured a scream might bring assistance. If I needed it.

For now, I'd be brash. Bold. Let my litigator side take control. Gee, if I could convince Leon never to darken Amanda's doorstep again, I'd erase her excuse for chasing Jeff.

As if she wouldn't pencil in another . . .

"I'm Kendra Ballantyne, Leon," I told him. "I'm a lawyer. And I'm aware that Amanda obtained a temporary restraining order from the courts to stop you from harassing her. That means you can't come close to her home, let alone trespass on her driveway. If you leave right now and promise not to come back I won't have you arrested. Deal?" I lifted my cell phone and waved it as if it was a talisman against evil.

"Tell me where she is," he growled again, his face no less contorted with rage than a minute earlier. I couldn't even guess his age — somewhere between hormone-excessive adolescence and the age of reason. His sleeveless shirt really showed off his muscles. Big, rippling biceps — might have looked sexy, if I hadn't been concerned about how strong he might be if he grabbed me.

"She's not here," I said, hoping he couldn't hear the hammering of my heart. "She isn't anywhere that you can find her." Besides, I had no idea where she was, either. "And I'd suggest you not be here when she gets home — whenever that might be." I flipped my phone open and held it visible to him as I started to press in 911. "Bye, Leon."

"Kendra Ballantyne? I'll remember that. But, sure, I'll go . . . now. Tell Amanda I'll see her soon."

With that, he turned his back and sauntered slowly toward his car. He opened the driver's door but stood there for a moment longer as he turned back toward me. His insolent eyes roved up and down my body, and I shivered as if I could feel their creepy, crawly progress.

And then he slid inside and sped away, peeling rubber with a screech that additionally iced my blood.

I remained still, clutching my phone and catching my breath. Who should I call? Phoning 911 without the presence of the vile TRO violator would do no good. I had a contact of sorts at the LAPD — homicide detective Ned Noralles. But there'd been no death here today, except, perhaps, my sense of security.

Amanda? Maybe. In fact, I'd absolutely have to tell her all about what had occurred. But with her, I'd want to think first about what to say and how to say it.

And at the moment, uninhibited venting was what I needed.

Almost instinctively, I scrolled down my

list of most recently called numbers.

And sighed with a sort of relief when the welcome male voice at the other end said, "Hi, Kendra."

Jeff.

Sagging sideways against my Beamer for support, I quickly told him what had happened.

"Damn!" he exclaimed into my sensitive ear. I winced.

"Yeah," I said. "That goes double for me."

"You called the cops, I presume."

"You presume too much. What good would they do now? Besides, for the police to enforce a TRO, it has to be on file. I'd have to talk to Amanda about whether she followed appropriate procedure, which cops have copies, that kind of thing."

"I know she did things right, since I advised her and so did her lawyer."

"Who is . . . ?"

"A guy named Mitch Severin. I got his name from another P.I. You know him?"

"No, but there are a lot of lawyers in L.A."

"Wait a minute," Jeff said, sounding suddenly peeved. "Did you say you'd have to talk to Amanda? You called me before you called her?"

"Well . . . yes." I noticed a couple of big guys strutting down Amanda's tree-lined street walking a couple of big dogs — looked like mastiff mixes. Where had they been five minutes ago?

"You'd better let her know. And when you talk to her, you can find out who her contact regarding the TRO is at the LAPD, which stations have copies, and where you can get one, too. Maybe also call her lawyer, in case there's anything useful he can tell you."

"Sure." I attempted to sound all together despite how disjoined my rattled nerves still felt. "Soon as we hang up. Bye, Jeff."

"You're okay, Kendra?" he asked — which is what he should have done in the first place. Okay, so now I was peeved as well as unnerved. Maybe the peeved part was an especially good thing, since it had started to overshadow my anxiety.

"Of course. Bye."

"You called me first because you needed some comfort," he said softly. "And here I was acting like a P.I. instead of someone who loves you. I'm sorry. Kendra, I wish I'd been there with you."

Me, too, I thought. His sudden attitude amendment had caused a rush of moisture to my eyes. He loved me? I'd thought I'd heard him say that a few months ago, but hadn't followed it up once Amanda had interjected herself back into his life.

50

And me? How did I feel?

Who knew?

I stood straight, no longer relying on my Beamer to boost me up. No way was I going to give in to emotionalism right now. *Any* kind of emotionalism. Especially after being confronted by someone else's stalker, a situation I'd handled just fine.

"I'll let you talk to Leon next time," I said in a tone I intended to sound joking.

"There'd better not be a next time," he said angrily.

"I agree," I replied. "At least I'll be prepared from now on, while I'm caring for Amanda's cats. I'll know just what to do if Leon shows up again."

"What's that?" he asked.

"Run like heck into the house and call the cops," I replied. "But you know what?"

"What?"

"For the first time since I learned she existed, after meeting Leon I feel a lot more empathy for your ex."

I'm not a coward. No way. No how.

But I always insist on taking a reasoned approach. Which was why I didn't follow Jeff's irritating instructions and immediately contact Amanda on her cell. I still hadn't decided how to play out that phone call. I considered it as the Beamer and I headed for our next pet-sitting stop.

Jeff had dangled the little tidbit that he loved me. And still I searched my own heart for a hint of how to respond.

I stared up at the darkening sky through my dirty windshield, hoping to see some stars I could startle by asking their advice.

Ha! In overpopulated-L.A.'s atmosphere? With all the lights glowing at ground level, I'd be lucky to see the beams from a low-flying helicopter.

No matter. I wasn't the superstitious sort anyway. No astrological forecast would fix my fate.

I cared for Jeff. Probably *could* love him. But did I at this uncertain instant?

With Amanda still dangling between us like a black widow spider sliding insidiously along a particularly sticky strand of web?

Well, heck, maybe she really had just attempted to rely on Jeff because of her fear of Leon.

Sure.

Still, stopped at a traffic light in a commercial area on Burbank Boulevard, I pondered the possibilities of how I'd inform Amanda of Leon's latest.

Should I act all matter-of-fact? "Hey, Amanda, just wanted to let you know the cats are cool today. Oh, and by the way, your stalker Leon showed up and suggested that I let him know how to find you."

Or how about horrified? "Why didn't you warn me that your stalker was likely to appear and menace me?"

Lawyerly? "I am not your attorney, so please put me in contact with Mr. Severin." Wasn't that the name Jeff mentioned? "I'll let him know that Leon isn't complying with the TRO and suggest that he counsel you accordingly."

These options and others barraged my already frazzled psyche until, before I knew it, I'd already tended all my pet-sitting clients and aimed the Beamer back toward Jeff's, where Lexie and Odin awaited me.

And still I hadn't sought out Amanda.

"Okay, I admit it," I said to Lexie and Odin after we returned from our late-night walk beneath the streetlights on Jeff's blessedly flat avenue. Odin's an Akita. They're good guard dogs, so I'd only looked over my shoulder a scant dozen times as we strolled. "I've been procrastinating. Now, don't look at me that way," I instructed Lexie, who regarded me reproachfully with cocked head and accusatory eyes. "If Amanda had been anywhere near here, somewhere Leon could have located her,

I'd have let her know immediately."

Lexie's tail wagged her understanding and exoneration.

"I'll call her first thing in the morning. I promise."

Only I didn't have to. As soon as I'd exited the shower and stuck on my nightshirt, my cell phone rang.

The caller ID informed me it was Amanda.

Almost before I could utter a hello, she started shouting. "Leon was at my house? Are Cherise and Carnie all right? Why didn't you call me?"

Not even a hint of, "Gee, Kendra, I hope he didn't hurt you." But what did I expect from her? Certainly no sympathy, let alone any compassionate concern.

And then reality slapped me nearly silly.

There were only two ways Amanda could have known Leon accosted me in her driveway. I didn't imagine that the selfsame stalker had suddenly unearthed his prey's unlisted cell phone number and called to describe his day to her.

That meant she'd been speaking with Jeff.

"Didn't Jeff tell you?" I responded sweetly, settling my butt on the bed to prevent myself from slithering beneath it in sorrow. "He told me to wait until tomorrow morning, so the news wouldn't interrupt your *sleep* tonight."

I swallowed my outraged gasp as I heard a stifled conversation somewhere in the background, as if Amanda attempted to hide its contents from me. Or the identity of the other person, which suddenly seemed quite apparent.

Jeff? With Amanda? That SOB! Now I knew just why she'd conned me into caring for her cats — all the better to push his duplicity smack into my face.

In moments, Amanda's voice resumed its scratching of my sore eardrums. "He said he didn't —"

A pregnant pause, and then another voice assailed me. "Kendra, I'm with Amanda, as if you didn't know by now, but whatever you're thinking, it's not that. I'm —"

"Who said I'm thinking anything, Jeff? You were right to let Amanda know immediately about Leon. Tell her I apologize for not informing her myself. At least Leon's unlikely to figure out she's followed you to Chicago. Oh, and by the way, Odin sends his love. He's doing fine. Good night to Amanda. And you, too."

I flipped my phone's flaps back together decisively. Tears trying to torment my eyes? I insisted on their immediate evaporation.

Well, so much for love, and Amanda out of his life. They were trysting in the Windy City.

And the body of water she'd mentioned? It had to be Lake Michigan.

In my mind, I conjured a cyclone that struck their shared bed and blew away some mighty critical body parts. The growl I evoked in my head must have emanated from my mouth, since both dogs sat up at attention on the floor beside me.

And then my phone dared to intone "It's My Life" again.

Yet again, it was Amanda.

"I'll come home early, Kendra," she said with no preface. "I'm worried about my cats."

"They're fine, and whatever I may feel toward you, I've already assured you I won't take it out on them."

"Not you. Leon. He's threatened them since I got the restraining order. And since he knows I'm not around, he may harm them to get to me."

I couldn't discount that possibility. And even if Cherise and Carnie were not my favorite cats in the cosmos, I most certainly wouldn't want Leon to harm them. Plus, as a lawyer, I had to consider the possibility of my own liability if I failed to keep my charges safe.

Still, I had to add, "But if you come back and Leon learns about it, it's you he'll go after."

"For my cats' sake, I'll take my chances," Amanda said.

For that instant, as a fellow animal adorer, I almost stopped abhorring Amanda.

Until I heard Jeff's muffled voice engaging in a similar sort of persuasion.

"How soon do you expect to be home?" I inquired coolly.

"I've checked about changing my reservations," she said. "I'd like to leave right now, but I've promised my doctors to stay through Monday morning since they paid for a class for me here. I'll be home late that afternoon."

"Glad to hear it." This was Thursday. If she was *that* worried, why wasn't she ignoring her bosses and barreling back home?

"You'd better keep my cats safe until then, Kendra."

"I will," I assured her, hoping it was so.

When Jeff called back a half hour later, I stayed amazingly pleasant. "You were right," I acknowledged, resting my back against his bed pillows, Odin and Lexie curled up at my side. Okay, so I hadn't the heart to be a hound-dog disciplinarian. And their cuddly presences gave me a heck of a lot more peace of mind. "I should have called her in the first place. Good thing she joined you in Chicago so you could let her know what was happening on her home front."

"It didn't happen that way, Kendra. I never told her I was heading for Chicago, let alone where to find me here."

"Sure," I said.

"She called around to some of my long-time clients till she learned where I'd be traveling this time. In any event, she's booked her own room, and I just sent her off to bed."

"Good idea," I agreed. But my bad old brain snapped imaginary digital photos of him sneaking there in the middle of the night.

"Kendra." He drew out my name as if he was exasperated. He probably *was* exasperated. "We resolved this weeks ago. It's you I care about now. Amanda simply doesn't take no for an answer. And you know she claims she didn't trust the other P.I. I sent her to, even though he's an old pal."

"I understand, Jeff. And I can also comprehend why Amanda doesn't want to let go." Hot damn! Didn't I sound reasonable?

If only it weren't mostly an act.

Well, hell. I'd known forever what a loser I was in selecting men for meaningful relationships. I'd nearly convinced myself that Jeff was different, especially after he'd asserted — or at least implied — to Amanda that he was ousting her from his existence once and for all. He'd done this before my very eyes.

My very gullible eyes.

"Anyway, don't worry about it," I added airily. "When you and she are both home, let's all talk about the best way to ensure Leon is out of her life for good."

Too bad I didn't know how prophetic those words would prove to be.

CHAPTER FOUR

Did I fret and fume over the following few days, waiting for Amanda and Jeff to hurry home?

Hardly.

The next morning, I handled my pet-sitting rounds efficiently, as always — enjoying every moment of romping with my mostly canine charges and ensuring they knew they'd had some intense human attention.

Heck, once I'd gotten my law license unsuspended a few months back, I'd considered whether to give up pet-sitting and concentrate on attorneying, including pet advocacy. But the truth was, I found visiting others' babies a treat, not just a business. So here I still was, happily juggling both vocations.

Right now, though, I spied around a lot for the white sedan that had previously kept me stuck in the driveway — just in case.

Fortunately, it wasn't anywhere near Amanda's.

"You haven't seen that creep Leon, have you?" I asked Cherise and Carnie as they strutted into the kitchen to see me — blessedly without any rodent present this time.

If they'd any suspicion that Leon had been lurking, they didn't deign to inform me.

I'd left Lexie locked in the car, but not for long, with Leon's possible neighborhood presence and the threat he'd made to Amanda's cats — which he could expand to canines. Feeling guilty for leaving her alone at all, I decided to treat her to a nice, safe day at my good friend Darryl's Doggy Indulgence Day Resort.

Which might not have been a good thing, since Darryl's immediate and gleeful appearance from behind the entrance desk suggested he'd been hoping to see me.

The resort was essentially one huge room with several areas to please the most finicky pup, plus Darryl's office and a highly active kitchen.

I let Lexie off her leash, and she bounded to the doggy play portion — an area filled with an assortment of canines plus balls, flyable disks, and lots of other delightful doggy toys. Kiki, another movie star hopeful and my least favorite of Darryl's staff,

61

was leading a game of "find it and fetch" with some fuzzy rag bones.

Darryl, standing beside me, said, "I have an emergency pet-sitting referral for you, Kendra. Can you take it on for me?"

Tall, thin, and spectacularly softhearted, Darryl appeared almost studious in his wire-rimmed spectacles, yet a perpetual twinkle lit his huge, puppy-dog eyes. He'd been my buddy from when I'd been a well-paid litigator in the large law firm — and had handed me my new career as a pet-sitter to assist me in paying my bills when my law license was temporarily suspended.

Did I have time to take on a new client? Not really, especially since Rachel's audition had extended into several days. But for Darryl —

"Sure," I assured him.

He immediately swept me into the area that contained human furniture and introduced me to Stromboli, a shepherd mix, who was there with his owner, Dana Maroni. Dana was a petite human female who looked too little to handle rowdy and rambunctious Stromboli. Even so, a soft "Sit" from the slender brunette, who was clad in a long-sleeved shirt and short black skirt, immediately brought the big dog to his haunches — even in the midst of a half dozen other pups who didn't elect to obey.

"I'm so glad to meet you, Kendra." Dana held out a slender hand. Her grasp was as firm as any attorney's. "Darryl said he was going to call you, so it's really serendipitous that you came in. My dad's ill up in Seattle, so I'm leaving town this morning unexpectedly and I simply can't bring Stromboli."

Said dog looked up lovingly at his mistress.

"He seems like a sweetheart," I said.

"He is," Dana assured me, and we went into the details of where Stromboli and she lived, and how I should care for her big canine baby while she cared for her ailing dad. I retrieved from the Beamer a standard contract for my pet-sitting company, Critter TLC, LLC, and she eagerly signed it.

"I'll take Stromboli home now," she told me. "You'll visit him this evening, take him for a walk, and feed him?"

"Sure will," I assured her. "Twice a day till you call and tell me you're back. Or my assistant will, if that's okay."

"If you trust your assistant, that's fine with me."

A minute later, Darryl walked me to the door. "Once again, you're a lifesaver, Kendra," he said. "I owe you."

I stood on tiptoe and slipped him a kiss on his long, smooth cheek. "Enough, Nestler," I rejoined with pseudo crabbiness. "Or I'll have to start singing my own chorus of who owes whom."

"With your voice? Talk about off-key. No, forget it, Kendra. Especially if you expect me to say 'whom.' "

I laughed and left, heading for my law office. Our suite sat in a long, low building that senior partner Borden Yurick had bought, a one-time restaurant in the Encino area of the San Fernando Valley.

Inside, I returned the effervescent greeting of Mignon, the young and exuberant receptionist. Then, head down, I headed for my office, where I quickly got to work. At lunchtime, I ducked out once more to go walk Widget, then hustled back to the office to end my law day by finishing the complaint I'd started drafting for Borden's clients, the Shermans.

As with many of Borden's closest friends, including most of our firm's attorneys, the Shermans were active senior citizens. Their case? They were resolved to recoup rent overpaid at a brand-new Santa Barbara vacation resort where the amenities were highly overstated.

The place was promoted as a dream retreat, a delightful assortment of rooms that had access to golf, tennis, and the beach, with gourmet meals included.

But the couple had brought back pictures proving the inn was miles inland from the beach, and the closest amenity, if you could call it that, was a public park full of noisy kids. Oh, and yes, it had tennis of the table kind, plus golf of the miniature version. Meals? Sure, if one didn't mind grabbing fast food at the nearest Mickey D's — vouchers included. And the clients' complaints had thus far fallen on decidedly deaf ears and e-mail-immune eyes.

Before I sent the Shermans my draft complaint for comment and consent, I brought it to Borden. They were, after all, his clients. And the main condition for my junior partnership in his firm, with the right to have fun practicing law as I pleased, was that I also helped him with the cases he brought in.

Our sweet senior partner's office was the largest, and farthest from the door, of the building. Its walls were covered in attractive oak paneling, and one held a bevy of bookshelves filled with — what else? — law books. His desk looked like a lawyerly antique, but his other furnishings, mostly a mishmash of chairs, were so oddly assorted that I'd concluded they'd been bought with the restaurant building.

Sitting behind his desk, he looked up behind his big bifocals as I rapped on his door. "Hi, Kendra," he greeted in his high pitched but hearty voice. As usual, the lanky elder lawyer wore one of the floral inside-out-appearing Hawaiian-style shirts he favored. This one was beige, covered with big and pointed bird-of-paradise blossoms.

Borden had been a senior partner at Marden, Sergement, & Yurick, the high-powered L.A. firm where I'd worked before the ugly, and untrue, accusations about ethics violations had resulted in my resignation. About the same time, rumors had been rampant that Borden had had a mental breakdown.

Turned out that he'd simply needed a cogitation break, and when he returned from an extended and enviable expedition abroad, he'd made his decision to dump the Marden firm and start his own, extending employment offers to some of his retired counsel cronies. That caused the Marden folks to actively assert Borden's bonkerness, since he had also dared to abscond with his own client base — nearly half the whole firm's business.

And then he'd hired me, once my law license was restored, with the freedom to practice law as I loved it. I could continue my pet-sitting business, and take on pet advocacy cases of my own — my latest law-practice passion.

In fact, I'd been doing amazingly well with my own form of ADR. Those initials were usually interpreted in the legal profession as "alternate dispute resolution," but in my case they stood for "animal dispute resolution."

"I drafted the complaint in the Sherman matter," I said, stepping forward to hand him the printed copy.

"Good going! Thanks, Kendra. I'll take a look. I've already assured the Shermans they're in the best of legal hands." He bobbed his head so his silvery shock of hair glimmered in the light. "Aren't you late for this afternoon's pet-sitting?" he said. "You'd better get on your way, with all those precious pets in only your hands for the moment."

Good old Borden! I slid out of the office with a totally unencumbered conscience. Where else could I have had the cooperation of a firm's senior partner in such a situation?

I headed first to see to Stromboli. The sweet but energetic shepherd was clearly delighted for the company. I let him romp in his own small Burbank backyard to work off some energy before he took me for a walk. While watching him, I noticed his neighbor, an adorable medium-sized, wire-haired mutt who observed Stromboli's frolic from his own back porch.

I fed my latest friend Stromboli, walked him once more, and again got a peek at his cute and quiet neighbor.

Then I hied to some other clients', and finally to Amanda's.

Again I scanned the street for a sign of Leon or his car. Fortunately, I saw none.

Only . . . when I got inside the house, I found the refrigerator door open.

Horrified, I hurriedly checked the large appliance. Fortunately, Amanda had apparently, in anticipation of her trip, cleaned it out, since the only stuff inside consisted of things that wouldn't perish fast — salad dressing, packaged cheeses, and the like.

Most important, Cherise and Carnie were not inside, either.

The two leopardlike cats strolled into the kitchen as I surveyed it — and Carnie carried a mouse. Cherise greeted me with a mew.

"Gee, thanks, ladies," I said with solemn false gratitude. "By the way, do you happen to know how the refrigerator door got open?" Their water came from the filtered tap on the kitchen sink, and I'd never had to refrigerate their canned food, since between them, and with their daily kibble, each small can was emptied as soon as opened.

I'd had no reason to open the door. I doubted that the felines had done it.

So who, then?

The obvious culprit was the cad who'd no business even being on the property let alone in the house.

Leon.

This time, it didn't take Jeff's prodding to get me to call Amanda — after I'd gingerly deposited the gift mouse in its proper receptacle . . . outside.

Decoration-derived seasickness only added to my queasiness as I strolled down her hallway into her den. I sat at her desk and used her phone. When Amanda answered, I quickly related my concern. "It's possible the door was somehow opened accidentally," I admitted, "but I don't see how."

"And you'd turned on the security system?" she asked. Her voice sounded as quivery as mine.

"Yes, and it was still set. Does anyone else have a key, or permission to come in?"

"Only Jeff," she said, "and he's still here."

I chose not to react to that. And then I heard a sound from somewhere down the hall. I drew in my breath with a nasty gasp. "There's someone here," I managed to say.

"Get out of there, Kendra!"

I only half noticed that this time Amanda had expressed a shred of concern for my welfare. I hung up and prepared to hurry out — when I heard the noise again.

Slowly, my back to the seascape-decorated hallway, I slid in that direction. Foolish? Most likely.

Only I was certainly glad I'd done it a minute later, when I heard the noise again.

This time, I was peering surreptitiously into a bedroom — just as the slightly larger Cherise, observed by her housemate Carnie, leapt up onto a chair and attempted to bat down a pull chain that hung from an antique-looking floor lamp. She thumped back down to the floor without achieving her goal.

My latest scare had been caused by a cat's cavorting.

Laughing, I called Amanda back and told her.

"Could the cats have accidentally opened the refrigerator door by some kind of game?" she asked.

I returned to the kitchen and looked

around. I saw no errant pull chains nearby, but the refrigerator stood next to a window with a curtain askew.

"Maybe," I told her. "Have they ever leapt like that at any curtains?"

"No, but they've never gone after a lamp cord, either. Or brought mice inside the house."

In any event, I felt relieved — all the more so when Amanda confirmed she'd be home in three days. When I returned outside, I once more looked for Leon's car. I even peeked into Amanda's two-car garage, but the only vehicle there was one I recognized from her visits to Jeff's, a cherry-red Camry.

As I drove my Beamer down the street, though, I thought I saw a shadow duck behind a neighbor's garbage can. I slowed long enough to watch it some more but saw nothing alarming.

Nothing *not* alarming, either.

Still, that day ended quietly, and the next two, over the weekend, seemed filled with much of the same.

Finally came the day that Amanda was to return. She called in the late afternoon and said she'd just landed at LAX, as I was preparing to exit the Yurick offices.

"I'm heading to my place soon, Kendra," she told me. "Were my babies all right this morning when you visited them?"

"They sure were. And no more open refrigerator doors or games with dangling strings."

"I'm glad. Oh, and Jeff said to be sure to say hi for him. He promised to be back in another week or two."

Nothing like a reminder of whom she'd been with over the last few days to spoil my otherwise magnificent mood.

I threw myself into my final pet-sitting program for the evening, refusing to dwell on the Jeff-and-Amanda enigma, or where I fit into that particular puzzle — even with Jeff's somewhat surprising suggestion lately that I'd helped him pick up the pieces of his life post-Amanda. As if I believed it, especially now.

Once again, when I visited Stromboli at around 7 p.m., his fuzzy canine neighbor sat alone on the porch. This time, I may have been reflecting my own mood in that direction, but the pup appeared a mite morose.

As I left Stromboli's home, my cell phone rang. The caller ID identified Amanda. We'd already determined that I'd drop by late the next day to hand her back her keys and receive my check.

"Hi, Am—" I started to say, but she interrupted immediately.

"Kendra? Where are you? You'd better get over to my house right away."

"But wh—"

"Now," she insisted. Was that hysteria or rage in her voice? Whatever her state of mind, it wasn't one I especially wanted to visit. "What did you do? You have to take care of this. Now."

What did I do? my mind echoed equally frantically. Had I inadvertently accomplished something that had harmed Cherise or Carnie? The two leopard-cats had grown on me. I even almost appreciated their mousy gifts.

"I'll be there soon," I responded into the phone, and turned the Beamer toward Amanda's street. I wasn't at all certain what I'd expected, but I prayed the felines were fine.

Which they were. But what I'd heard in Amanda's voice turned out absolutely to be hysteria, a fact I learned ten minutes later when she wrenched open her door and yanked me inside.

"What's wrong?" I asked as she shrieked at me and sobbed.

"Why did you do this?" she screamed. "How could you?" Her grasp was incredibly

73

potent as she pulled me down her seascaped hall.

She turned on the light in the bedroom where I'd seen the cats toying with the floor lamp.

And there, lying beneath it, lay the bloody, apparently deceased, body of Leon Lucero.

CHAPTER FIVE

Only then, beneath the latest illumination, did I notice Amanda had been wearing a long, checkered apron. Standing to one side of the bedroom's door, she slipped it off and let it slide to the floor.

Her shirt and slacks beneath were soaked in blood.

I gasped, then asked, "Are you hurt, too?"

"No." She sounded huffy in the midst of her histrionics. "I didn't want my neighbors to see this mess on me. I told you I work at a doctors' office. When I first found Leon, I checked for vital signs and tried to revive him."

"Was he still alive?"

"No!" She shook her head vehemently, causing strands of blond hair to escape from her updo. Or maybe they'd already been hanging down. Other than her apron, I hadn't really paid attention to Amanda's appearance . . . before.

And now, staring sideways at her was a whole lot better than staring forward toward the corpse that had become her houseguest. Or, more likely, her trespasser with a whole lot of unwanted baggage.

Himself.

"I had to try, though," she continued. "My doctors would expect it of me. He was one of our patients, after all — even if he kept coming because he was after me." She choked on her last couple of words and covered her face in her hands.

The bedroom wasn't especially small, but for the moment it seemed utterly cramped. The lamp I'd noticed before, the one Cherise and Carnie had cavorted around, still stood across the room.

Past the bed.

And the part of the floor at its foot where Leon lay.

Amanda huddled herself against the room's closest wall — yes, beneath yet another original seascape. Tears rained from her eyes as she aimed them beseechingly at me. Only I hadn't any idea what they asked.

Time for some inquiries of my own.

"You did call 911, didn't you?"

"Of course not. I called *you.* Jeff would be awfully mad if I didn't give you a chance to come up with a good excuse. Did Leon attack you?"

"Me? Amanda, this is your house. The guy was your stalker. Was he here when you arrived? Did he attack *you?*" My mind had immediately morphed into "think like a lawyer" mode. Not that I was a criminal counsel. But the guy had been harassing Amanda. If she'd been the instrument of his demise, it was logical that he'd have attacked first. She could assert a perfectly good argument for self-defense. And a homicide caused by self-defense didn't result in a murder conviction.

"Didn't you hear me?" She squealed, her back still pressed to the wall. "He was here when I came home. Lying there. Bloody."

"Okay," I said, ignoring the questions and the possibly unwanted answers that had started to bloat my brain. First things first. "I'll call 911 since you didn't. The longer we wait without doing anything, the worse it'll look for you." Amazing. I was considering ways to keep Amanda from being unjustly accused — and I hadn't even a hint as to whether she was guilty as hell.

Guess it had become second nature to me, since I'd turned into a murder magnet and started helping others who were innocent get off the hook.

Heck. *Murder magnet.* Was the appellation

I'd piled on myself after all I'd gone through in the last months a self-fulfilling prophecy? If so . . . enough already!

Only, standing here with a trembling suspect across the room and a corpse on the floor wasn't the time to talk myself out of the mess.

I pulled my cell phone from a pocket in my big purse and pressed in those weighty numbers. I kept my description to the dispatcher minimal — although I mentioned my name, and told her that if Detective Ned Noralles happened to be on duty at the North Hollywood Police Station, which had jurisdiction here, he would recognize it.

And then I flipped the phone shut.

"Are they coming?" Amanda rasped.

"They'll be here soon, I'm sure."

"Oh, Kendra." This time, her tone started off as a whimper and ended as a moan. She buried her face in her hands.

Where was the woman who'd been so brash in her attempts to con me into cat-sitting and wrest back her ex-husband?

Had her brazenness been slain by her own hands, along with Leon?

No, wait. Hands alone couldn't have elicited such a massive amount of blood from the man. Could they?

I aimed my eyes toward where Amanda's

fingertips were curved over her face. Her nails were long and polished but didn't look like lethal weapons. Well, that was for the crime-scene team to determine.

Then again, I hadn't exactly searched for an obvious murder weapon.

I forced my gaze back along the floor, toward where Leon lay crumpled by the bed.

The guy was again wearing a muscle shirt and jeans. Maybe he never wore anything else. From this angle, I could just make out the expression on his face: angelic, compared with the angry grimaces he'd aimed at me during our single ugly encounter.

I felt a flicker of pain and realized I'd just bitten the inside of my lower lip. I loosened my teeth and looked away.

Which was when I spotted the first thing on the floor by Leon.

He'd ended up flat on his back, at least after Amanda allegedly attempted to save him. Way off, beyond one shoulder, lay something small. And furry.

And apparently as dead as he was.

A mouse.

Deposited by Cherise or Carnie? Probably. It was unlikely Leon left it there himself.

That gave credence to Amanda's explanation for what I'd first considered a kindly cat gift. Her felines left dead rodents near people they didn't like. I mean, how could they have enjoyed having a guy around who menaced their mistress? They'd probably dropped the mouse near him as a threat of their own.

Which meant that the mice they'd given me also constituted an indication that I was an interloper here, as Amanda had said.

Oh, well. And I'd thought we were getting along reasonably well. At least the mice were only given to me early on during my cat-care visits. Maybe I'd grown on the kitties.

Maybe they'd eventually decided not to threaten the hand that fed them.

I then noted that, closer to Leon's athletic shoes encasing his large, immobile feet, lay something else.

Something long. And horribly bloody.

The probable murder weapon.

A big, sharp screwdriver.

Did Amanda own a tool kit? Maybe so, especially if she hung those dozens of seascapes on her wall by herself.

Suddenly, the cats zipped from under the bed and hied themselves hurriedly out of the bedroom. Had they been there all along?

I noticed little bloody paw prints as I viewed their exit down the hall.

Which was when the pounding started from the other end. The front door?

A muffled shout announced, "Open up. This is the police."

Amanda slid to the floor with a sigh.

Ned Noralles wasn't the first LAPD detective to arrive at the scene. But arrive, he did.

The tall, nice-looking African-American with the less-than-stellar personality had been my would-be nemesis when I'd been accused of murder. Plus, he'd made it his personal mission to point his fingers toward some of my friends being framed in subsequent cases, and attempt to prove they were killers.

"Well, Kendra Ballantyne," he said, stepping into Amanda's small living room where the first cops who'd come had exiled us. "What a surprise, seeing you at a homicide site."

"Well, Ned." I remained seated on the sofa. "Sarcasm has never become you." He did, however, look sharp in his black suit, gray shirt, and blue patterned tie.

"Will I have the pleasure of investigating you as a suspect again?"

"Not hardly," I huffed.

"Then which of your buddies is in trouble

this time?" He scanned the room until his eyes lit on Amanda, its only other occupant except for the uniformed officer who stood in the doorway staring stonily. Guarding us.

As if we'd flee. I knew better. And Amanda seemed too shaky even to walk.

She'd taken an unobtrusive seat on one of her loveseats in the conversation area formed by her sofa. Its white pillows contrasted with the couch's bright red blatancy. It also emphasized the dried blood on Amanda's outfit. The crime-scene team from the Scientific Investigation Division had arrived only a little while earlier, and the cops hadn't ordered her to hand over her clothes yet.

"I gather you'd like an introduction." My droll tone elicited a sardonic smile from Ned.

"You gather right," he replied.

The epitome of etiquette, I rose from the sofa. "Amanda Hubbard, this is Detective Ned Noralles."

Amanda hardly reacted. She barely even looked up, and certainly didn't do the polite thing and offer her hand. Not that Ned was likely to want to shake it anyway. With all that blood about, it was likely to be evidence.

But . . .

Oops! No wonder the detective's dark eyebrows shot way the heck up his forehead. My recollection hadn't veered in that direction before, but Ned had a long history with Jeff Hubbard, who'd once been a cop himself. The two of them had allegedly gotten into a heck of a fistfight once upon a time, one that had resulted in Jeff's resignation from the LAPD.

On top of that, Jeff had been Ned's pet suspect in the last murder investigation where he and I had butted heads.

Not that Jeff had done it, of course. And I'd proven it.

Which had caused Ned jokingly to offer me a job.

"Well, hello, Amanda." His syrupy voice sounded scads too friendly to me. The subtext shouted excitedly in my ear: *Wouldn't it be a wonderful thing if I could get to your ex through a back door, by proving you're a murderer, since I couldn't pin the last killing on him?*

"Have you two already met?" I asked a little too casually. Like years ago, when Ned and Amanda's ex were competitive coworkers.

"I know his name," Amanda responded frostily, her first sign of spunk since she'd risen off the floor before.

"And I know yours," Ned practically purred, which made me want to shove his face into some used kitty litter.

A noise from the doorway attracted my attention. The two other detectives who'd arrived earlier stood there. One was Howard Wherlon, Ned's sometime sidekick who often showed up at scenes of Noralles's investigations. He had large bushy eyebrows and short, receding hair. As always, when I'd seen him, he was garbed in a drab gray suit.

The other had enthusiastically introduced himself as Detective Elliot Tidus. He looked maybe half the age of the fortyish Wherlon, and in his checkered sport jacket appeared more like an eager pre-owned car hawker than a professional cop.

"Detective Noralles," said Tidus as he strode into the room. "We're ready to start our interrogation." He smiled eagerly, as if awaiting his superior's blessing to pull out the rubber hoses and whip the truth out of these two suspect civilians.

"Very good," Noralles responded. "Detective Wherlon and you may take Ms. Ballantyne outside and question her. I'll ask Ms. Hubbard a few questions."

Whatever color Amanda had, besides the blood on her clothing, faded fast from her face. I wondered if she was about to faint. The uniform at the doorway, who'd stepped aside to allow the detectives to enter, must have wondered the same thing, since he strode forward as if to catch her when she fell.

Instead, she rose and looked absolutely regal as she stared down her nose — hard to do at her height compared with the taller Detective Noralles — and said, "Under the circumstances, I'd prefer that one of the other detectives question me."

"Under what circumstances?" asked the obviously naïve Tidus. Or maybe he was simply uninformed. He was clearly too junior to have been around during the Noralles-Hubbard bout.

"I'm totally objective," Noralles said, clearly stung, "but to avoid any appearance of impropriety I'll allow Detective Wherlon to question you, Ms. Hubbard. Detective Tidus, you come with me. You, too, Ms. Ballantyne."

Detective Tidus practically skipped from the room behind Ned and me, obviously itching to ask questions about the situation. Which might be a good thing. Maybe I could turn their focus back to why Amanda didn't want Ned to question her, and away from any incisive inquisition of me. Not that

I had anything to hide. I simply hated being subjected to a police interrogation.

I'd gone through way too many lately.

A result of being a murder magnet.

As we stepped outside onto Amanda's well-lit front porch, I heard her offer Detective Wherlon some tea. How polite, to entertain one's police examiner. I imagined his response would be negative, since serving refreshments might mean a sojourn into the kitchen, still under scrutiny by the SID.

Ned motioned me to the sole lawn chair on the wooden deck. He planted his behind against the railing and motioned for Tidus to take a similar spot.

"Okay, Kendra," Ned said. "Will you tell me what you know? Or do we need to play games again and let me extract the information word by word?"

He was referring to the fact that, as a lawyer, I knew to instruct a witness to answer questions only as asked, and not volunteer extraneous information. That could lead to long interrogations, where questions answered by "yes" or "no" were followed up by queries requiring more informative responses. In our prior course of conduct, Ned had been treated to some of my single-syllable replies, which drove him nuts.

Of course, the fact that we had a course of conduct for homicide interrogations didn't exactly cause me to turn cartwheels.

"No games, Ned. I'll tell you what happened." And I did, mostly ignoring young Tidus beside him and editing only a little. I told how Amanda had first invited me to her home, where she'd asked me to pet-sit while she fled her frightening foe, Leon.

But I didn't reveal to this sometimes snide cop how I'd recognized that Amanda had intended to manipulate me into caring for her calculating cats, or that I'd given in due to her tale of potential kitty-calamity.

Or that I'd finally figured out why she had done such a dastardly deed: She'd determined Jeff's destination, and planned all along to call me while with him. Her intent was to imply they'd arranged a Chicago assignation, leaving me in L.A. cleaning kitty litter.

Which should make me loathe the scheming bitch even more. Except that, when she worried about her pets enough to return early, alone, and to potentially brave her horrible harasser if he showed up again at her home, I'd discovered a soft spot inside for Amanda.

Of course, rot also resulted in soft spots . . .

"So Ms. Hubbard said she was leaving town because she felt threatened by Leon Lucero?" Detective Tidus interjected as I wound my story down.

"That's right," I said. "And I absolutely understood her rationale when the slimeball showed up and blocked my Beamer right in Amanda's driveway."

Ned ricocheted from the porch rail, sailing toward me and stopping only inches from where I sat. "He was here before? You talked to him?"

I nodded. "I figured out fast who he was. He demanded that I tell him where Amanda was. I was honest when I told him I wasn't sure, except that she wasn't at home. Wrong answer. He threatened not only Amanda, but me, too."

"Are you trying to hand me a motive why you might have killed that miserable so-and-so?"

"A fairly flimsy one, don't you think?"

"Could be. So, I assume you called 911, or at least whoever at the North Hollywood Station is managing Amanda's TRO."

I stuck my hand in the air, stopped it from shaking, and started counting my responses on my fingers. "One, I didn't call 911, since I didn't consider the situation life-threatening. Call me naïve, but I figured he

88

wouldn't hurt me, only Amanda."

"Okay, Ms. Naïve. Go on."

"Two, I don't know who at the station had a copy of Amanda's TRO, or what cops she'd spoken with to enforce it. I could only guess its contents, so it might have allowed Leon to be on the street but not on her property. Three, I didn't have a copy of the TRO to wave at Leon and your enforcement guys, and that's supposed to be necessary even when a TRO's on file. Four, he'd have been gone anyhow even if I had called you cops."

I paused for breath, allowing Noralles to get a word (or several) in edgewise. "So what's five?"

"Who says I have anything more to say?"

"You're still holding up your hand."

"Oh, right." I bent my final finger down, forming a fist that I quickly lowered. No sense getting Ned concerned I was about to kayo him — as Jeff had many years ago. "Finally, five. Even if I'd done all that, who's to say you cops would have paid the puniest bit of attention? The TRO's to protect Amanda Hubbard, which isn't exactly my name."

"They're sometimes worded to keep the stalkers certain distances from places generally occupied by their victims," Tidus intoned from over Ned's shoulder, as if quoting from some kind of cop manual.

"True," I acknowledged. "And that absolutely would have been my argument, if I'd had a copy and sought to have it enforced. But I didn't. Oh, one more thing you might be interested in knowing. I can't tell you how Leon got into Amanda's house last night, but I suspect it wasn't the first time." I explained how I'd found the refrigerator door inexplicably open a few nights earlier and patiently responded to his ensuing inquiries. Soon, I figured I'd conveyed all I could. Even so, I asked, "Any other questions?"

"Actually, yes." Ned had moved slowly back to where he'd stood before, and again he rested against the wooden porch railing. Tidus also scooted back and scowled in concentration. "One. Do you think Amanda killed Leon Lucero, and, if so, do you think it was in self-defense?"

"That's two questions, Detective. Or one compound one." I pondered for a prolonged moment how to respond. Not that my word would count as irrefutable evidence, but if I replied yes and no, in that order, would I help to put Amanda away for the rest of her life — and keep her the hell out of Jeff's?

Perhaps.

But I was still and again an officer of the court. Despite the alleged ethics violations of which I'd been unjustly accused, I didn't lie easily. Even when it gave me an advantage.

"I don't think she did it, Ned," I said. "In self-defense or otherwise."

He shook his head and sighed. "One day you'll agree with my assessment of a case, Kendra. You know I can still consider you a suspect here?"

"Only if you're really reaching for one," I responded while my insides plummeted at the mere idea.

"We'll see. In any event, I'll want to hear Amanda's answers. And though I sometimes want to kick your butt, I have to admit you've been right in some of my cases lately. If you don't think it was Amanda, who's your favorite suspect?"

"I don't have one yet, Ned."

"And if I asked you to stay out of this investigation and not even think of coming up with a suspect of your own . . . ?"

"Even if I agreed, you wouldn't believe me."

"You wouldn't believe yourself, either, Kendra." His head was still shaking as he disappeared into the house, Tidus behind him.

CHAPTER SIX

I considered chasing the two cops inside the house and checking on Amanda.

Bad idea. They'd officially dismissed me. And Lexie was waiting.

Carnie and Cherise? No sign of the clever cats. If not with their beleaguered owner, they'd made themselves scarce.

Besides, hanging around a murder scene was never my idea of a rollicking adventure, no matter how much experience I'd had with such situations lately.

I headed for Darryl's.

On the way I attempted to call Jeff to impart the latest events, but his cell phone was apparently turned off. I sighed at the sound of his outgoing voice message. I kinda missed the guy — or at least I missed what I'd assumed we had together till this latest Amanda mess. I hung up fast, leaving no message. His caller ID would let him know I'd tried, and though I wasn't at a loss for words — I never was — I admitted to myself some uncertainty about how relieved I should sound about Leon's demise, and how pleased I should be that Jeff's execrable ex was a suspect.

I was greeted at the doggy resort not only by Lexie and some other pups who'd escaped from their play areas, but also by another familiar state of affairs these days.

Darryl had collected yet another law client for me.

She sat in his office with her Pomeranian on her lap. Darryl stood at his establishment's big front desk, near where I entered.

"Her name is Mae," he whispered, then unobtrusively waved toward the large indoor window he'd installed so he could watch his world from the sanctity of his hideaway.

"The owner or the Pom?" I asked.

"The owner. Mae Sward. Her pup is Sugar."

As I entered Darryl's office with him right behind, I noticed that Sugar had one of those plastic cones cupping her head, the kind that kept dogs from gnawing stitches and skin after surgery.

"Kendra, meet Mae. Mae, this is the attorney I've told you about, Kendra —"

Mae Sward didn't dally for further introductions but stood, securing her dog under

93

her large left arm. She was more than a little bit chunky, with curly hair in an orange shade that suggested she'd tried hard to resemble her cute little Pom. She wore an oversized silky blue top over well-filled jeans.

"Oh, Kendra, I'm so glad to meet you." She stuck out her right hand, and I shook it. Her grip was businesslike. "Did Darryl tell you what happened?"

Her eyes, somewhat hidden beneath the flesh of her face, overflowed with tears. The poor lady's pain was nearly palpable. That spurred my sympathy.

"No, he didn't. Let's sit down, and you can fill me in."

"It's Sugar," she wailed. She settled back in her chair while removing the fluffy pup from under her arm and sticking her back on her ample lap.

"I'll leave you ladies to your legal discussion," Darryl said from the doorway and hastily retreated. Okay, he was a guy and so far this promised to be a girl thing, a session simmering with emotion. Only, I wished he'd stayed, at least till I understood the issues. I might be the one seeking emotional support. And a graceful out, if I didn't decide to take the case.

Sugar sat on Mae's legs, staring morosely. I admit to having an overactive imagination, especially when it comes to assuming I understand what an animal is attempting to convey, but I swear that Sugar was glumly attempting to tell her side of the story. Whatever it was.

I soon learned it from Mae, who had no compunction about revealing the terrible truth: "Sugar has been spayed," she moaned, as if that was the most horrifying sentence in the English language. Or in Pomeranian.

Mae stared with teary eyes as if anticipating my equally appalled reaction. But so far, I'd heard nothing especially revolting. In fact, pet neutering was usually considered to be necessary, both for ultimate health reasons and because of the excess of unwanted pups in shelters everywhere.

Not that I'd neutered Lexie yet. I still harbored hopes of her having baby Cavaliers someday. But I'd need to plan that day soon, if at all.

Unsure how to react, I simply reflected the woman's words back to her. "So Sugar has been neutered. I see."

"No, you don't. She's had three litters so far, and several of her puppies were promising show dogs. I'd hoped for more."

"So you had her spayed . . . why?"

"I didn't," Mae barked. "That's the whole

point. That horrible vet operated on her without even asking me. Look, my daughter is watching Sugar's latest litter now. They're at my house — three of the cutest little Pomeranian puppies imaginable. I wanted to hurry home to them, but I stayed a little later because Darryl said you'd pick up your dog around now, and I wanted to meet you. Long story short: I had to take Sugar to the vet this time to have her puppies since they were coming out slowly and I was worried about her. I left her overnight, and when I returned the next morning, there she was, nursing her pups — but she'd also been spayed!" Mae's eyes watered up all over again.

"If her birthing was especially difficult, maybe she needed the surgery for health reasons," I suggested reasonably.

"Did he talk to you already?" she spat. "That damned vet? That's what he said, but I know better. He did it out of spite. I'll tell you more about it later. But that's why I need a lawyer. That horrible doctor sawed my poor Sugar open and put her through all that trauma for no reason, and I want to sue the bastard."

"Sorry about that, Kendra," Darryl said a short while later. He had reclaimed his office, and I sat in a chair across from him, observing him over the mounds of materials cluttering his desk. I'd left Lexie outside the door before so as not to disturb Sugar and her overemotional owner, and now my little Cavalier curled contentedly on my lap, resting after her active day at Darryl's resort.

"I'm still unsure why Mae's so upset," I said.

"She obviously loves Pomeranian puppies, and now her little Sugar won't be able to have any more."

"Yeah, I got that. But since the vet said it was for health reasons —"

"She insists there's more to it. Look —" RMy lanky dog-loving friend leaned across his overcrowded desk and regarded me over his wire-rimmed glasses. "She's a relatively recent customer and has brought some of her other Poms in — older ones, not puppies. She was so excited about this impending litter, and then when things went wrong afterward, she started crying on my shoulder — figuratively, thank heavens. But she was really upset and asked if I knew any lawyers who understood dog lovers. Who would I recommend besides you?"

"Thanks," I said. "I'll look into it more, though I'll reserve judgment about whether I'll take the case. If there was a nefarious reason, and not just the poor mama-dog's health involved, as Mae implied, she might have a valid legal claim."

"And if it involves someone making a pooch suffer, I know you'll take it on. You're the world's greatest champion of pet problems, you know. The go-to attorney for animal dispute resolution."

"Flattery won't earn you forgiveness if this is a total fiasco of a case, Darryl, my friend. Right now, I don't have time to waste on frivolity and debacles."

"Enough stuff of your own going on? I figured. Pet-sitting without being sure of your assistant's assistance. A full plate of legal cases from your boss, Borden. And . . . any idea yet who slew Amanda Hubbard's stalker?"

Of course, the murder had already made the news. But I'd divulged it to Darryl first, while driving here earlier.

He, of all people, was well aware of my murder-magnet status. And I'd wanted him to learn of this latest one from me, not some terrible tabloid news-type.

"Not yet. And despite what I've said to my buddy Ned Noralles, I can't completely rule her out yet."

Darryl smiled a toothy grin that lit up his whole lean face. "Well, whoever dunnit, I know that my buddy Kendra Ballantyne will figure it out."

"That's not exactly a reputation I want to have," I told Lexie in the Beamer heading back toward home. "On the other hand —" I considered the deep satisfaction I felt when I ferreted out a murderer ahead of Detective Ned Noralles, who'd been so set on seeing me prosecuted for a couple of killings of which I'd been innocent. And —

My phone started singing "It's My Life," and I grinned. It sure was my life, and these days it was a pretty good one — with some obvious love-life and murder-magnet exceptions.

I immediately regretted having tempted fate by such a positive cogitation when the person who called — with a caller ID I didn't recognize — identified herself. "Hello, Kendra. I'm so glad I caught you. This is Corina Carey."

Oh, shit. She wasn't someone I'd ever met — nor had I ever wanted to. But I knew her only too well.

She was a news reporter on a local network affiliate TV station who seemed to hog air time by taking on the world's most notorious stories. Plus, she often wrote articles for local papers that were picked up by national news services.

I chose to stay silent. Hanging up might only result in another call. Or multiple messages if I chose not to answer.

And maybe on-air insinuations I wouldn't even be able to sue about, since they'd doubtless fall short of the legal definition of defamation.

But I did pull the car to the nearest curb. If my wrath rose as it was apt to, I didn't want to add a car accident to elevated blood pressure.

"Kendra? We must have a bad connection. Kendra Ballantyne? Can you hear me now?"

Unfortunately, I could. "Hello, Ms. Carey," I finally responded frostily.

"Oh, good. I'm a reporter, largely for the *National NewsShakers Show*." RAs if I didn't know. "I've started a story on police investigations in L.A. and your name came up regarding a homicide that just occurred today. You've been mentioned in broadcasts before, plus I looked you up on the Net and . . . well, this isn't the first murder investigation where you've been involved. I gather you're a lawyer but not in law enforcement. I'd love to come and interview you. Can we set up a time and place?"

Hoping my voice didn't shudder as much as my body, I searched my mind for an immediate reason to be unavailable for the next fifty years. Well, hell. I was a litigator. And a former murder suspect myself. I was used to unpleasant surprises, and knew how to handle every situation.

Almost.

My experience with the raft of reporters who'd covered my circumstances before had been anything but pleasant. Same went for those who'd sniffed around and spouted stories when I'd looked into murders to help friends.

"I'm sorry, Ms. Carey, but I'm really not interested." As if this pushy reporter — a redundancy in expression, of course — was prone to take no for an answer.

"I understand," she said much too smoothly. I stared at Lexie, who sat shotgun and regarded me with sympathetic yet curious brown eyes. "But if I don't get to talk to you, I'll only have your story from other people, who'll give me their perspectives, which may not be yours."

"If the story you're talking about concerns the apparent murder that occurred earlier today in Sherman Oaks, then I really don't have a perspective. Goodbye, Ms. Carey."

"Goodbye for now, Kendra," she responded, and I heard a smile every bit as snide as one of Amanda's in her voice. "I'll talk to you soon. Count on it."

My cell phone didn't ring again until we'd reached our garage-sweet-home and I'd settled down after organizing what apparel to take along for the next day and taking time to veg out in our compact living room.

I had laid my cell on the coffee table near my comfy beige sectional sofa and it both sang and vibrated on the glass surface, startling Lexie and me.

I peered at it suspiciously, having hated to hear from the last caller. This time, though, I nearly grinned in pleasure.

Jeff.

"Hi," I said perkily after flipping the phone open. I eyed the table where I'd balanced my dinner, knowing that Lexie's nose would nudge it, followed by her eager tongue, if I didn't watch it. "Did you see that you missed my call before?" He could have called back earlier. "There's some stuff I wanted to tell you about, but right now Lexie and I are heading to your place to keep Odin company tonight. How are things?" Like, are you surviving Chicago alone now, without having Amanda there to comfort?

"What the hell is going on, Kendra?" he demanded, startling me. "How did that jerk

Leon wind up dead in Amanda's house? And with all your experience dealing with such things — not to mention the fact you're a goddamned lawyer — why the devil aren't you helping her?"

Chapter Seven

I couldn't quite respond for a few appalled instants. Then my words dripped so frostily from my lips that I might have been sipping a Frappuccino. "I'm delighted to speak with you, too. I really don't have any specific information to impart to you about the recently departed Leon and your dear Amanda. I merely attempted to call you earlier to let you know what had occurred. And even though Amanda isn't exactly my favorite person, if it appears that she didn't commit murder, then I'll commiserate with her — figuratively. I'm not exactly eager to subject myself to her difficult presence again. You're the investigator, Jeff. Utilize your license and come back to L.A. to help your beloved ex, if that's what you want."

This time, the pause wasn't from my perspective. Back stiff despite the comfortableness of my soft sofa cushions, I waited for Jeff to jump in and say he'd take control.

Or better yet, to apologize.

And waited.

And was finally rewarded with something substantially less than an admission of contrition. But at least it wasn't accusatory this time, either.

"You're right, Kendra," he said slowly. "That wasn't fair. After all the good work you did to help me clear myself of murder, I guess I started taking too much for granted."

I'll say. But I kept that thought to myself.

He continued, "You know how I feel about Amanda now, and —"

"No, Jeff, actually I don't," I interrupted. "So what if you made a huge pronouncement telling her to use another P.I., presumably choosing me over her? Talk, as they say, is cheap — and my pet-sitting and legal services aren't. I've only acted as an intern P.I. when it was the only way I could get information to assist in cases *I* chose. Amanda's isn't one of them."

"I understand." His soft voice smacked of remorse at last. "And I will be home soon. I only hope you'll understand if I try to help Amanda through this. It doesn't mean there's still anything between us —"

"Except history. I get it." But I didn't believe it.

As we hung up a minute later, after good-byes that were more uncomfortable than amatory, I couldn't help recalling all over again what a loser I was in the long-term lover selection process.

Well, Odin wasn't to blame for his master's treachery in dealing with females. That was why I gathered my clothing and Lexie within the next five minutes and hustled us out the door and down the steps from our apartment.

Just in time to see Rachel pull her small, recently acquired blue sedan through the security gates and into the driveway. The new, used car had been her dad's gift to allow her to assist me in pet-sitting. She opened the garage door remotely and drove inside, and was out of the car almost immediately.

"I did it, Kendra!" she shouted with exuberance that left no doubt what she was talking about. She'd landed a speaking role in a film — major or minor, it didn't matter. In her mind, at least, she was on her way to a substantial starring career.

"I'm so happy for you," I gushed, almost meaning it, as she stopped near enough to bend and stroke Lexie, then rose with a huge grin. She squeezed me in a healthy hug, bumping her huge shoulder bag against my side.

"It's a chick flick about a mother and three daughters," she explained as she pulled away, "and I play their next door neighbor who's the same age as the oldest. Daughter, that is, not the mother. I'm on camera four times, and I have at least a couple of lines, too. I'm so excited!"

"Justifiably."

How could I do anything but feel happy for someone so young and optimistic? Was I ever there? At her age, I'd been intensely immersed in undergraduate studies, since I'd planned all along on law school. But surely I'd been as certain as she that every nuance of my fondest dreams would come true and my life would be spectacular.

Well, hell. Most of the time it was. Or had been. And these days it was absolutely getting back on track — even if my caboose was headed in a way different direction than I'd initially anticipated.

"So when does shooting start?" I asked.

"Soon. Not right away, so I'll still be able to do some pet-sitting. But for when I can't, here's some help — I hope." She reached into her tote bag and extracted what appeared to be a tabloid news-simulator . . . er, newspaper.

Instinctively, I yanked my hands away, causing a gleam of indignation to appear on Rachel's gamin face.

"It's for you," she insisted. "Look." She yanked the pages open and scanned down some columns until she spied what she was searching for. "Here." She pointed to something in a calendar section.

I looked at the top of the page first. This wasn't a tabloid but a throwaway sheet from a neighborhood on L.A.'s west side.

And the entry to which Rachel was pointing?

It was a notice of the supposed second meeting of a group calling itself the Pet-Sitters Club of SoCal, claiming it was a new professional organization. The group would get together this Wednesday evening.

A professional pet-sitters' group? Hey, what an intriguing idea!

Rachel must have read the interest on my face. "See? If you go there, maybe you'll meet others who can help you out when I can't."

"Rachel, you're the greatest." And this time, I was the initiator of a huge hug.

Causing a jealous jump from my currently ignored canine. Both Rachel and I bent to rectify that sorry situation.

"I'll walk Widget tomorrow," Rachel said.

"Any other pets you'd like me to check on?"

"Sure," I said. "Come up to our place, and we'll work out who goes where."

And so Lexie and I got an even later start on our late-day pet-sitting service, which didn't much matter since Rachel took over two of the visits.

Adorable assistant!

Especially since she'd given me a hint on how to recruit her replacement — if necessary.

I'd kept the Stromboli assignment to myself. I really liked Dana Maroni's well-trained shepherd mix. And my insatiable curiosity and canine-loving led me to want to check on his apparently lonely next door neighbor.

Sure enough, Stromboli seemed excited to see me. Or at least his supper. With Lexie waiting patiently — I hoped — for me in the Beamer, Stromboli and I took a nice, exercise-energizing walk through his flat residential neighborhood.

I peered through a back window into the neighbor's yard before and after our evening stroll. Sure enough, that middle-sized wire-haired pup was there both times. Alone. Tethered to something near his back door.

Didn't the people who lived there ever let

him in? Or even, if he was a dedicated outside dog, didn't they show him some occasional appreciation in that large, lonely yard?

I'd have to ask Dana on her return, scheduled for later in the week.

Meanwhile . . . well, okay, I admit it. I'm a big softy, especially when it comes to apparently abandoned dogs. After settling Stromboli back in his abode, I went into his backyard and looked at the neighbor's dog.

He looked back at me, ears down and dejected.

"Can you come here?" I asked him.

He appeared to perk up a whole lot at the attention, and he did extend his lead far enough to reach the yard-dividing fence.

I looked around, in case his owners were around and interested enough to chastise me for calling him.

No movement at all from that house.

So I reached into my pocket and gave the pup a biscuit. Bad form for a professional pet-sitter? You bet! How would I know if this particular pup had a major biscuit allergy?

I doubted he did, and this was a fairly vanilla kind of doggy cracker.

The dog obviously appreciated it. I noticed, close up, just how skinny he was, too.

Was someone starving him, not only for attention, but for food, too?

I'd have to find out. If I called Animal Control, though, they might remove him and then not be able to find him a suitably loving home.

And what if I was wrong, and all was right with this neighboring dog?

For now, I'd just wait and see what happened as I continued to visit Stromboli.

Finally it was time for Lexie and me to head to Odin's place. Jeff's place, too, although we went there for the lonesome pup that night, and not his mind-taxing master.

The adorable Akita was delighted to see us, and we three engaged in a fast-paced tramp beneath the streetlights in the Sherman Oaks neighborhood, both to settle the pups' evening evacuation urges and to exercise my beleaguered brain into exhaustion.

The last part didn't work too well.

Even so, I took my shower and prepared for bed. Good thing I'd brought along a folder full of cases downloaded from the Yurick firm's online legal service. Since elder law was the firm's focus, I was determined to learn all I could about how courts viewed senior citizens. I've recognized, after long experience, that case law isn't the most stimulating of reading material, unless one concentrates on the human aspect of who did what to whom. Even then, clerks assigned to appellate judges tend to be detailed and dry in their writing — and they're the ones who do at least the initial drafting of published decisions.

As anticipated, my eyelids started sinking after only a few minutes of studying the pages.

I'd nearly fallen asleep, canine companions snoring on the floor beneath the bed, when my cell phone sang.

I stared at it, charging at its place on the bedside stand, for a few seconds. This was the time that Jeff usually called to make some sexy insinuations before we both dropped off to sleep, but our last conversation had surely snuffed out any sizzling embers between us, at least for now.

But as I glanced at the caller ID, I saw that it indeed was the owner of the home and the bed in which I reposed.

"Hi, Jeff," I said in a soft yet neutral tone. I didn't need further verbal abuse to disabuse me of the idea of sleeping that night. I wanted my rest.

"Hi, Kendra. Are you in bed yet?" His soft, suggestive tone didn't even hint that he recalled our earlier fiasco of a conversation. Did I want to play this game now, when my mind, apparently unlike his, was hung up on our dismal dialogue?

"Yes, I am." My tone stayed businesslike, avoiding any semblance of sensuality.

"Good. Me, too. I'm sleeping in the nude tonight, and I plan to dream of you. And, Kendra? I'm coming home early so we can talk. See you the day after tomorrow."

Chapter Eight

"Hey, Borden," I said second thing the next morning, popping my head into my senior partner's office. "Have a minute?"

"Always for you, Kendra," he replied. "Almost. Unless I've got to talk to a client. Or another attorney at the firm. Or —"

I laughed. "Okay, I know where I rate. But I caught you between crises, so I'm sneaking in." Which I did. I slid into my current favorite of the diversely styled chairs facing his attractive old desk — complete with rococo carved back and arms, and blue embroidered upholstery.

Borden's Hawaiian aloha shirt du jour was muted aqua covered in a print of large pineapples.

"How was your pet-sitting this morning?" he asked as soon as I was seated.

"Just fine," I responded. It had been the first thing I'd accomplished that day after Lexie, Odin, and I completed our morning routine. My rounds had been abbreviated since I still had Rachel's assistance for now. I'd left Lexie with Odin, since I had one more night to care for Jeff's Akita. And tomorrow, when he came home, where would my Cavalier and I sleep?

At our own digs, I felt certain.

Almost, my mind echoed Borden's earlier word.

"I didn't get back to you yesterday on the complaint you drafted for the Shermans." His senior citizen clients with the big beef with the small and shoddy Santa Barbara resort. "I think it's fine. Okay if I ask them to come in this afternoon to go over it?"

"Sure," I said. "Oh, and I wanted to tell you about another possible pet law matter. Darryl referred me to someone else, Mae Sward, who said her Pomeranian was spayed by her vet without her permission. I'll need more info before saying yes or no, since the neutering was done in the aftermath of the poor little dog's birthing some pups. Mae said the vet's motive was an ulterior one, and he didn't spay strictly to preserve the mama's health."

"Sounds potentially interesting. Any chargeable fees?" Borden knew full well that many of my animal dispute resolution cases were less than lucrative, and not because I could dispose of them by spending minimal time.

"Unknown so far, but I wouldn't count on redoing the office décor on our receipts."

"What redecorating are you talking about? Don't you like our ambiance?" I was sure his apparent affront was a put-on. At least I hoped so. No way did I want to injure this kind and generous man's very deep feelings.

"Couldn't love it more, Borden. That's why I don't want to earn the firm too much bread, or one of the other attorneys might want to apply some of the dough toward alternate decoration of our former restaurant digs."

"Who'd want to do that?"

"You tell me."

"No one," he insisted.

"I agree," I agreed.

We smiled at one another.

"Troublemaker," he accused.

"If the shoe fits . . ." I stared down at the black leather loafers on my feet, which fit just right. I'd dressed down just a little, since it wasn't a court day, in nice charcoal slacks and a silky blue blouse.

"Okay, then," he said. "Go to it, kid. I love your form of ADR. I'll be eager to hear how this one turns out."

I grinned all the way down the hall toward my office, turned the corner and headed down the next hall.

"Hi, Kendra," said Geraldine Glass, heading the opposite way from me with a cup of coffee in her hand. One of Borden's former law school buddies who'd joined the firm as a partner, she was as senior a citizen as he was. Her curly brown hair was decorated by her reading glasses snugged up on her head today and acting like a headband.

"Morning," I responded, inhaling the rich caffeine as we passed one another. The next person I noted was the firm's receptionist, perky young Mignon who sat at a big desk at the entry where the hostess had once greeted diners at this former restaurant.

"Hi, Kendra," she said, a lot less perkiness than usual in her singsong tone. Even her auburn curls seemed a smidgen droopy.

"Everything okay?" I asked immediately, stopping beside her chair.

"Absolutely," she sang, somewhat off-key. Her eyes met mine and her head tilted sideways in what appeared to be a signal.

I looked in the direction she'd indicated, toward the room that was once a bar and was now the firm's main conference room.

My breathing suddenly stopped, then started again. Fast.

"Hello, Amanda," I said. "What are you doing here?"

We sat in my office, as Amanda requested. A good call, I thought. If we got into a heated exchange, I'd no desire to allow all my coworkers their daily dose of fun by eavesdropping. Not to mention ammunition to ambush me with if ever they needed blackmail material.

"This is very nice," Amanda said, looking around my cluttered but comfortable environment, with its lived-in law office look. My desk was Early Litigation style, with lots of stacks of papers on top. My chairs were ergonomic, upholstered in blue, and my rug was rugged Berber.

I was unsure how to react. Amanda acted humble, not haughty or hysterical. She wore a tailored skirt and blouse that bordered on conservative, instead of underscoring how attractive she was.

What did she want, inserting herself so moderately into my milieu? I sure as hell didn't trust her.

And how had her latest contact been with Jeff? In between his two phone calls to me yesterday, shading from insults to almost apology, had she somehow determined to dump him?

Well, sitting at my desk, waiting till she got good and ready to speak her piece, wasn't exactly my style.

"Why are you here, Amanda?" I echoed my earlier startled greeting.

"Cherise and Carnie sent me." Her smile almost seemed tentative, as if testing whether I enjoyed her attempt at humor.

"How are they?" I played along. "Have they left any more mice as presents? I've been wondering whether their gifts to me were really intended to be threats. Maybe they gave Leon his, then screwdrivered him to death."

Amanda's lovely face faded to ashen. "That's not a joke," she rasped, then dropped her gaze to her lap. "It isn't my kitties the cops think did it, but me."

"If so, you have defenses, Amanda," I responded seriously. "Have you spoken with your attorney?"

"Yes, but I'm not sure Mitch feels comfortable handling a possible capital criminal case." She swallowed hard, and when she lifted her eyes to stare into mine, they were definitely misty. "He might refer me to someone else. And with your background in helping innocent people who're accused of murder, I told him I want you both to get together and agree on who I should hire.

Will you help me, Kendra?"

Why should I? my mind immediately shot back. *You've been a barbed thorn in my side from even before I knew you existed.* But the remainder of my brain ordered that edge of my mind to stay open, at least a little.

"What's in it for me?" I heard myself demand. "You haven't even paid me for pet-sitting yet." Oh, well. So much for remaining even a nuance neutral.

"I will," she said with a sigh. "And if you help clear me of killing Leon, I promise I'll get out of Jeff's life, forever."

"You're willing to put that in writing?" I shot back.

"If you want."

"I want," I said. "It's an old saying among lawyers that verbal agreements aren't worth —"

"The paper they're written on. I've heard it." Her tone was taking on its old edge once more. Which made me feel a teensy bit more sure she was serious.

At least for this moment.

I turned to the computer sitting on the side of my desk and typed up a short yet official-looking contract, inserting boiler-plate by copying and pasting from a fine form I'd previously created for a very differ-ent purpose. Not only did it appear binding; it *was* binding — once we'd both signed it. In duplicate. Assuming a court would enforce it in the event of a breach.

Dumb? Decidedly. Even so, it assisted me with arguable leverage over Amanda if I ever wished to assert it — in the event she truly was innocent, and I assisted her in extricating herself from this mess.

"Good," I said, handing Amanda her fully executed agreement. "So now I'll need more information about anyone you think could be a suspect, and whoever else you're aware of who knew Leon. Plus, we'll need to set up a meeting with Mitch Severin. Want me to come to your home later this afternoon? Or have you been permitted to go back, since it's a crime scene under investigation?"

"Not yet. Cherise, Carnie, and I are staying with one of my coworkers for now."

"Okay, then, when and where should we meet with Mitch?" The logical location popped into my mind. "How about at your medical office? Tomorrow. You can introduce me to some of the folks you work with — notably, those who knew Leon, too."

Amanda's turn to seem startled. "You don't really think anyone there killed him, do you?"

"My mind is open to every possible perpetrator, and yours should be, too. Right now, you need to prepare that list of everyone you're aware of who knew Leon, and that means doctors, other assistants, any of your neighbors who might have had run-ins with him . . . anyone."

"You're right," she said. "Of course. You've been through this before."

Yep, that's what murder magnets do. Not that I let her in on that definitely disquieting thought.

She stood and held out her hand. "Thanks, Kendra. I can't tell you how much this means to me."

"Me, too," I said. "I'll let Jeff know." But I couldn't quite manage a snide smile at her sad look as she exited my office door.

I managed only one more meeting that Tuesday. The Shermans with the Santa Barbara beef were unavailable until Thursday. But Mae Sward, my new client with the Pomeranian problem, had called and spoken with Mignon, who'd set up a time later that day.

She arrived with Sugar, still clad in her surgical collar, on a rhinestone-studded leash matching Mae's sparkling handbag. Her large figure was well-hidden behind the long jacket of her elegant gray suit.

My non-court attire, though nice, didn't match her chicness, but I didn't feel over-shadowed, either. "Come in, Mae," I told her. "You, too, Sugar. How's the mom business?"

"Her pups are getting along just fine," Mae said, beaming, as she followed me into my digs. But her pleasure paled as she took her seat. "It's so hard to believe this is her last litter." A tear escaped the edge of one brown eye and she swiped it away with a gesture suggesting determination. "I want you to sue that terrible vet," she said. "And it's not just for the money. If I could turn back the clock and have Sugar the way she was, that's how I'd be happiest."

"I understand," I said. Interesting idea. I wondered briefly how much litigation could be avoided if the parties could simply march backward in time and amend critical incidents like accidents that caused suable situations.

Well, heck, that could put poor litigators like me plum out of business. Good thing sci-fi couldn't be integrated into real life. Unless one counted all the stuff of one-time fiction that eventually entered our lives . . . Submarines. Space travel.

Okay, I hardly had time to philosophize with an eager client occupying my office.

"You were going to tell me why you thought Sugar's vet decided to spay her for nonmedical purposes."

"He hates me. He's always telling me how to take care of my little darlings, then bawling me out for feeding them treats and making sure the mommies have lots of babies."

"Those could be health reasons for Sugar," I rationalized. "We'll need something more."

"Well, I reported him to the state one time before this for how he treated Sugar and a couple of my other Poms. He insisted that one of his assistants hold them when they got shots, and even had one muzzled when she nipped at him. He treated them like . . . well, dogs. And he was really mad when an inspector came to check him out."

Somehow, I couldn't quite get excited about this terrible veterinary behavior. And I hadn't yet done any research on the kind of claim I could make for involuntary neutering of one's pet. But I would.

"What is it you want out of a lawsuit, if we file it?"

"I'd love to have his license pulled, but the board didn't seem inclined to do anything before, so I don't trust them now. I'd like a lot of money from that horrible man, enough that it'll hurt. Okay?"

"We'll see what we can do. One question, though. If you didn't like this vet, why didn't you go to another one?"

She regarded me as if I'd suddenly grown stupid. "Because he's the best in my neighborhood. His reputation is great, and everyone else loves him. I wouldn't even think of taking my babies to someone less well regarded."

"Of course." I mentally shook my head. Mae might have an arguable claim, but I figured she wouldn't exactly impress a jury with her emotionalism over her Pom and against her vet. That meant a possible ADR situation, resulting in some kind of settlement that would satisfy her.

Did I like her case? Not really. But I also despised the idea that her vet could have harmed her pet out of revenge against her.

"Okay, then," I said. "Give me the particulars."

Over the next fifteen minutes, we discussed names, dates, and details. Then I said, "I'm going to call Dr. . . ." I looked down at my notes. "Dr. Thomas Venson. I'll ask if he has an attorney, and if so request a meeting."

"You mean I have to see that horrible man again?"

"You'd have to face him in court anyway,"

I reminded her.

"Well, all right." But she seemed utterly disconcerted.

The vet did indeed have an attorney, not that the receptionist revealed who. Even so, she promised to set up a meeting for the next afternoon and suggested a time that her boss wouldn't be busy with a patient.

What with my planned visit at Amanda's medical office in the morning and a meeting with a new pet-sitters' society in the evening, tomorrow would be a thoroughly intense day.

Was this day done with surprises? No way! My phone rang just after Mae and Sugar had skedaddled.

"Hi, Kendra," said a voice from my not-too-distant past. "This is Baird."

Judge Baird Roehmann was a jurist with roamin' hands whom I'd known well in my days as a litigator with the Marden law firm. He'd gotten a temporary restraining order against *me* when he'd believed I was stalking him a few months earlier.

Ergo, hearing from him was one huge surprise.

"Are you busy for dinner tonight?" he asked. "I have an issue I'd really like to run by you."

As always, when I'd not needed something

from him, my gut reaction kicked into negative mode. "I'm sorry, Baird. It's great to hear from you, but —"

"Please, Kendra? I'm really sorry about how things were left with us before, and I'd really like to talk to you."

Would wonders never cease in this amazing day? First, Amanda's agreement to leave Jeff forever — at least if I helped her.

Now this. There was a humbleness to Baird's tone that I'd never before imagined even existed inside him.

If nothing else, it stoked my curiosity.

"I don't have a lot of time, Baird, but if you can meet me at seven-thirty in the Valley . . ." Past my prime pet-sitting time.

"Done. Tell me where and I'll be there."

CHAPTER NINE

Despite an inclination to dash through my pet-sitting duties that evening, I couldn't help it. I knocked on Stromboli's neighbor's door.

As my shepherd-mix charge had cavorted in his own backyard, that poor wiry pup had slunk as close as his lead would allow, wagging his tail and entreating my attention. I, of course, heaved a treat over the fence as my sympathies soared. Sure, the canine could be a skilled con-dog, but I'd always seen him leashed outside without an iota of human notice — either for the dog or for my interference.

So as soon as Stromboli was through inhaling his dinner and had a final frenetic foray into his yard, I said my good nights to him and hied my irate self next door.

The house was quaint and cottagelike, but looked as if no one had mowed the front lawn or trimmed the rosebushes for eons.

To my amazement, I got an answer to the doorbell — and not just the dog's "someone's intruding on my turf" barkfest. A middle-aged woman pulled open the door. "Yes?" she asked with a somewhat fearful frown. Her loose blue jeans and Universal Studios sweatshirt didn't say much more about her than her suspicious brown eyes, but her short, well-styled hair, complete with pale highlights, suggested she gave some consideration to her appearance.

I held out my hand. "Hi," I said in a tone assumed for its friendliness, to throw her off guard. "I'm Kendra Ballantyne. I'm a pet-sitter, and I'm taking care of Stromboli next door, while Dana Maroni's out of town."

She said nothing during my pregnant pause.

"I noticed you have a dog. I've seen him in your yard."

Still not a word.

"Do you ever need a pet-sitter to walk him during the day, or take care of him when you're not around?"

"No," she said solemnly and started to shut the door.

I stuck my vulnerable toe out and levered it, in my nice black loafers, to keep her from closing me out altogether. "The thing is, he

looks lonesome sometimes, and I'd —"
Surely my accusation hadn't been especially
harsh . . . yet.

Even so, tears welled in the woman's eyes.
"Aren't we all?" She sounded so bitter that
the words I bit back tasted terrible in my
mouth. She again attempted to shut the
door, but I hadn't removed my shoe, nor
the toes within it. She stared down at the
offending intrusion, then back into my face.
"I know you mean well, Ms. Ballantyne, but
taking care of Meph is the least of my
problems now."

"Meth — as in methamphetamines?" I
tried to keep her talking.

"Meph, as in Mephistopheles. That cute
little terrier is actually a devil."

"He still doesn't deserve to be shut in the
yard with no attention twenty-four/seven."
Okay, could be I'd blown it by my inability
to keep my criticisms curled inside.

The woman blinked and allowed her bot-
tom lip to sag, as if amazed at my effrontery.
She immediately closed her mouth, and the
action apparently created a pump that set
her tears flowing.

"Sorry," I said hastily. "It's not really my
business. Except that it is. Pets, I mean, are
my business, and I hate to see one seem
neglected."

"People can be neglected, too, Ms. Ballantyne." She threw up her hands and attempted to erase the residue of her words from the air. "Never mind. You didn't come here to hear about me."

"Even so, if there's anything I can do . . . I'm sorry, I didn't get your name."

"I didn't give it, but it's Maribelle Openheim. And I'll try to pay more attention to Meph, okay? Now leave me alone."

"Sure," I said softly. "But obviously you have something on your mind. If there's anything I can do to help . . ."

"There is. Get your foot out of my door."

I did, and she closed that door firmly in my face.

I squeezed Lexie in an extra-loving hug later after retrieving her from her daily delights at Darryl's and driving her home with me. Then I deposited her gently back on the floor. "I won't be long, I promise," I vowed as I prepared to abandon her for a couple of hours at our garage-top home while I joined Judge Baird Roehmann at a restaurant.

Near the door, my adorable tricolor Cavalier cocked her head and regarded me solemnly as if attempting to assess my veracity.

"We'll get together with Odin afterward, okay?"

As if understanding and agreeing, she wagged her tail.

I had to hustle from our hilltop abode down the sloped street toward Cahuenga Boulevard. After further discussion with Baird, I'd selected one of my favorite neighborhood bistros, one that served both great food and delightful wine.

On the way, my cell phone sang. Amanda. Of course. "I have everything all set up at my office tomorrow," she said.

"Good. See you then."

"And you'll figure out who killed Leon?"

"I'll try."

"Well, succeed!" she exploded. "We have a contract now, and that damned Detective Noralles won't leave me alone. He just called again. All those questions and insinuations, and —"

"That's his job, Amanda," I interjected irritably. Not that I enjoyed defending Ned.

"Well, yours is to fix things for me. Fast." Before I had a chance to shove some reality toward her, she hung up.

I considered calling back and telling her exactly where to go — like, to court and to prison, sans my investigative assistance. But I absorbed my anger instead — this time.

That didn't leave me in the best of moods to meet Baird.

The tall, silver-haired jurist waited for me in a wooden-backed booth, a small candle glimmering in a multifaceted glass on the table. He stood as I joined him . . . and shook my hand.

Shook my hand? And immediately released it? This from the judge who'd always given me the once-over, his look lingering on my bust, every time we met outside a courtroom?

Something was obviously up with him. Since he'd invited me to dinner, I suspected I'd soon find out what it was.

I slid into the booth, then allowed Baird to order a bottle of wine. He was the smooth sort, and although I'd seldom allowed him to treat me to meals, the few times we'd eaten together I'd been impressed by his expertise in vintages.

I'd not been impressed by his assumption that plying females with wine led to bedroom gymnastics later. That was one reason I clothed myself conservatively that night: a sexless beige shirt with a high collar that skimmed my chin, and loose navy slacks.

"So how are you, Baird?" I inquired after our server, a nice young man surely too homely to be one of L.A.'s usual wannabe movie stars, had served our wine, taken our orders, and obsequiously sailed toward the kitchen.

"I've been better, Kendra." Although his voice held the peal he'd practiced to allow its resonance through any courtroom, it lacked its usual verve.

Knowing a cue when I heard one, I asked, "What's wrong?"

He sighed, staring with solemn brown eyes over his slightly misshapen nose. Rumor had it that he'd broken it while boxing as an undergrad, but I'd never confirmed if that was myth and part of his mystique, or an actual occurrence. "I asked you to join me tonight since I knew you'd understand. Daisy is gone."

Daisy. A recent lover who had succumbed to the judge's charms? A particularly skilled court clerk who'd grown tired of Baird's lustfulness and left?

"I'm sorry. But I didn't know Daisy." And wasn't sure I should have.

"She was so beautiful. So loving. And I simply don't know what I'll do without her." He gulped down a goblet of Merlot, then filled his glass again.

Okay, he'd handed me a hint with the word "loving." That surely couldn't apply to an assistant. Had Baird been married all this time? If so, Daisy's defection, with all the sexual harassment Baird foisted on females on and off the job, didn't seem a stretch. Or was she a longtime, long-suffering lover?

"I'm sorry," I repeated, then, still searching for a clue, said, "Tell me about her."

"You never met her?" He glared as if I'd insulted him, but then his expression mellowed. "I guess not. We've known each other more professionally than personally, haven't we?" I nodded, and he continued, "Well, Daisy was the most beautiful damned Dalmatian you could ever imagine."

Oh, so that was Daisy's pedigree!

For the next forty minutes, over appetizers, salads, and entrées, Baird all but bawled on my shoulder about his dear, departed dog. And I absolutely sympathized with him, which mellowed my post-Amanda mood.

His mourning didn't appear to injure his appetite. Or maybe it was the tastiness of the excellent French cuisine that kept him eating. In any event, over coffee, he finally ended his extolling of Daisy's virtues.

"I'm really sorry, Baird," I said yet again. "I know how hard it is to lose a pet you really care about."

Poor Daisy's problem had been simply

growing old. And I honestly did share Baird's pain. I'd had pets before Lexie that I'd lost, and each time I'd felt I'd never get over it.

That thought triggered a suggestion. "Have you considered adopting another dog?"

He glared as if I'd told him to dine on Daisy's remains. "No. How could I? It would feel . . . disloyal."

This from a judge who hopped from one willing female to the next without compunction, flirting shamelessly with unwilling ones in between.

"I understand. There's no way to replace her. But having another pet might help to ease your pain."

"I'm lonely Kendra," he asserted, then appeared aghast at the revelation. He inhaled a final swig of wine, then shook his silver mane. "I know what you're thinking. A man as well-liked as I am, who never lacks for female company . . . how could I possibly feel lonely? Well, if I had one woman I really cared about, one who'd be good company every night, then it might not feel so bad to go home without Daisy to greet me."

"Sure, Baird." Surely he wasn't suggesting that I could be that sole eternal female. Was he?

No, thank heavens. "If you've any lady friends that you think might be worth introducing me to, ones with looks and brains" — I noticed which he'd fed out first — "please introduce me. Meantime, I'll consider adopting another dog. I still can't get over the fact you decided not to return to your rightful place as one of this city's premier litigators to join Borden Yurick's firm and stay a pet-sitter, too. That's why I thought you might understand about Daisy."

"I do, Baird. I'll think about who to introduce you to."

"And if you have any ideas about another dog . . . well, give me a little time, but I'll want to hear your suggestions."

Which was one heck of a first. Baird Roehmann agreeing to listen instead of grope?

Not that he totally disabused me of my recollections of his penchants for pinches. When we eventually said goodbye beneath the lights outside the restaurant, he enveloped me in a judicial bear hug — followed by an unambiguous feeling up of my butt.

That night, I elected to take the offensive. Instead of waiting for Jeff to call after the pups and I had prepared for bed, I phoned him. "Have you spoken with Amanda today?" I asked.

"Yes, and she says you drive a hard bargain, Kendra."

"Well, you're the P.I. If you want, you can investigate Leon's murder on her behalf, instead of me. That way she won't be contractually obligated to remove herself from your life." And perhaps she would stop provoking me . . . please!

"I was serious when I chose you over her, Kendra," Jeff said. "None of us could have foreseen Leon's murder, and I appreciate your trying to help her. And I apologize for yelling at you for *not* helping her. Once this is behind us, I really will insist that she stay out of my life. Okay?"

"Yes, but —"

"I'm lying here in the nude now, thinking about you . . . and how things'll be when I'm back home tomorrow night."

Which was exactly what I thought about as I attempted to drop off to sleep after we hung up. Only . . . I realized I was far from sure about how I wanted things to unfold after Jeff's return home.

CHAPTER TEN

I'd have overslept the next morning, the clock radio's crooning notwithstanding, if Lexie and Odin hadn't leapt onto my bed and let me know it was time to eat and walk, not necessarily in that exact order.

I obeyed their instructions, then gave Rachel a call from my cell phone to ensure she was on duty that day. She assured me she was, although she issued a warning that she'd need to go to some readings and rehearsals next week.

With luck, I'd have a backup assistant figured out by then.

Odin appeared so sad when Lexie and I started to depart that I decided to provide him with a special treat. It meant I'd need to return to Jeff's in the evening, but, especially after his speech last night that I nearly believed, I had assured myself I could handle seeing him again if I happened to be there dropping Odin off when he appeared.

"It's been awhile since you've visited Darryl's," I told Odin. "How about a doggy resort for today?"

He exuberantly wagged the enthusiastic, fuzzy tail curled over his back, and the decision was made.

I couldn't spend much time at Darryl's though.

"Busy day planned?" my lanky friend asked from his front desk after greeting the pups and me.

"Absolutely." I listed the rundown: Amanda's office, a visit to the potential defendant vet, and a pet-sitters' conclave. "Not to mention the usual."

"Pet-sitting and playing lawyer," he finished for me. "No wonder these two can't keep up with you." He bent to stroke Lexie and Odin, whom I hadn't let loose yet, despite their fascinated observation of the doggy resort's multiple pup-play areas.

I accomplished the items Darryl had delineated first. Borden also appeared amused at my many irons in my well-stoked fire that day, as did receptionist Mignon and a couple of the senior-citizen attorneys who lingered around as I explained them all.

Then I was off to Amanda's office.

The address she'd given was on Third Street near Cedars-Sinai Medical Center.

There were lots of doctors' offices in several nearby buildings, many served by the same overstuffed parking lots. Nevertheless, the Beamer and I found a spot, and I hurried inside and up an elevator to the designated suite.

The reception area was decorated with a plethora of original paintings — big surprise after Amanda's description of her doctor's patients. What was unexpected was that few were seascapes. Apparently Amanda's affinity was not everyone else's.

When I gave my name, an efficient-looking Asian lady behind a big, glass window scanned a sheet of paper. "Which doctor are you here to see? I don't find you on the appointment list."

"I'm here to see one of their assistants, Amanda Hubbard."

Was it my imagination, or did the woman's expression morph a mite into irritation? In any event, she was too much of a pro to say anything, nasty or nice. "I'll let her know you're here."

"You're Kendra Ballantyne?" asked a voice from behind me.

I turned to see a moderate-height man in a yellow button-down shirt standing behind me, holding a large black briefcase in his left hand. "I'm Mitch Severin," he said.

"Amanda's attorney."

"Good to meet you, Mitch." We shook hands and assessed one another, as opposition attorneys often do. Except we were, at least nominally, on the same side. Perhaps only I assumed so.

He was maybe mid-thirties, like me, with a wide mouth that dominated his facial features. His pale brown hair grew sparse both on his head and in thinnish brows over oddly inexpressive eyes. He must have practiced the latter as part of his litigator repertoire, at least when he interviewed witnesses.

"Come over here a second," he said, gesturing with a wide shoulder toward a window between a still life and a portrait of children at play. I joined him obediently, curious as to what he intended to impart at this end of the reception area where no other patients awaited their examinations.

"Look," he said sternly. "It's one thing for you to want to help Amanda, but to make it a media event — well, that's not in her best interests, and I really must insist that you stop."

"Media event? What are you talking about?" But I had a sinking suspicion I already knew.

"This, of course." He lifted his briefcase

to lay one edge along the windowsill while he popped the clasp and opened it. He extracted a newspaper: this morning's edition of the *Los Angeles Times.* The second page included a teaser leading to an article further inside, about the ongoing murder investigation of an alleged stalker named Leon Lucero.

When Mitch turned to that article, not only was Amanda mentioned as a possible suspect, but several paragraphs were devoted to my knowing her — plus my own recent forays into far too many murder investigations.

The byline? You guessed it. The reporter who'd attempted so assertively to interview me: multimedia maven Corina Carey.

I didn't actually owe Mitch an explanation. Even so, I said, "She wrote this without my input or cooperation." Time to turn the subject to something different — fast. Although I made a mental note to pick up a copy of the *Times* somewhere, later. And hope I didn't get heartburn from sizzling over the contents of that article. "Anyway, I assume you're here so we can discuss potential attorney referrals for Amanda during the police investigation of Leon's death, in case they continue to regard her as a person of interest — or, worse, a suspect."

"Well, sure, we can talk about it." Mitch appeared a little affronted. Or maybe that pallor was created by the hazy light haloing from the window. In any event, he placed his reclasped briefcase on the floor and faced me with a frown. "But there's been a little misunderstanding. I told her that while I'm mostly a civil litigator, I do criminal work, too — although I've never represented a defendant in a possible murder trial. I handled her temporary restraining order against Leon, you know."

"So she said. But are you suggesting that you represent her now? If you've no experience in potential first-degree murder cases, maybe that's not such a great idea." I folded my arms, unsure whether I intended to do battle, but preparing at least for a protracted disagreement. The guy's ego was definitely overflowing into our conversation.

"You'd be right, Kendra, if I didn't take all the steps available to educate myself and do a great job for Amanda."

"What steps are those, Mitch?" I inquired with an ingenuous smile, as if I expected him to spout a good answer.

To my amazement, he actually did. "I've found myself cocounsel of impeccable credentials." The name he dropped was that and a whole lot more. Quentin Rush was the most recent lawyer to get celebrity murder suspects exonerated in high-profile criminal trials. "He's promised to go over all evidence with me and sit second chair in the unlikely event this matter winds up in court."

Well, hell. The wind was definitely out of my anticipatory sails. I admitted to myself how impressed I was with this guy's gumption.

"That could work well," I admitted, relieved despite myself. I mean, I'd committed to assist Amanda in exonerating herself. I'd certainly not volunteered to act as her criminal counsel, since all the litigation I'd ever done was on the civil side. And I hadn't wanted to hand her a referral to my own excellent criminal attorney, Esther Ickes. I liked Esther way too much to wish Amanda on her. I'd come to today's meeting prepared to provide an alternate referral, to Martin Skull. He'd represented one of my two original tenants when they both were murder suspects and their interests had started to diverge enough to require separate counsel.

"Kendra. Mitch. Hi." The female voice reverberated through the reception area. I turned simultaneously with the other attorney to face Amanda.

Her pretty features seemed drawn and dismal — perhaps as a reaction to the LAPD staying steadfastly on her case. But did she apologize for taking that out on me? Hardly.

"Come with me," she directed. "I've reserved a small room where the doctors usually counsel patients and their families. It's got a table and chairs — maybe a little like an attorney's conference room."

"Sounds good," Mitch said.

The chamber to which she ushered us was indeed very small, and smelled of something antiseptic. The examination table in the middle of the room was no larger than one that could be found in a compact kitchen, and around it were packed six plain wooden chairs. About the edges of the room were several sorts of medical equipment I couldn't identify, all full of tubes and wires and gauges. Beyond them, on the walls, was another assortment of original watercolors.

Mitch and I sat while Amanda left us alone again for five minutes, returning with plastic cups and a bottle of mineral water. I didn't even want to imagine what those cups might alternately be used for in a doctors' office. I decided I wasn't an iota thirsty after all.

"So," Amanda said brightly. "I guess, first

thing, since I'm surrounded by lawyers, is to talk about who I should hire to represent me. Fast. When I heard from that Detective Noralles last night, he told me to come to his police station later today just to talk."

"Without counsel present?" Mitch asked angrily. "He should know better."

So should Mitch, I imagined. As long as Amanda was simply being questioned as a possible witness, and wasn't in custody, she wouldn't be read her Miranda rights, which would inform her of her right to counsel.

No matter. If she wanted to bring a lawyer along from the get-go, the cops shouldn't tell that attorney to get gone.

"In any event," Mitch went on, "I was just explaining to Kendra that there might be a misunderstanding that I've easily corrected." He went on to tell her what he'd just enlightened me about — including the name of the illustrious media-impressing attorney whom he'd enlisted as his assistant: Quentin Rush.

Amanda's gray eyes glowed in apparent optimism. "That's great. Now I won't even have to think about hiring anyone else." Nevertheless, she shot a gaze to me as if questioning my concurrence.

"Mitch's solution sounds fine to me," I said.

That settled, Amanda said, "If you can wait just a few minutes, I've told some people that you'd be here and that you needed their opinions on whether I could have done anything to Leon." She leaned conspiratorially toward us over the table. "What I think, though, is that these people really disliked Leon. Not that I believe either one killed him," she interjected hastily. "At least I don't think so. But, Kendra, you asked for me to introduce you to at least a few potential suspects that you could start investigating, right?"

Her change of mood from last night annoyed me. In the interest of accomplishing something, I played it commensurately cool and nodded. "Even if they don't seem murderous to me, their answers to questions could point to other suspects." I turned to Mitch. "I hope Amanda informed you that she asked for my assistance this way. But if you feel I'm treading on your toes, I'll stop." Which would in effect breach our semiserious contract and give me a great excuse to walk away — which I could always do anyway. But, hey, I didn't want to hand Amanda the satisfaction of seeing me quit.

"No," Mitch said. "Go ahead and help Amanda, Kendra. She told me your agreement, and if I wasn't already aware of your expertise in handling homicide investigations, that newspaper article gave a lot of interesting details."

Oh, joy. Seldom had I wanted to throttle someone more than I did reporter Corina Carey. But maybe all she'd shoved into her story was nothing but the truth.

"I'm sure," I said acerbically. Then, to Amanda, I said, "Okay. Bring on your first Leon-loather."

That happened to be Amanda's direct boss, Dr. Henry Grant, a cardiologist extraordinaire, if his description of his credentials was to be believed. And who was I to doubt such an illustrious physician — notwithstanding the fact that he resembled Jonesy, a Welsh terrier whose acquaintance I'd once made, with his short, neat brown hair and matching, close-cut wiry beard.

He entered the room with his white lab coat open and his eyes on the watch on his wrist. When he looked up, he smiled all around. "So this is Amanda's defense team. I'm delighted to meet you. This is all such a travesty. First the poor woman is hounded by that terrible man, and then she's accused of killing him."

"By 'that terrible man,' I assume you're referring to Leon Lucero?" I asked. At his nod I said, "Wasn't he your patient?"

The doctor unexpectedly slumped into a seat. "Yes, more's the pity. The man was a malingerer. I have too many genuinely ill people to see to spend time with someone like him, and yet with all his complaints I couldn't simply throw him out. What if there was something wrong with him that I hadn't yet found? Not that I truly believed there could be. And, well, I'm much too thorough for that really to occur."

"So why didn't you just tell him to get another doctor?" Mitch demanded, as if extracting the words right out of my mouth.

Dr. Grant's hairy face turned furious. "The bastard threatened me," he growled. "Said he'd make sure everyone knew what a lousy doctor I am — that I couldn't diagnose the heart condition that made his chest hurt and the rest of his body weak. He'd publicize it to all my patients. Make sure the media investigated me. Sue me." His voice had risen until the last words erupted in an enraged shout.

I couldn't help sliding a slightly triumphant gaze toward Mitch, whose pleased nod was nearly imperceptible. Motive? Maybe. But it would absolutely merit further investigation.

"I understand how frustrating that could

be," I responded mildly.

"And I know what you're thinking," the doctor shot back. "That I was a wimp. The SOB was stalking one of my own employees, but I let his threats overshadow that fact and allowed him to keep coming back. And I knew about that stalking, and how he wouldn't leave Amanda alone, so maybe that gave me a reason to kill him myself. Well, I didn't." He swiveled his glare from me to Mitch and back again, and then turned it to Amanda for good measure.

She'd been sitting still in her chair nearest the window, simply watching our exchange and letting the putative pros deal with her doctor. Now, she blanched and brayed, "Of course not, Dr. Grant. No one would ever accuse you of that."

She looked toward me first for confirmation.

"We're just after the truth," I equivocated. "Investigating the facts. That's all."

"Well, I've told you all I know. And I've a room full of patients waiting."

"Thanks for your time," I called after him as the last vestige of his white lab coat vanished from the room.

"Interesting possibilities," Mitch mused when the three of us were alone once more.

"If he can use medical instruments, he

probably knows his way around a screwdriver," I asserted in agreement.

"But he said he didn't do it," Amanda dissented. "And I believe him."

"But disbelieving him gives us another avenue to explore to absolve you from any murder charge," I pointed out.

"Well . . . he's not your boss. Go ahead and disbelieve him. Wait here, though. There's a patient who's always here at this time every week, and I want you to meet him, too." A pause that seemed saturated with unspoken meaning, and then she said, "I dated him for a while, after I stopped seeing Leon." With that, Amanda followed her boss out of our presence.

She strolled back in only a few minutes later with a guy who appeared to be exactly Amanda's type: tall and a Chippendale's candidate — at least he appeared so with his clothes on. Nice clothes, too: a snug black T-shirt tucked into gray slacks, with a casual charcoal sport jacket overtop.

I sucked my own tongue back into my mouth and smiled a pleasant greeting as Amanda said, "Kennedy McCaffrey, this is Kendra Ballantyne and Mitch Severin."

"Glad to meet you," he said, and held out a hand that, inevitably, provided a firm-gripped shake. His hair was blond, his complexion tanned, notwithstanding the L.A. winter, and his features were film-star gorgeous.

Perfection!

And yet . . . "You're a regular patient here?" I heard myself blurt out. Well, I hadn't promised to stay tactful, though the health of this amazing specimen of mankind was likely to be irrelevant in my pursuit of who slew Leon.

"Unfortunately," he said, shrugging one massive shoulder as he took a seat. "Long story, but I'm likely to wind up with a heart transplant someday."

Wow, looks could be deceiving! If I'd had to guess, I'd never have imagined this man to be anything less than in impeccably perfect health.

"I'm sorry," I said. Then, sizing him up as I spoke, I said, "Do you have enough strength to wield a screwdriver?"

I expected him to act as affronted as the previous potential suspect had. Instead, he laughed.

"Sure. In fact, I'm in the contracting business part time — when I'm not painting or writing screenplays. I take as good care of myself as I can in a body with a failing heart. And I hated that asshole Leon Lucero, if that's your next question. But did I use a screwdriver on him? Nope. As much as I'd love to see the heat off Amanda, it doesn't belong on me."

"Okay," I acknowledged, my head suddenly swimming with questions his mini-speech had generated.

But before I could issue any, Mitch Severin slung one out. "You hated Leon? Why?"

"For one thing, I like Amanda." He inched his fingers along the table toward where her hand lay and gave it a squeeze. They shared a smile — one that illuminated the entire room. Two striking people beaming at one another. Electric!

But then Kennedy returned his attention to Mitch. "Plus, the guy was an outright thief. In my spare time, I like to do creative stuff. No one has ever bought any of my screenplays yet, but my watercolors are becoming kind of popular, at least around here."

"Seascapes?" I had to insert.

"Yes. You've seen some?"

"At Amanda's," I acknowledged.

Again they looked caringly toward one another, but this time only for an instant. Even so, if I'd captured those couple of moments on my cell phone camera, I would have had a great time letting Jeff in on where he stood.

Now, now, I admonished myself. Hadn't he already promised to prove the veracity of his earlier ousting of Amanda once this was all over? If he followed through, no photos would be necessary — and keeping my end of the ditsy devil's bargain I'd dived into with Amanda would only act as icing on that very sweet cake.

"That asshole Leon liked to paint, too. Only what he did was totally unoriginal. He'd study something I'd done, then do one just like it. Only . . ."

"Only?" I encouraged.

Kennedy drew in a deep breath — and his next several minutes were spent in a coughing fit.

When he'd stopped, his face was white and his fingers were shaking.

It was terrible to see how awful this man felt — he was genuinely ill. And this interview surely couldn't be helpful to his health.

"Only," he said, this time in a totally raspy tone, "the bastard's stuff wasn't bad. Some people considered his style childish, but there was a freshness to it. It was definitely different. But would I kill him for that?"

His coughing recommenced, and Amanda, obviously alarmed, ran out to hail one of the doctors.

Mitch stood and appeared nervous.

I stood, too, and rubbed Kennedy's back. Help him? I wished I could, but how?

What I did know was that his last question was intended to be rhetorical. Any answer he'd have given would have to be "no."

Even so, I moved poor Kennedy McCaffrey up near the top of my suspect list . . . even as I wondered whether his ailing heart could have survived the excitement of his slaying someone.

CHAPTER ELEVEN

Amanda returned to the room where Mitch and I sat uneasily exchanging comments and suspicions about the two men she'd introduced us to.

"Suspect or not, I didn't get a chance to ask that Kennedy for his card," Mitch was saying sadly. "I've a little improvement project at home that needs to be finished, but I'm too busy. I could use a contractor, and maybe if I was around the guy longer, I could get a confession out of him. Only —"

"Kennedy will be fine," Amanda said, interrupting from the doorway, then sighed. "I guess I should have known better than to bring him in here for you to harass."

Her glare as she resumed her seat was at me, not Mitch, even though the other attorney had acted quite adroit at leveling accusations of his own.

"No one wanted to harm him, Amanda," I said. "But in the event he's Leon's killer, it'll be a whole lot better for you if that little fact becomes known now, instead of after you're in custody."

"You're right," she agreed. And then, "So, now what will you do?"

"I'll check the backgrounds of the guys you brought in here today. Anyone else you'd like for us to meet — like others you dated, or additional doctors who rubbed Leon wrong?"

"Maybe, but they're not here now."

"Give me their names, and I'll ask Jeff's folks to do a background check on them, too. If any seem like likely suspects, then you can arrange for me to meet them. Us," I amended as I noticed Mitch open his mouth.

I have to admit that Amanda was gracious enough to utter a thank-you as Mitch and I exited the office into a full waiting room.

"Please keep me informed about Amanda's situation," I said to her attorney as we prepared to part ways at street level.

"You'll let me know if you uncover anything potentially useful?" he inquired, holding out his hand for a final shake.

"Done," I agreed.

A short stint back at the Yurick offices, and then I was off again, traveling west toward my next meeting of the day.

My nose was going to grow extremely tired of medical office odors — my upcoming conference was at a veterinarian's, in Tarzana, along Reseda Boulevard.

Mae Sward met me there, sans Sugar. She wore a businesslike blouse and plain skirt, and appeared ready for bear. "My baby gets so upset even when we just drive by here," she said. (Wasn't that what shrinks called transference?) "I don't want to subject her to That Man's presence anymore." I heard the capitalization in her angry tone. "At least I was finally allowed to remove that horrid collar he put on her."

The veterinary office was a stand-alone gray building with parking behind, which was where we rallied. Together, we stomped inside.

Along with an assortment of nervous dogs and their soothing owners, someone I'd met before on a pet-related matter sat in the waiting area: Attorney Gina Udovich. In the prior situation, we'd reached an almost-amicable settlement as to placement of a pooch — an adorable Scottish terrier called Glenfiddich — but the money his deceased owner had left for his care was still in dispute. Litigation over it remained likely.

Gina rose. As I remembered, she always

made the most of her appearance, dressing impeccably in designer duds. Today, she wore a lilac pantsuit with ornate embroidered purple frog closures holding the jacket closed. She was dressed as if she'd headed for court instead of a conference to hopefully stave off future litigation.

"Kendra, hi. I'd have called to let you know that I was the attorney representing Dr. Venson, but there wasn't time."

"Good to see you, Gina," I said. I almost meant it. Even though we'd butted heads on the prior matter, the fact that we'd reached at least a partial resolution boded well for possibly resolving this one, too. "This is my client, Mae Sward."

Gina's close-set eyes narrowed assessingly, but all she said was, "How do you do?"

A young lady with a large lizard on her shoulder and a friendly smile on her face ushered us through the waiting area and into a tiny room. It resembled the one in the human doctors' office I'd visited that morning, only the table in the center was a raised one of gleaming metal, where pets could be elevated for examinations. Around the room's edges were several chairs, which the three of us settled into. Mae crossed her arms, conveying her continued anger by her body language.

Since Gina was apparently new to the situation, I decided to start speaking even before her client came in. "Did Dr. Venson explain what happened, Gina?"

"Sort of," she said. "Something about a claim of having injured a dog in his care."

"You make it sound like he didn't do it on purpose!" Mae raged.

"May I speak to you outside?" I asked Mae, staying supremely calm. I'd warned her ahead of time that casting accusations was unlikely to result in anything constructive.

"No need," she huffed, aiming a full-fledged pout at me before switching her stare down to the shiny linoleum floor.

As I'd assumed, this place smelled somewhat like the other medical location I'd been in, only the antiseptic aroma couldn't quite mask the scent of animal accidents. I started again to open a discussion with Gina, but just then the door opened.

A man in a long white lab jacket strolled in. "Hello, ladies," he said. His smile seemed both rueful and lopsided as he continued, "It seems strange to me not to have an animal in here, too."

"You —" Mae began in her accusatory roar, but she quelled it at a cautionary frown from me.

"Dr. Venson?" I inquired.

"Tom," he responded. "You're Ms. Bal-lantyne?"

"Kendra," I replied in kind.

"Good to see you, Tom," Gina said, approaching her client with her hand held out.

Preliminaries ended, I intended to start right in — diligently representing my client. Only we were minus one seat to allow everyone to start out on an even playing field. "Do you have another chair, Tom?"

"I'll stand," he said. I couldn't tell for sure from this vantage point, but I guessed he was of average height for a guy, an inch or two below six feet. He had dark hair that pointed to his face in a widow's peak, deep brown eyes beneath straight, solid brows, and an amiable, if ordinary, face.

"Well, all right," I agreed. "Why don't we begin? We're here because —"

"May I speak first?" Tom interrupted. He asked his attorney's okay by a glance, and Gina nodded. "First, I want to apologize to you, Ms. Sward."

Mae's brown eyebrows lifted haughtily beneath the bangs in their unnatural shade of orange. Her full lips pursed as if it was all she could do to stay silent. My turn to nod at my own client, encouraging her attempt at prudence.

"There was definitely a terrible misunderstanding about Sugar and her puppies. I know how much you love your dog, but by the time you brought her here, she was having trouble with the delivery."

"It wasn't my fault," Mae shrieked. "You acted like it was."

"Let my client have his say first," Gina asserted. "Then you'll get your turn."

"But —"

"That's a reasonable way to handle this meeting," I said in a soft but insistent tone to Mae. "If we interrupt each other, it'll take a lot longer and we may not accomplish as much." Although, in the short time since we'd started, I'd all but relinquished any hope of a positive outcome from this day's endeavors.

"All right," Mae agreed irritably.

"Thank you," Dr. Venson said, aiming a slight smile toward me. "Ms. Sward, that litter was the third Sugar had delivered in less than two years. Some dogs handle that well, but Sugar didn't seem to. Maybe she was just exhausted. In any event, she was in pain, and I had to deliver the last puppy by C-section. While I was in there, I noticed trauma to her reproductive organs. I'm not certain whether she could have conceived again anyway, but I made an on-the-spot determination that it was in her best interests to spay her."

"You should have asked me."

I couldn't disagree with Mae's assertion, but I despised this latest interruption after my earlier admonishment. "Let's let Dr. Venson finish, Mae," I said, speaking slowly and clearly, like a mother correcting an especially obstreperous child.

"I am finished," Tom Venson said. "Except to agree that I wish I'd had time to check with Ms. Sward. But though I consider it important to please my patients' owners, it's even more important to me to make the best medical decisions I can for the animals."

Hear, hear, I wanted to say. I'd always been an unqualified advocate for my clients, and yet this time I found myself siding with what the vet at the opposite end of the table had to say. Sort of. It was self-serving stuff, of course, but it made perfect sense to an animal advocate like me.

Not that I'd admit it to anyone else in this room. Mae was still my client, and I owed her the same superior support that I gave to all I represented.

After several seconds of silence, I realized that the vet had finished speaking.

"Do you want to add anything, Gina?" I asked.

"I think my client has said it all," she replied.

"Mae, it's your turn."

Which she turned into a tirade against the vet's allegedly awful judgment. "Sugar is devastated that she can't have any more pups," Mae concluded. "Me, too. And I think you're full of shit. You'd told me the last time we came in for a checkup and vaccinations that you didn't think Sugar should have any more puppies for at least a year, and then when you found out she was pregnant again, you hollered at me. Spaying her was your revenge for me not listening to you. You're just one egotistical, horrible damned vet!"

No surprise that we didn't settle the dispute that afternoon. Mae drove away in a huff soon after making her statement. I stayed near the clinic's back door and spoke with Gina for a short while more.

We were joined by Dr. Venson.

He looked me straight in the eye when he said, "She's not entirely wrong, I'm sad to say. But I was mad, not because she chose to ignore my advice, but because I was concerned that Sugar would suffer for it.

And she did. Plus, she was likely to suffer more if she continued to have litters at the same rate in the future."

Damn. I liked this guy's attitude. I liked the sincerity in his gaze. I liked that, even though he wasn't extremely tall, I had to look up at him. I also liked that, despite the fact he wasn't extremely handsome, he was a nice-looking guy who really gave a damn about what he did — about the animals in his care.

But I was an attorney and an advocate. And I had some advocacy to accomplish here. "I'll discuss the situation with my client," was all I could say. "I'll be in touch with you soon, Gina. Goodbye, Dr. Venson."

"Tom," he repeated his earlier request. "Bye, Kendra."

Okay, so I'm a fickle female. Or at least my mind insisted on being inconsistent right about then, as I drove my Beamer east from Woodland Hills toward Darryl's doggy care.

Well, what the heck? It wasn't as if Jeff and I had any commitment to force me not to fantasize about the really nice Dr. Venson. And Jeff had been the one who'd sort of spoiled what we had, thanks to his ongoing fixation with his ex-wife, whether or not he'd committed to cut it off.

Maybe I was rationalizing.

Or allowing myself to consider yet another mistake in the arcane arena of relationships, since those sorts of errors engorged my life. Kick Jeff out before giving him a final chance to make good on his promise?

Let another guy attract my attention simply because he loved animals like I did?

I turned on my car radio as I determined to think of other things, like growing irritable over the usual, miserable, hardly moving freeway traffic.

Instead, I nearly started singing along when the unmistakable intro to "It's My Life" started. Only it wasn't the radio but my cell phone.

I reached across my seat and pulled it from my purse. I was traveling slowly enough to have no trouble glancing at the caller ID.

What a surprise. It was my kinda investigative client, Amanda.

"Hello, Amanda —" I began.

"Kendra, you have to come here. Now. I'm getting scared that when I go to the police station to get questioned this time, that terrible detective won't ever let me leave. You have to tell him your list of suspects. Better yet, can you prove who Leon's killer was yet?"

I swallowed the malicious retort that rose into my embattled mind. "It's been less than a day since your last demand, Amanda. I haven't even had a chance yet to ask Althea to do an online search about all the potential suspects you gave me today. And with a horrible person like Leon as the victim, I figure the list we have now is far from complete. Have you called Mitch yet to tell him how worried you are?"

"No. I called you first."

"Well, he's your lawyer." I paused as a big bruiser of an SUV bullied its way into my lane. "He's the one who'll represent you at the police interrogation. Contact him now, tell him about our conversation, and let him reassure you." If he can. "Got it?"

"Yes." She sounded sullen, sweet person that she was. "But we have a deal, Kendra. You promised to help me."

"And I will," I assured her.

But as I flipped my phone shut, I considered yet again shredding that symbolic shackle of a silly contract.

CHAPTER TWELVE

A few hours later, I stood in the small reception area in Jeff's Westwood office, the central hub of a suite composed of rooms radiating off it.

Lexie was with me. I'd already picked both pups up from Darryl's and dropped Odin off at home. His master wasn't there, sadly for the Akita but fortunately for me. Then Lexie and I had done our pet-sitting visits a bit early. And now, here we were.

"This is everyone?" asked Althea, the amazing Hubbard Security computer guru. She'd joined me and my Cavalier, who'd sat down obediently by my feet.

When I'd met Althea face-to-face a bunch of weeks ago, I'd been surprised to see how pretty and well preserved the slender, blond grandma was. Sure, as Jeff had suggested, she was middle-aged in years, but for a lady in her fifties, she looked damn good. Her image was dynamically assisted by how she dressed, like someone decades younger.

"That's all I've got so far," I said. "But I know you looked Leon up before. If there's anyone else on your list of people he's harmed, who could have hated him enough to off him, please pursue those strings, too." Of course some of the threads Althea chased weren't precisely public domain as provided by standard Internet search engines. There were those databases paid for by Hubbard Security.

And then there were those that Althea accessed by avenues of her own devising. Hacker? Who, her?

"Will do. I'll update you by e-mail. Oh, and by the way, what's the ETA for our fearless leader? I gather he's coming home early because of the situation with our dear Amanda."

"I'd thought I had a monopoly on sarcasm when it came to Jeff's ex."

"No way. There's so much to despise."

"Amen," I said.

"I knew you felt that way."

"He'll be home tonight. And our friend Amanda is why I need info from you." I described my devil's bargain to Althea. She might be Jeff's employee, but she'd become my buddy.

"I get it," she said. "And I'll feed you all

the info I can. So . . . what's the real 411 behind that *L.A. Times* story? The hype says there'll be a follow-up on TV on that *National NewsShakers Show.*"

My grimace undoubtedly qualified for Halloween gremlin status. "Just another nasty reporter who tried to bully me to tell my side."

"Considering her innuendoes against you and your possibly acting as an unlicensed investigator in a whole lot of murders lately, can I assume you didn't give in?"

I cringed. "You sure can." Maybe it was a mistake. Only . . . how could I be sure the relentless reporter would get things right even if I explained my involvement? Or at least the part I didn't mind the world knowing about — if there was such a part.

"Anyway, thanks, Althea," I called over my shoulder as Lexie and I dashed out. "We'll talk again soon."

Next stop: the back room of a chichi pet boutique in West Hollywood where the Pet-Sitters Club of SoCal was scheduled to meet. I'd brought Lexie without asking if pets were permitted. I mean, come on. Of all associations imaginable, this one, composed of an assortment of animal lovers, had to allow members to bring their own best friends.

As Lexie and I strolled into the store, the barks from its rear, combined with human chatterings, told me the meeting's actual location. The sales clerk's directions confirmed it.

Sure enough, the thirty or so people who milled around, caught up in at least a dozen conversations, all appeared to have brought their buddies along: a couple of macaws, but mostly dogs — mutts and purebreds — and among them, another Cavalier!

That was the direction in which Lexie and I headed, of course. I quickly introduced us to Wanda Villareal, who in turn presented herself and her pup, Basil, who was the Blenheim coloration — red and white — so characteristic of the majority of Cavaliers. "The breed's of British descent, of course," she explained, "and I've always been a Sherlock Holmes fan."

"Basil Rathbone," I asserted approvingly. "The actor who epitomized Holmes in all those early black-and-white films."

"Exactly." Wanda's heart-shaped face beamed as her Basil and Lexie exchanged interested sniffs. She was a particularly petite person, and I couldn't imagine how she handled some of the larger or more robust animals that might come under her charge as a pet-sitter. Wanda wore a loose-fitting pink gauzy top over blue jeans, and her brown hair was pulled loosely into a clip at her nape. "You're new here, aren't you? I've never seen another Cavalier at one of these events."

I gave her a grin. "It's a lot easier to keep track of pets I've met, too, than the people who own them."

"That's for certain," said someone else who'd approached from behind Wanda. "Hi. I'm Tracy Owens."

"The originator of this august organization," said Wanda.

"You could say that," Tracy admitted modestly as we shook hands. She stood around my own stature of five-five, and appeared as if the exercise she obtained as a pet-sitter didn't quite keep her in shape. Or maybe her chubby cheeks and full lips were what gave that impression, since she was far from fat.

Attached to the end of the brown leather leash she held was a small, short-haired sweetie of a pup. "Is that a puggle?" I guessed. I'd never before seen one of the touted designer dogs that were hybrids between a pug and a beagle.

"Sure is. This is Phoebe." Who also got along famously with Lexie and Basil.

Tracy soon called the meeting to order — after we'd all helped ourselves to cheese and crackers for us and gourmet biscuits for our babies. She introduced the store's owner who graciously allowed the group to gather there, and who also gave a sales pitch for her darling canine duds and other merchandise.

I could wax eloquent for an amazingly long time about what went on at the meeting — introductions and discussions of who pet-sat where and why, where the organization hoped to head, that kind of thing.

Suffice it to say that my spirits soared! Here were all kinds of kindred souls, including some who also saw clients in the San Fernando Valley. One of them was Wanda, and afterward she and I exchanged contact info as fellow Cavalier lovers.

"Maybe we could meet for coffee someday," she said, "and you could tell me how you got into all those messes that the media talk about. Or not," she added, after I emitted a rueful sigh.

"I'd hoped no one here would associate me with *that* Kendra Ballantyne," I explained.

"It's an unusual enough name that you're out of luck," said Wanda.

"Amen," I agreed and started to mingle.

And stopped short as I eavesdropped on a conversation in which one pet-sitter complained to another. "Trust someone else to take care of a client now and then? No way. Just guess who stole three of my customers after I asked for her help." I turned to see Wanda talking with someone I hadn't yet met.

Sigh. One of my major reasons for joining was jeopardized from the get-go. Lexie and I headed for the door.

We were stopped by Tracy. "Are you leaving, Kendra?"

I admitted I was, then bent to give Phoebe a parting pat. Basil, too, as Wanda and he joined us.

"Glad you came," Tracy said. "Oh, and by the way, we're looking for a slate of officers for the organization for the upcoming year. Are you interested?"

"Most likely not, but I appreciate your asking."

Seeing the look exchanged between the two women whom I'd just met and shared a simpatico situation with, I suddenly had a sinking sensation that my polite but less-than-firm refusal could lead to my affiliation with this new organization sucking in whatever was left of my overextended time.

Like a good citizen and possible pet-sitters club member, I'd had my cell phone turned off in the meeting. I turned it back on again when Lexie and I sat inside the Beamer. It immediately beeped — I'd received a message. I checked the missed-call list first.

Amanda.

If I'd thought I'd hate being subservient to that nasty lady as her cat-sitter, that was nothing compared to how overused I felt now. But unless and until I dumped Jeff, her, and investigating, I'd have to respond. "Hang on a sec," I said to a bouncing Lex as I called in for the message.

Amanda's habitual hysterics came across in her recorded voice. "Kendra, all their questions — terrible! I'm on a potty break now. And, yes, Mitch is with me at the police station. It looks like they'll keep me here all night. Please check on Cherise and Carnie for me. They'll be so lonesome." *Click.* Once again, no thank-yous, not that I'd ever observed the slightest evidence of etiquette from Amanda.

I couldn't let her cats suffer as a result of her insufferability. But I still needed some info before I could go care for them. Would she be able to answer her phone?

I would only find out if I called her back.

Her voice, when she answered, sounded drained. "You didn't need to call back, Kendra. Unless — you are going to look in on my kitties for me, aren't you?"

"Yes, but you'll need to tell me if they're at your house. Has the crime scene been released back to you?"

I heard a strangled sound. "Crime scene? Yes, my home's mine again now, and the cats are there. And with all the confusion before, I never got the key back from you."

"True." *You never paid me, either.* I didn't say that out loud — this time. I'd insist on pet-sitting payback, though, whether or not I exonerated her of Leon's slaying. "I'm on my way now." With only an instant's hesitation, I added, "Good luck with Ned Noralles."

Her laugh was cynical. "Yeah. Oh, and . . . Well, I know Jeff'll be back tonight. Please tell him what's going on. For now, at least, he may be interested."

Translation: *You haven't earned my obligation to leave him alone, Ballantyne, so I'll twist the screwdriver in your stomach — ersatz this time — until you fulfill your end of our bargain.*

Lexie wasn't exactly elated when I left her

in the Beamer in Amanda's driveway. I almost parked on the street after recalling all too well being blocked in there by the loud and angry Leon.

That was one occurrence I no longer had to fear.

Both leopard-cats came straight out to see me as I entered the seascape-lined hallway. Their striped tails waved in the air airily, as if they felt utterly nonchalant in my presence, and one issued an irritated meow.

"How are you two doing?" I asked somewhat anxiously. I mean, even though they were Amanda's charges, they had sensibilities as much as any other pets. All the upset and excitement in their lives couldn't have been good for them.

Their response was to stick a lot closer to me than usual during this visit, which was indeed an answer. "Poor ladies," I said to them, and they even purred and rubbed up against my legs as I prepared to pour out their supper. "If you'd known I was coming, would you have caught a special mouse for me?" I still wasn't certain whether it was a sign of affection from these particular felines, or whether conveying rodent corpses was a threat to trespassers.

The media, including Corina Carey, had picked up on the mouse near Leon's corpse

178

and seemed also to speculate on its significance.

While I watched the cats glance into their dinner bowls and grudgingly each grab up a morsel, Amanda's kitchen phone rang.

Knowing that she had a message machine, I pondered whether to answer it.

Well, why not? I was supposed to be assisting her in finding who really did Leon in, in this very house. Anyone who knew where she lived could theoretically become a suspect.

Amanda's kitchen phone was a handset sitting in a cradle on the tile counter, near the sink. I picked it up and pushed the button. "Hello, Amanda's home." Even after all this time, I sometimes had a hard time using her last name, since she still shared it with my own sometime lover.

"Who's this?" demanded the male voice at the other end.

"Who's *this?*" I responded.

"Bentley," he said.

"Bentley who?" I asked sweetly, even while despising how this conversation was degenerating into a weird game of "knock-knock."

"Bentley Barnett." The name sounded squeezed through clenched teeth. "Amanda's brother. And you?"

"I'm Kendra Ballantyne, her pet-sitter."

I'd headed across the shiny hardwood floor toward the square table in the corner, where I pulled out a squat chair and sat.

"Oh, yeah. She told me about you. The one who's after ol' Jeff these days."

My turn to grit some teeth. "They're divorced," I said. Then, more brightly, I added, "Unfortunately Amanda can't come to the phone right now. She's under police interrogation."

"Damn! That's why she didn't answer her cell phone."

She must have been ordered to turn it off after our conversation. Either that, or she noticed the caller ID and chose not to speak with her sibling.

"That bastard Leon's getting to her even now that he's dead," Bentley continued. "Why she even went out with that slimy muscle-shirted son of a bitch in the first place —"

"Oh, then you met Leon?" And hated him? And killed him?

Amanda might not like it if I pinned the murder-tale on her apparent jackass of a brother, but better than her, right?

"Oh, yeah, I met him. I was even hanging out at her place one night when he did some of his stalker routine. I got him to leave. Fast."

"Then why didn't you hang out with Amanda more, scare him off her back permanently?"

"Because my job's in San Diego, not there. I convinced her a few months ago to move in with the folks for a while up north, near Bakersfield. But did she stay? No. She just had to go back to L.A. She wouldn't even think of coming down to stay with me. Not with your buddy Jeff there."

"Of course." Now, how was I going to extract the information I intended? Oh, what the hell? I dove into the direct approach. "I don't suppose you were in the L.A. area yourself late last week . . . say, Friday?"

I heard a semblance of a sardonic laugh. "You asking if I killed the guy? Well, if I'd happened to have been there when he snuck into my sister's home, I might have done it — strictly self-defense, of course. I know how those things go, and what defenses there are in murder trials. I'm a bailiff down here, in the San Diego Superior Court. Do I have a great alibi for the night the bastard died in Amanda's house? No. I went out early with some buddies, got drunk, drove home, and went to bed, all by myself. I could have had time to drive to L.A., kill the bastard, and get back before anyone noticed. Will I admit to you that I did it? Hell, no. I wish you luck finding out who did, though. One thing I'm sure of is that it wasn't Amanda. She's too prissy to get blood on her hands. Poison . . . maybe. But I heard it was a screwdriver. Anyway, tell her I'll call her later. Nice meeting you, Kendra."

"Likewise, Bentley," I lied.

I checked once more on Carnie and Cherise, then headed out toward my Beamer and Lexie, musing every moment.

Interesting conversation I'd had with Amanda's brother. Was I convinced he didn't do it? No way. Did I assume his filial devotion would force him to confess to save his sister if he did do it? Nope.

I stuck Bentley Barnett on my mental list of further candidates for Althea's online research.

Chapter Thirteen

On my nice, narrow, twisting residential road up in the Hollywood Hills, I aimed my Beamer toward my driveway and pushed the button to unfurl the security gate.

That was when I noticed motion from the corner of my eye, activity in one of the vehicles parked slightly uphill.

A big, black Escalade.

And in it? Jeff and Odin, of course.

Of course? Here, sitting uninvited on my street?

Who crowned you queen of the block, Ballantyne? scoffed a nasty inner voice.

Buzz off, my conscious thoughts shot back.

Lexie had no such conflict in her cute little mind. As soon as I'd parked beside our garage and we'd exited the Beamer, she noticed her pal Odin approaching and immediately started yanking on her leash and yapping. That encouraged an echoing bark-fest from inside the big house — Rachel and

Russ's Irish setter. Neither father nor daughter quieted Beggar or watched through a window, so I assumed they weren't home.

I'd no urge to bark at seeing Jeff approach, although my impulse was suddenly to bolt up the steps to my apartment and lock the door behind me. His promises and protestations notwithstanding, I had too much soul-searching to do about our relationship to know whether I wanted to spend time in Jeff's company just then. Which was why Lexie and I left Odin at their home earlier and didn't head there after our pet-sitters' soiree.

"Hi, Kendra," Jeff said solemnly as he neared me, while Odin and Lexie traded sniffs. Damn, but even when I was conflicted the guy was one good-looking dude, all six feet of him, a picture of craggy features and shadows beneath the motion-sensor light hanging from the garage. His muscle-hugging dark T-shirt tucked into snug jeans only added to the ambiance. "Odin and I were both hoping Lexie and you would be at our place tonight."

"Oh, really? Well, we were just at a meeting of the coolest new organization for pet-sitters, and Amanda wanted me to check on her cats afterward, and it was getting late and I didn't want to bother you, so we came home." All that exited my mouth in a single, falsely cheerful string.

"It's never a bother to see you two, no matter how late." When I couldn't quite think of a response to that and stayed silent, Jeff continued, "Could we come in for a while?"

"Of course. I've a busy day planned for tomorrow, though, so I can't stay up too late." At that moment, I didn't know exactly what my next day's plans happened to be, so I held my breath in the hopes he wouldn't ask.

"That's fine. We won't stay long . . . unless you invite us."

No way, I thought. *Way*, contradicted my incorrigible libido as I followed Jeff up the outside stairway, my view mostly of his firm, denim-encased butt.

As soon as dogs were inside with us in my tiny tiled entry and the door was closed, Jeff enfolded me in his arms and against his hard body. Lord, but that felt good. His hot lips and sexy kiss felt even better, getting parts of me sparking that clearly could squish down my good sense, if I let them.

I savored the moment along with Jeff's searching tongue, but as his hands started roving to places that could drive me even crazier, I carefully stepped back.

"We need to talk," I said.

"I know. Later."

"No, now." I preceded him into my kitchen where I flicked on all the lights. There were times, like now, that I wished my teensy yet comfy rooms were instead the humongous and formal size of those in my great house. I wanted space between Jeff and me as we spoke. At least I got the round mini kitchen table to intercede, after I poured us each some ice water. I, for one, needed chilliness to inject perspective between us.

I did the next best thing — introduced his ex's name even as our conversation started. "Do you know where Amanda is right now?" I asked.

"No, and I don't care."

Was he serious, or was he simply hoping to seduce me?

How could I think such nasty thoughts about the guy staring at me sincerely with his gorgeous blue eyes? The one who'd shared my bed often during the last few months, each time he was in town.

"She's being questioned by your buddy Noralles at the North Hollywood Station, even as we speak."

For someone who professed not to give a

damn, he sure gave a fierce frown. He also recovered fast. "I assume her lawyer's with her, so everything's under control. Let's talk about us."

I wondered if he'd act so nonchalant if I contradicted him and said she'd chosen to represent herself. Well, lying wouldn't get us anywhere, so I instead said, "What is there to say, Jeff?"

"A lot. When Amanda told me about your agreement with her, I wanted to dump you both for trying to arrange my life. But once I cooled down and considered it, I realized I hadn't really made good on what I'd told you: my intention not to see her anymore. Of course I hadn't considered something happening like Leon's murder, but even so, I'm sorry."

"No need. Since she's a suspect, I'm sure she's scared, so she'd turn to the one guy she thought she could trust." Hey, whose side was I suddenly on? Besides, she'd followed Jeff to Chicago before the murder occurred.

Jeff's solemn features relaxed into a smile. "I knew you'd understand. And I promise I won't do much to help her out of this mess unless you ask me to do something. I know you've got Althea researching stuff on Amanda's behalf, and that's just fine." He reached across my table — maybe its small size wasn't so awfully bad — and took my nervously shaking hands in his strong and still ones. "Kendra, you know I love you. I still want us to live together when this is all over. I recognize this isn't the best time to get into it," he inserted hastily as I attempted to snatch my fingers back, "but once Amanda's in the clear, we'll talk about it again."

Which could be never, of course. I didn't believe she'd deleted Leon, but who knew how successful I, or anyone else, would be in discovering the honest-to-badness actual slayer? Or if no one else was unearthed, how long it would take for her to go to trial and be found, with luck, not guilty?

That train of thought made me smile. Not that I wished anything worse on Amanda than I already had, but I at least had a reprieve in talking to Jeff about too much togetherness.

Maybe I'd make up my mind how I really felt about him first.

"Okay," I agreed seriously. "And you know I care about you, too. But I really need to get to bed, because —"

"Me, too," Jeff agreed huskily, rising right across the table from me. He moved so fast that suddenly he was on my side. Pulling me again into his arms . . .

I could blame giving in to baser instincts that night on relief at having any decision delayed. But, hell, his sexiness was way too hard to resist — at least when we weren't feuding.

So, after one final foray outside with the dogs — one filled with longing looks and tantalizing surreptitious touches, we hurried back upstairs and went to bed.

And, yes, I even, eventually, got a little sleep.

I was awakened by a ringing. "Damn!" I whispered. "Did I accidentally push the button too far?"

Only I hadn't set the alarm to ring if the sound of my clock radio failed to roust me out of bed. Ergo, what I heard was my landline phone.

I reached toward the table to answer, and rolled over Jeff.

Who grabbed me and rubbed some interesting body parts against some other ones of mine . . . and I almost decided to let my machine answer.

Almost. But when I said hello, I felt even more that my answering had been a great gaffe.

"Kendra? I just spent the most miserable

night in the police station with that horrible detective, and even though Mitch did a good job objecting to questions and making sure I only answered what I was asked, I'm sure they're convinced I killed Leon. Why didn't you come after seeing to my cats? And tell Jeff he could have come, too. I know you're together. I tried calling his home and didn't get any answer."

"Good morning to you, too, Amanda."

I watched Jeff's eyes react as I spoke, widening, narrowing, blinking in clear concern.

Damn! I'd done it again. Last night, I had allowed my understandable and undeniable sexual attraction to Jeff overshadow my common sense.

"Why don't you tell Jeff yourself?" I suggested sweetly and handed him the phone — even as I rolled off him and clambered toward my closet. I required an all-concealing robe to cover my sudden embarrassment at being caught clothesless.

Not, fortunately, that Amanda could see. But she was too smart to assume otherwise.

Ignoring my urge to eavesdrop, I allowed the dogs to follow me into the kitchen, where I started a pot of coffee. Then, I slunk into the bathroom, where I showered . . . after peeking in and seeing that Jeff was still on the phone.

I dressed and accompanied the pups on a short walk while Jeff showered. When I joined him for a quick breakfast of toast, jelly, and java, I attempted not to shout out my sudden remorse. Not that I had to. Jeff obviously sensed it.

"You didn't have to hand me the phone, Kendra," he said in a stilted voice. "Since you did, I had to talk to her."

"Mmm-hmm," I assented, my mouth conveniently full.

"Damn it, Kendra, you —"

"Sorry," I said, swallowing my food. "Got to run. I'll drop Lexie off at Darryl's. Bye, Odin. Bye, Jeff." I knelt and leashed Lexie, grabbed the coffee I'd conveniently poured into a portable plastic cup, then dashed out the door.

At least, since Jeff was a security expert, I could be sure he'd lock the door and set the alarm. But alarms were going off already in my head. I was really making a mess of this relationship. Or, rather, Jeff already had. Or —

"Hi, Kendra."

No need to turn to see where the welcome distraction came from — especially since Beggar bounded up and began leaping around the delighted Lexie.

"Good morning, Rachel."

My waiflike young tenant pranced up to us along the driveway with as much vigor as her adorable big pup, her open pink jacket almost flying behind her.

"You done good, kid." I described the joys of attending the pet-sitters' club last night without mentioning my doubts.

"Glad it worked out. Er, Kendra?" She suddenly stooped to start petting Lexie.

"Yes?" What was on her mind? Was she about to quit my part-time employ altogether? She certainly seemed uneasy. Those big brown eyes of hers had barely glanced into mine.

"How's your murder investigation going?" she asked, still squatting on the ground. "I mean the one where the lady's accused of killing her stalker. The one where you were mentioned in the paper."

"Oh, *that* murder investigation. Well, I haven't looked into it much, that miserable reporter notwithstanding."

"Really? Oh, no!" Rachel rose fast, and those eyes of hers appeared aghast.

"Why do you care?" I queried, since she obviously did.

"Well . . ." Once again, she looked away, but this time only for an instant. "See, I've been bragging about knowing you at my initial readings for the new film. And . . . and . . ."

"What?" I encouraged, sure I'd be sorry. Which I was.

"Well, I've bet a bunch of the others that the lady didn't do it, and you'd find out who did, way before the cops."

"Rachel, I'm not even a licensed investigator," I admonished almost angrily.

"But your friend Jeff is, and you always work with him when you're investigating, right?"

"That's right," said that very man, who'd snuck up behind me. "Good wager, kid. I'll bet you'll win."

"Cut it out, you two," I all but shouted, sprinting, with Lexie, for my car.

I grumbled the whole way to most of my pet-sitting clients that morning. Though I treated them all equally amicably, I was irritable enough to confront Meph's owner, Maribelle Openheim, when I reached Stromboli's and found the poor pup again — still — tethered alone and lonely in his backyard, but she wasn't home.

I brought Lexie with me to my law office, needing the friendly company that day, and even managed amiable greetings to my cohorts at the Yurick office before slamming my door and sitting down at my desk.

I'd barely begun trying to settle down to my legal work when my cell phone sang. Ignoring Lexie's baleful, fearful stare, I yanked the phone from the drawer and studied the caller ID.

I took a deep breath to conceal my miserable mood from the perceptive person at the other end.

"Good morning, Althea," I managed to say cheerfully.

"What's wrong, Kendra?" she responded. "No, wait, hold it a minute. I've got something that'll make you feel better, whatever it is. Guess what I have for you on Leon Lucero."

CHAPTER FOURTEEN

The woman was a whiz! But, of course, I'd learned that in multiple past interactions. "Got a pencil?" she asked.

"No, a pen."

"Lord, you're obviously a lawyer — so literal. Or should I say anal? Anyhow, take this down. Better yet, hold on a sec." In a moment, she said, "Now, check your e-mail."

Good old cyberspace. I immediately received Althea's proffered lists. One contained Leon Lucero's former employers. He might have been a painter and professional heart patient, but he'd also held jobs in retail, mostly as a manager in department stores. Another displayed names, dates, and court-case numbers for numerous TROs and even permanent restraining orders that other stalking victims had obtained against Leon all over Southern California, plus a few in Arizona. Althea had done her homework before, when Jeff assisted Amanda in hiring an attorney, and we already knew the guy was essentially a serial stalker. Now, I scrambled to absorb every chapter, verse, and potential villain — or vindicator, depending on how one looked at it.

"With all that wonderful info," I said after I'd scanned it, "I don't suppose you found some indication online that one or more of his victims happened to be in Amanda's neighborhood the night Leon was offed? I mean, a parking ticket, use of a credit card in a nearby store, a murder confession in a blog . . . ?"

"What do you want, Kendra — for *me* to be the one to save Amanda's butt? What would that do to your contract with the bitch?" If she learned you weren't the one —"

"Yeah, yeah. I know. She'd use that as yet another excuse to try to stay tied to Jeff's hip."

"And a nice hip it is, if I'm any judge," she said suggestively. "Not that I've ever seen it except in his slacks. Care to deliver any details?"

"Hey, Althea, you're his employee. Not to mention that —"

"I'm more than a decade older than him. That doesn't mean I don't notice such things. Wait until you're my age."

She had at least fifteen years on me. I shuddered. "I'll do that. Wait, I mean . . ."

"It's not so bad. In fact, you worry about a lot less stuff when you get older. Anyway, if there's anything else you need from me that makes sense for an old computer hack to get —"

"That's hacker."

"Whatever."

"One more thing," I said. "Could you check whether any complaints of pet malpractice have been filed against a certain veterinarian?" I gave her the particulars on Dr. Thomas Venson. "Thanks," I finished. "You're a wonder, Althea."

"Tell me something I don't know." With that, she severed our connection.

I stared at a wall near my office door. There wasn't much room above the multiple file cabinets comprising my sole decoration. But what if I started collecting genuine seascapes like Amanda . . . ?

Where was my mind? I moved my eyes back to the computer screen and printed the page.

Then I called Mitch. Amanda's attorney had undoubtedly received the fruit of Althea's prior Leon searches. Had he spoken with other attorneys who'd obtained TROs against the guy? If so, he hadn't shared any tidbits to assist me in aiding his client. I called him.

"No," he said, "I didn't figure anyone would share something important to Amanda's situation, thanks to attorney-client privilege with whoever they represented. Do you think one of them could have killed Leon and is now letting Amanda take the blame? Great job, Kendra."

Good thing he'd have serious backup in any homicide case against Amanda.

I hadn't exactly been fully focused on any of the other matters I'd attempted to do that day, such as delving even further into the Santa Barbara resort scandal for Borden's clients the Shermans. Even Mae Sward's Pom-neutering problems hadn't stayed centered in my concentration.

So, without changing my current subject, I started calling suspects on Althea's handy-dandy little list. Reaching voice mails, I left some vanilla messages about being an attorney researching an unspecified case.

The first genuine person I reached lived in Oxnard, nearly all the way west of the San Fernando Valley to Ventura. Her name was Betty Faust, and she unsurprisingly surmised immediately what case I happened to be researching. In fact, she seemed to know my name — courtesy of Corina Carey, I was certain.

"You're calling about that horrible Leon Lucero, aren't you?" Betty said so hoarsely that I could hardly hear her. "I wondered if anyone would remember what he did to me."

With my monster of a mood that day, I had a sudden urge to get out of Dodge . . . er, Encino. "Betty, would you mind much if I came to see you? I could be there in about . . ." I checked my watch. "An hour, if traffic is on my side."

"It never is, coming this way," she said with a sigh, "but that would be fine."

Betty's address actually led me to an exclusive community called Channel Islands Harbor, where small homes along a man-made waterway to the Pacific abutted boat-laden docks.

I made it there, as I'd aspired to, in a little over an hour — even with the detour I took to take Lexie to Darryl's. Betty was waiting apparently not far from the entry. When I rang the bell I heard a scuffling, and then the wooden door swung open. "Ms. Ballantyne?"

"Yes — Kendra. Ms. Faust?"

"Betty. Come in."

After my assessment of Amanda's physical prettiness — notwithstanding her pitiful personality — I'd assumed Leon stalked lookers. Not necessarily. Betty Faust was short, with a thick neck and squat build. Her black hair was beautiful, though — thick, wavy, and long enough to reach her waist in the back.

Maybe Leon had a hair fetish. Or maybe, since he'd painted seaside scenes, he also stalked ladies who lived near the ocean.

Passing a central stairway in the hall, Betty led me into a very blue living room. Not that it rendered me morose, but everything seemed nautical and picked up the shade of the sea.

She motioned me to a vivid blue settee, and I sat.

"Are you trying to help that poor lady who finally had enough and killed Leon?" Betty dove in sans preamble.

"I'm looking for facts that will help in the defense of Amanda Hubbard," I corrected as a lawyer should. "I'm not her attorney, but I haven't seen any indication of evidence that would prove her guilty."

"I see." Betty ran her fingers through the part of her hair that had slid over the side of her face. Her skin was an olive tone, her cheeks prominent. The more I stared at her, the more attractive her appearance seemed. Beautiful? Maybe not, but absolutely arresting. "Well, if she did it, I applaud her." Which she did, and the staccato of her clapping reverberated through the small room. "If not her, I still congratulate whoever did it. The man was a menace. He hurt people." She paused. "He hurt me."

Her pale brown eyes suddenly studied the blue rug beneath the chair facing mine that she had taken.

"Tell me about it," I encouraged.

That was all it took to get her to spout out a horrendous story of how she'd met him at a friend's birthday soiree. She'd learned later that Leon had been a crasher, but he'd acted so sweet and romantic that she'd provided him with her phone number. "And then he'd call all the time," she said with a shiver. "Somehow, though I never told him where I lived, he found out and showed up nearly every night. I lost two jobs because of him, since he kept coming into the gift shops where I worked and followed me around."

"But you got a temporary restraining order against him?" I prompted.

"As if those ever help. I read in the paper about how your client Amanda got one, too, and how Leon ignored it."

"Unfortunately," I acknowledged, recalling all too well how he'd confronted me at Amanda's house. "When did Leon stop stalking you? I assume he ultimately did, right?"

"Yeah, when I started seeing Betty," boomed a deep voice from the doorway. Startled, I turned that way. The man who stood there filled the space, an Incredible Hulk look-alike except for the sweetly human face. The guy, dressed in jeans and a dirty workshirt, was huge, and Leon would have been a wimpy shrimp in comparison. "I told the jerk hands off. He listened."

"I bet he would," I said. Only, had he honestly? Betty's guy clearly could have taken on Leon in any kind of physical contest. If Leon hadn't listened, who's to say that Mr. Muscles wouldn't have decided to do something final about it?

As if he knew exactly what I was surmising, the guy said, "I'm glad the creep's dead, too, like Betty. And if it helps, I'll give you a check toward the cost of that poor lady's legal defense. I'm Coprik, by the way. I own Coprik Marine — sell lots of boats and equipment at the harbor. Fix stuff myself, too."

That I believed.

"Kendra Ballantyne," I said, introducing myself. "I'm —"

"A lawyer. Yeah. Betty told me you were coming, which is why I'm here. I wanted to be sure you didn't try to pin anything on either of us. Sure, neither of us is sorry the jerk's gone, but we didn't do it. Hear?"

I heard, and after only a little further discussion I soon took my leave.

Did I believe Coprik and his Betty? Not necessarily — especially when they spoke so often and explicitly about their delight in Leon's demise.

I kept them on my list of potential people for Mitch Severin to depose in the event his illustrious cocounsel and he needed additional suspects in Amanda's defense.

By the time the Beamer and I sailed out of Channel Islands Harbor, it was mid-afternoon. I could head back to the office for a couple of hours before commencing my evening's pet-sitting chores. Or, I could make a stop along the way — to further check out Dr. Thomas Venson's veterinary prowess.

I settled on the latter. After all, I hadn't spent as much time as I should have on Mae Sward's Pom-battery case.

This time, instead of taking up a spot in

the lot behind the building, I parked along the street, not far from the front entrance. First, I watched the caliber of client who entered the clinic. No one seemed especially noteworthy, and their pets appeared essentially standard: big dogs and little dogs on leashes, and handheld cages that I assumed held mostly cats.

This wouldn't get me any information I required to make a case for Mae. I needed to talk to those normal people and see what they thought of their regular vet.

I exited my car. I'd be too obvious if I entered the waiting area and began badgering folks with questions, so I sauntered down the driveway into the parking lot. Standing outside might not be fun, since it was a cool February day, and I'd dressed for legal success, which meant that my outerwear was a light jacket — more attractive than functional.

The first person I saw was a twentyish lady wearing an all-weather coat and carting a cat carrying case. "Hi," I said jauntily. "Mind if I ask you about the vet? I'm thinking of starting to use Dr. Venson's services for my own cat." I bent and peered through the bars at an irritated-appearing feline who hissed. "Guess he doesn't like confinement." I forced a smile.

"No, *she* doesn't. She doesn't like Dr. Venson at all, but, then, what animal does like coming to the doctor?"

"True. And what's your opinion?"

"He's really nice to the animals. Seems to care a lot about them. I'd recommend him." With that she hurried past.

My next victim — er, target — was an older Asian fellow with a large mixed breed on a short leash. The dog lunged at me as I neared, and the guy struggled to keep control.

"Hi," I said and attempted to start my spiel about researching the vet for future pet care, but the man and mutt just passed me by.

"The doctor's a good one," the fellow shouted over his shoulder.

Two for two. But what did I expect? Anyone who came to see the vet was likely to consider him competent, or why bring a beloved pet for torture instead of treatment? Except Mae, of course, who'd claimed she'd continued coming because of the vet's good reputation.

I decided on one more volley of veterinary inquiry. I headed back into the parking lot, avoiding a car that was exiting and eyeing a second for a possible subject.

That meant I wasn't paying enough attention to the rest of the crowded surroundings.

"Ms. Ballantyne, what are you doing here?" came a familiar and forceful masculine voice from behind me.

Cringing and pivoting at the same time was no mean feat, but I managed it, along with a sheepish smile.

"Hello, Dr. Venson," I said to the man who'd come up behind me. "Fancy meeting you here."

CHAPTER FIFTEEN

"My sentiments exactly," voiced the vet. He'd come outside in his white lab coat, which contrasted nicely with the darkness of his hair. I'd recalled how sincere his eyes had appeared to me in our prior meeting. Now they were wary.

An intelligent potential defendant.

"Who, me?" my own tone shrilled. "I was just looking around to see —"

"To see what my assets appear to be, so you'll know how much to sue me for on behalf of Mae Sward?" He didn't sound happy. I shrank at his continued assessing stare — right against the nearest Mercedes sedan. A lot of people don't like strangers leaning against their cars, and I'd no idea who this one belonged to. I stepped sideways toward the next auto in the row, a smallish SUV.

"I can't talk to you about that," I responded primly. "You're represented by counsel, and your lawyer isn't present."

"That's because you appeared here with no warning, Ms. Ballantyne. Why? What's the real reason?"

Damned if I knew. Or maybe I did, not that I wanted to express it to him, let alone myself.

The truth was, I'd found the guy an iota too attractive the other day.

There. I *had* thought it. Nothing appeared from the sky to strike me down.

Jeff didn't drive up in his big, black Escalade and start browbeating me. At least not the real Jeff. The one in my mind's eye didn't appear exactly thrilled.

I realized I was shivering slightly, and it had nothing to do with the lightness of my jacket. I'd been caught. And Tom's question was pending. Yes, I was thinking about him on a first-name basis, even if that hadn't been his means of addressing me this day. I'd liked him and his apparent attitude about animals.

But had he committed actionable battery on Mae Sward's prize Pom?

I wondered what it would feel like to have those skilled veterinary hands of his commit battery on me. I glanced at those well-trained digits and noted he wore no wedding ring. Of course, since he performed pet surgery, he might simply ignore such customs out of convenience.

Okay, so he wasn't as handsome as Jeff. Or as tall. Or as hunky.

But he seemed so genuinely nice and caring and . . . well, comfortable.

"Look," I said, hastily discarding my inner thoughts, "I'm somewhat sorry you caught me here, but maybe it was for the best. Of course I can't discuss the case, but you know I represent Mae Sward in a dispute with you. I've also developed a bit of expertise in legal situations involving pets, and my preference is always to attempt ADR. Do you know what that usually stands for in a legal context?"

His features segued from mistrustful to bemused. "How about if I ask you for the definition of a veterinary term instead?"

I laughed. He smiled. The tension between us seemed to vanish.

Not necessarily a good thing.

"Okay," I said. " 'ADR' most often means 'alternate dispute resolution.' With me, though, it's 'animal dispute resolution.' I always try to work out a way to craft win-win situations for parties on both sides of a pet-related issue."

"That's what you were doing here?"

"Just getting ideas," I said. Lots of ideas.

Ideas that didn't necessarily have to do with Mae Sward and Sugar. But he didn't have to know that.

Only, by the assessing and interested way he regarded me, I had a sense he already did.

"Anyway," I continued hastily, "I'll try to set up another settlement conference with your attorney, Gina Udovich. The best way to resolve disputes is for both sides to consider a compromise. I'd suggest you think about what you might be able to offer Mae in exchange for settling her claim, and I'll tell her to do the same."

"Good deal," he said. "I'll look forward to seeing you again, Kendra."

He *did* remember my first name. As I strolled bemusedly to the Beamer and got in, I tried to tell myself that he'd sounded so pleased about the prospect of our next meeting only because of the potential for ADR it would bring.

If I hadn't had a foot alternating between brake and gas pedal as I headed the Beamer back to the Yurick office, I might have kicked myself in my own behind. Assuming I was agile enough to do such a thing.

I had a relationship with Jeff that hadn't yet reached a resolution. I cared about Jeff.

Maybe even loved him.

And he'd said he loved me.

If I found Leon Lucero's killer and co-erced Amanda into honoring our written contract — and, better yet, Jeff did as promised and enforced his prior assertion of preference — she'd no longer loom between us as a barrier to what might be. Only, maybe her presence over the past months had already caused too much dam-age.

Did I want Jeff? Did I want to drop Jeff?

Heck, I'd known forever that I was a loser in the love department. I mean, what win-ning charmer lets herself be seduced by the senior partner of the first law firm where she'd worked? Not that I'd started sleeping with "Drill Sergeant" Bill Sergement with my eyes closed — figuratively, at least. I'd known how ill-advised and ephemeral it would be. But that had been several years back. He'd since seduced another associate, after marrying someone else altogether. My affairs afterward had been blessedly brief — till now. And —

I had to cease my silly self-flagellation to slip several lanes over on the freeway for my exit. Thank heavens.

In several more minutes, I'd parked the Beamer in my prize parking spot and scurried into the office.

"Hi, Mignon," I said to our exuberant and reliable receptionist. She wore a flowing silky top that day in shimmering red, festooned with decorative rhinestones. "The Shermans aren't here yet, are they?"

"Not yet," she sang. "It's only three forty-five. They're due at four, aren't they?"

"Sure are." I hustled myself down the open hallway to my office, where I speedily shuffled my files and notes together for the upcoming meeting. I was fully prepared when Mignon buzzed and bade me to come to the conference room. Or bar, depending upon how one regarded it. It was once the saloon side of this former restaurant building, and Borden had elected to retain the original décor. One end was lined with the large wooden bar, and the rest was filled with high-backed booths. Of course there was now a sizable and serviceable conference table in the center.

The Shermans, standing in the doorway, had already been schmoozed by my skinny, smiling senior partner. Like many of Borden's prized clients, they seemed like swinging seniors. Connie was slightly stoop-shouldered with a well-wrinkled face, but her smooth hair was a highlighted medium brown, as attractive as mine had been when

I'd been a high-priced litigator who hadn't thought twice about spending big bucks on the area's most sought-after stylists. Her husband Charley's physique suggested the Pillsbury Doughboy, and he grinned equally pleasantly.

After initial amenities, including the ritual pouring of libation — no, not liquor despite the décor, but rich, aromatic coffee in large white mugs — we sat around the conference table and dissected the complaint.

"You're sure this'll entitle us to lots of money for our suffering?" Charley demanded when we were done.

"There's no guarantee of winning anything," I cautioned, "since we can't completely predict what any judge or jury will do. But this is definitely enough to get the attention of that resort's management, as long as they hire reputable counsel."

"That's for sure," Borden seconded. "Especially that cause of action for fraud and misrepresentation."

"The one that lets us claim punitive damages?" Connie shrilled excitedly.

"Exactly," I agreed.

They soon signed their declarations and prepared to depart.

"Thanks so much, dear," Connie said, giving me a small kiss on the cheek. "Go get 'em."

"Yeah," Charley said. "I'm looking forward to using whatever we win here to take a nice, long cruise."

"Don't count your cruise before it's embarked," Borden admonished.

"We know," Charley said, and then they were gone.

"Cute couple," I said to Borden.

"Yeah, I've known them for years. Connie knows the odds of winning. She knows lots of odds. She used to be the head actuary for a huge insurance company."

"And Charley?"

"He's a longtime animal trainer for Hennesey Studios, semiretired now. I told him you're a pet-sitter on the side. You might hear from him someday as a client when you're wearing your other hat."

"Interesting idea . . . sitting for performing pets." And with that idea simmering in my skull, I headed back to my office to make the minor edits to the complaint that we'd collaborated on.

By the time I was finished and handed it to a paralegal for finalizing and filing, it was time for me to slide away for the day for my pet-sitting stuff.

In a couple of hours, I'd completed all of

my adored chores except seeing to Stromboli. I'd intentionally saved him for last. I'd no idea about his neighbor Maribelle's schedule, but I figured that if she worked what was usually considered typical hours, she might be home later in the day.

I was bound and determined to continue my monologue about her treatment of poor Meph.

When I slipped the Beamer into Dana Maroni's driveway, her automatic lights already glowed inside. There were lights on at the Openheims', too — home of Maribelle and Meph — automatic, or an indication the place was inhabited by human fingers?

I did my usual enjoyable romp with Stromboli, feeding and walking and playing with the exuberant shepherd mix. When I started out, Meph wasn't leashed in the lot next door! I was thrilled for the wiry little mutt. Maybe he was enjoying some attention after all.

But by the time I prepared to give Stromboli his exit hug and treat, there Meph was once again, seeming solitary and sad at the end of his leash.

Still . . . maybe I'd gotten through to Maribelle, since he apparently hadn't been exiled all day. If so, I decided to give her a pat on the back. I went next door and rang the bell. I heard some sound as the peephole was used, and then the door opened. The middle-aged Maribelle today wore dark slacks, dark shirt and a tentative smile. "Yes — Kendra, isn't it?"

"Exactly. I just wanted to tell you how glad I was not to see Meph hanging outside when I first got here. And —"

I saw tears slosh down her cheeks from brown eyes that today appeared more morose than suspicious. "You were right. I shouldn't have taken it out on him, only —" She stopped. "Never mind. But thanks." She started to shut the door.

Okay, I'm the nosy sort. At least where animals are involved. "If you'd like to talk, I'd like to listen," I said.

"Really?" She sounded startled.

"Really," I said, "although I can't stay long." Which gave us both an out if our conversation collapsed into crap.

Showing me into her sparsely furnished and somewhat shabby home, she led me into a kitchen where cabinets had once been painted white. She let Meph in to join us. The wire-haired honey was so excited he couldn't sit still. Instead, he boomeranged from slobbering on Maribelle, then me, then back again.

Meantime, Maribelle fed me hot tea, and I fed her sympathy.

"I never meant to take it out on Meph, you know," she said when she was finished telling me how she'd been widowed eighteen months earlier, left with a sizable mortgage when her husband had been the main breadwinner. "Our kids are grown and live clear across the country, and I didn't want to bother them. And I was . . . well, angry that Opie — that was my husband — died. Meph had been mainly his dog, so I guess I was taking it out on him. I didn't mean to, but I've been working extra long hours as a hairstylist at one of those discount salons to try to hold on here. Opie didn't carry life insurance, and we lived well while he was alive. I'm too young to collect his pension or Social Security, and I don't want to sell this place if I can possibly hold on, so . . . well, I'm sorry, Meph." She leaned down from where she sat to stroke the wagging-all-over pup. "I guess if I could find him a better home, I would."

I succumbed to shock. Toss out her sole housemate? "Wouldn't that leave you lonely?"

"Maybe, but if he'd be better off . . ."

"Well, think about it," I said. "Here." I gave her my card — the pet-sitter sort —

217

and said, "If you want to talk more, give me a call. Anytime. And I really appreciate how you're handling Meph now."

"I guess he is, too," she said with a somber smile, then saw me to the door.

After a sad story like that, I had to give Lexie a whole lot of extra hugs when I retrieved her from Darryl's. We headed home.

For the first time in weeks, we wouldn't see Odin. I told Lexie. Did she understand? Who knew? But she didn't seem to, since when we got to our upstairs digs, she sat at the door for a short while as if in anticipation of my usual collection of evening gear and taking off.

"Not tonight," I told her, hearing some sadness in my own voice, too. But I needed a break to think. Especially after the sizzling-hot sex Jeff and I had shared last night. It kept me from cogitating clearly over my future, and where Jeff might or might not be within it. I fed Lexie, then considered my own dinner. I peeked into the fridge and freezer. Not much there, after I'd spent so little time here lately. Well, okay. I'd take a sojourn to the nearest supermarket, and —

"It's My Life" reverberated through my apartment. I grabbed for my purse to retrieve my cell phone.

And saw the caller ID. Jeff.

I straightened my shoulders in preparation for an invitation, followed by an argument.

Only . . . Jeff said the one thing to get me to head to his place, at least for a while, that I simply couldn't resist.

"I've picked up takeout Thai, Kendra. Our favorites — Mee Krob and Pad Thai. Some sticky rice for the dogs, too. Come on over."

And so we did.

We'd barely begun to bite into our Thai delights when the dogs began barking. They barreled out of Jeff's kitchen and toward the front of the house. That's when the doorbell rang.

"Who's that?" I asked Jeff.

"You got me," he responded as he hurried from the room to find out.

Hustling along the hardwood floor of the hall behind him, I caught up in a jiffy — just in time for Amanda to stride haughtily inside.

The good thing about that was that she apparently had ceded Jeff's key back to him.

The bad thing was that she was *here.* And clearly unhappy.

Me, too.

She didn't allow me the opportunity to say something profound and pointed.

"You two are supposed to be helping me," she shouted. "Instead, everyone in the world is going to know I'm a murder suspect. You have to do something. Fast."

"Calm down, will you?" Jeff chided, grabbing her shoulder clad in a soft, white sweater.

"I will not." She slid her fiery gaze up his arm and into his face. He flushed and rapidly released her.

Far be it for me to suddenly step in as the voice of reason, but that's what I did. "Please tell us what's happened, Amanda." For I could only assume from her impulsive anger and erratic behavior that something new had triggered it.

She glanced at her watch, then grimaced. "Tell you? I'll *show* you." She stalked down the step into Jeff's sunken living room and made herself at home, sinking onto his sofa and aiming the remote toward his big-screen TV.

In a moment, the set was on, and she changed the channel.

Suddenly, the room was filled with a familiar too-glib voice, and the picture showed someone I never wanted to talk to again: Corina Carey.

"Tell me, Detective Noralles," the abhorrent reporter was saying, "are you looking into any suspects in the murder of Leon Lucero besides his alleged stalking victim, Amanda Hubbard?"

I stood petrified by shock as Corina shoved the microphone away. The camera followed it to the equally familiar face of my own personal police nemesis, Ned Noralles. "I cannot comment on that at this time," he said.

"Of course you can't, Detective," Corina responded in soft sarcasm as she drew the microphone back toward her own mouth. "But we will. This reporter has been conducting an investigation of her own, and I can say at this time that there are no other contenders for prime suspect as good as Ms. Hubbard. If it was her, was it self-defense or something else? Stay tuned, and we'll let you know what we've found out."

CHAPTER SIXTEEN

Okay, so Corina's words turned out to be more enticement than a herald of a show of substance. In fact, despite acres of innuendoes that she'd developed a slew of suspects yet Amanda remained best, her show mostly castigated the cops who refused to confirm that the cutting-edge reporter was on the right track.

Afterward, I turned to Amanda. By then, I'd somehow sunk onto the couch beside her, and Jeff was at her other side, as if somehow we'd tacitly agreed to flank her as fortification against what we viewed. The dogs lay protectively on the floor by our feet. Amanda's sweater drooped over her stooped shoulders, and her blond hair strung limply around her sad face. Even so, she managed to look sorrowfully lovely.

Since I'd anticipated facing my ambivalence about Jeff again that evening, I'd come in loose jeans and a sweatshirt. Really sexy stuff.

Sigh.

"How did you know that was going to be on?" I asked Amanda once the blare of the follow-up commercials was muted.

"There've been teasers about it for hours," she said, her big gray eyes filled with tears. " 'Death of a stalker. Who did it and why?' 'Who was Leon Lucero, and did he deserve to die?' 'Did the victim suddenly become the stalker?' That kind of stuff. I could have screamed!"

"You did scream," Jeff countered dryly. "The instant you walked in my door." He'd dressed down similarly to me. Was he equally ambivalent? But even if his loose brown T-shirt and tight, threadbare jeans made a statement of indecision, he still managed to look yummy in them.

"What did you expect?" Amanda shot back snidely. "If you'd done your best private eye and security stuff in the first place, maybe Leon wouldn't have kept on stalking me. Then I wouldn't be in this mess."

"Shove a sock in it, Amanda," I snapped. "Jeff did help you find the resources you needed — like a lawyer to get the TRO, and another P.I. to work with you, and —"

"And you?" she said, standing to stare down at me. "You signed a contract promising to help me clear myself in Leon's murder, and I'm still the main suspect. Even if the police have other people in mind, that TV show will make sure no one else in the world will believe someone else could have killed him."

"I'm still working on my side of the bargain," I said, also rising to face the frosty female. "But here you are at Jeff's. And —"

"I only promised to stay away if you got me off the hook in Leon's murder," she spat.

"I want you to stay away anyhow," Jeff said. He was on his feet by now, too, and at his six-foot altitude he seemed a lot more authoritative than either of us ladies. Odin, his Akita, stood at his side, as if seconding everything his master said.

Lexie sat beside me, looking a slight bit scared, obviously rendered uncertain by the vicious vibes circulating around the humans in this room.

"And if I don't?" Amanda demanded.

"Maybe I can help the cops show you *did* do it," he shot back.

She gasped and paled and looked so shocked that I considered illuminating a lightbulb from the hands she raised to ward off his awful words.

Good thing? He apparently seemed serious about averting further contact with Amanda.

Bad thing? Well, heck. Murder magnet that I am, I abhor seeing others accused of killings they didn't commit. And despite how I despised Amanda, I still doubted she was guilty.

Even though Leon had been found dead in her house. And she'd been his main stalker subject at the time. And —

Okay, if I kept that up, I might convince myself she *had* done it.

Would that be such a bad thing?

At that precise second, I was too confused to say.

But I was determined to dig out the truth, whatever it was. And not because of our farce of a contract. I'd do it for *me.* To meet and beat the formidable challenge. Yet I wanted Amanda to stay out of my way.

Endeavoring to sound utterly reasonable, I sublimated my ongoing irritation and said, "I understand how upset that Corina Carey and her tabloidlike reporting can make anyone. I'll make allowances for that, Amanda. I'll even delve deeper into your case tomorrow and talk to some of the people I didn't reach before. But enough's enough. Get out of our faces right now, or forget any further assistance from either of us."

I tossed a glance toward Jeff, who nodded his assent.

"Thanks, Kendra." Her tone tingled with ice. "Give me a call about whatever you find, and if I think of anything else, I'll let you know." She stormed out without even looking again at Jeff, slamming the front door behind her.

Which should have made me feel great.

But it wasn't just the fact that she'd narrowly missed catching poor Lexie's muzzle in the door that instead made me steam. Maybe, like my pup, I was traumatized by the negative atmosphere in this abode.

Jeff, after staying silent for several seconds, said, "I already knew she could be a bitch. That's why we got divorced in the first place. But blaming me — us — for not figuring out how to get her out of her own mess . . ."

"You said it," I agreed. I suddenly felt exhausted. "Come on, Lexie. Let's go home."

Jeff stood in front of me, his large hands clasped on my shaking shoulders. "Please stay, Kendra." His amazing blue eyes stared down into mine, sapping my resolve.

But after all the argument and emotion of

the last hour, I needed space. Time to think. And perhaps a good solitary session of sipping something strong.

"I'm planning a big day of investigating on Amanda's behalf tomorrow," I told him. "I don't want to be distracted by exhaustion from staying up too much tonight." I did stretch up on my tiptoes and give him one hot and sexy kiss good night. Then I headed to the kitchen, retrieved Lexie's leash, and left.

Good thing we'd slept at home, I informed myself the next morning after the conversation Lexie and I had with Rachel and Beggar.

My pet-sitting assistant, full of excitement, notified me that her next long days required for her movie shoot would start in less than a week.

"Can you believe it, Kendra?" the waiflike late-teen trumpeted. "I have to visit the filming location in Canada and stay there for a few weeks, while the first scenes I'll be in are shot. There'll be more later, too. I don't understand how they schedule things, but maybe I'll learn on the job."

"Sounds educational," I said, trying not to shadow her exuberance by my lack of enthusiasm.

"Oh, Kendra, I'm so sorry . . . but the people you met at that pet-sitters group will be able to help you, won't they?"

"Of course. We traded information and promised to backstop each other. It'll be fine." I figuratively crossed all my fingers. And made a mental note to call my new best pet-sitting friends Tracy Owens and Wanda Villareal today.

But recalling the conversation I'd eavesdropped on at the group meeting, I sighed at the idea I could wind up casting some of my client list to the competition.

I dropped Lexie off at Darryl's before heading for my first client of the morning. That happened to be Piglet the pug, whom I'd known for about as long as I'd been a pet-sitter. Not that I'd commenced being Piglet's sometime caretaker immediately, but he'd been the beneficiary of my first attempt at animal dispute resolution. I'd helped to ensure his continued ownership by Fran Korwald, who'd evinced eternal gratitude and now hired me to care for Piglet when she was out of town. She'd sent other customers my way, too — both for sitting and for ADR-ing. Even with my abbreviated sitting schedule now that I was practicing law again, Fran was one of those clients

I catered to myself, whether or not I had an assistant available.

And Piglet? A pug-load of fun as he waddled alongside me on our long walk.

Fortunately, Fran's home wasn't far from Dana Maroni and Stromboli's in Burbank, where I headed next.

I sucked in my breath in irritation when I noticed poor Meph alone and leashed once more in Maribelle's backyard. I'd thought she'd undertaken an improvement in her pup's situation, but apparently I was mistaken. I did my usual enjoyable routine with Stromboli, then hugged him and locked him inside.

From Stromboli's yard, I slipped next door to treat Meph to a biscuit and, more important, some attention — which was when I noticed the note tied around the wiry and excited pup's collar.

It had my name on it.

So, of course, I unlooped the string and scrutinized the surprisingly long missive of loopy letters squeezed onto a not-so-large piece of lined paper.

It read, *Kendra, I knew you'd see Stromboli so I left Meph out for fresh air. House unlocked. Please put Meph in, give treat, and pat head. I'll pay when I see you. Thought of someone I can give him to who'll love him? I'll miss him awfully. M.*

I smiled and shook my head as I complied with M.'s wishes. More than one pat on the head, of course, and Meph wagged all over. But, no, I hadn't thought of someone else to love this lovable mutt. At least not yet.

I pondered that, Corina Carey, Amanda, and more as I finished up a couple more pet-sitting visits and headed to the office. My conclusion? It was way past time for more proactive probing into Leon's death. Now.

Well . . . as soon as I'd dealt with my other duties.

First thing after exchanging hellos with chirpy Mignon at her reception desk, I noted Borden holding a conclave of firm attorneys in our bar-turned-conference room. I slid inside and gave my morning's greetings to the group of them: Borden in an aloha shirt I'd seen before, curly-haired Geraldine Glass, plump William Fortier, and classy Elaine Aames, all products of Borden's senior generation of attorneys.

I'd spent time over the last months bonding with silver-haired estates and trusts attorney Elaine and the amazingly intelligent Blue and Gold Macaw she'd adopted — Gigi. Poor Gigi was previously owned by a former attorney at this firm, Ezra Cossner, who'd been slain by a killer right in his office down the hall. Hey, I said I was a murder magnet.

"Borden, I'll be working on one of my own matters most of today," I said. "Okay?"

"Is your question rhetorical?" he responded with a smile. "You'll do it anyway, won't you?"

"Sure," I said, "but figured this was a good time to let you know, so if you had something urgent to attend to, the gang would hear about it here, take pity on you, and volunteer. Right?" I scanned the room, but no one's hands elevated. Lots of grins suddenly appeared, though. Gad, how I loved this group!

"Does this have anything to do with that stalker slaying?" Elaine asked. She'd been smack-dab in the middle of Ezra's murder investigation and knew how I operated — whether I liked it or not. "I read about it in the paper, and last night there was stuff on TV, too. That Corina Carey is some investigative reporter."

"You could say that," I said.

"I just did," Elaine jabbed back.

"She's a reason I have to delve deeper into who could have killed Leon Lucero besides Amanda Hubbard. Okay, gang?"

"I've got nothing pressing for you now

since you've got the Sherman case under control," Borden said. "Go to it, Kendra." He was seconded by the rest. I smiled all the way down the open restaurant hallway to my office.

Then I frowned as I tried to figure out how to approach my many possible suspects — literally or figuratively? I referred to the amazing list generated by Jeff's computer guru, my pal Althea.

The only prior stalking victim of Leon's I'd spoken to in person was Betty Faust. She was still on my list, as was her sweetheart, the incredibly hulking Coprik.

I considered calling some of Leon's other victims again, but none had returned my earlier messages. Many lived far enough away that sitting on their doorsteps to ensure they couldn't avoid me was simply too impractical. I chose a couple of locals, though, for follow-up.

I referred to my notes, which suggested that I look further into the doctors and others at Amanda's office. Might any of them have wanted to dispose of Leon at Amanda's expense?

Then there was Amanda's brother, Bentley Barnett. And . . . hey, there could be a whole universe of suspects out there.

Corina Carey had even suggested she had

a growing list. Neither the cops nor she were likely to share their thinking with me, of course.

Only — I dug out a phone number and called it. "Hi, Mitch," I said to Amanda's attorney when he answered. "Did you see Corina Carey's report on Channel —"

"Of course," he responded, sounding huffy. "I've even tried to talk to the woman about what she's found so far, but she only asks me questions and won't answer mine. She refers me to the attorneys for her paper and TV station. They're claiming journalistic privilege regarding sources, or something else that shouldn't work but is at least delaying things."

"Damn," I said. "I promised Amanda last night to push even harder to figure out who else could have killed Leon, and Corina made herself sound like an ideal resource. What does your cocounsel, Quentin Rush, think about all this?"

"I haven't reached him yet to ask," Mitch said. "Do you have any other information you can share with him and me?"

"Sure. You and I can get together and compare notes. Feel free to bring Quentin. I'd love to meet him and get his perspective. Meantime, I'll continue trying to talk to Leon's stalking victims. He was definitely a champion."

"Lots of people with motive," Mitch agreed.

Yeah, and if you'd done your homework, you'd be able to save me a whole lot of research right about now. "Absolutely," I said. "I've already talked to some and I intend to speak with even more."

"Great! Yes, let's do lunch and discuss it soon. Today's Friday . . . next week? I'll check Quentin's schedule, too."

"Great," I said.

Today *was* Friday, I realized as I hung up. I'd have the whole weekend to attempt face-to-faces with other local stalking victims. Wouldn't it be a kick if I could impress famous counsel-to-the-stars Quentin Rush with my snooping prowess?

Which made this an excellent opportunity to return to Amanda's medical office and see what I could learn.

Not much, as it turned out. Oh, her boss Dr. Henry Grant was in, and I was able to convince the receptionist to allow me a brief audience between patients in the disinfectant-fragrant hall near the waiting room. But the heart of the cardiologist seemed in the wrong place that day. His beard-laden chin twitched as he reiterated how he hoped the best for Amanda, but out of sight, out of mind, was how he now looked at Leon Lucero. He hadn't exactly wished his difficult patient dead, but now that he was gone things were much more serene around this office. And, no, he still hadn't any ideas who besides Amanda might have murdered the man. Not him, certainly.

When he stalked off, I was glad enough to find myself still in that hallway. For the next ten minutes, I hastily interviewed other doctors who looked alternately angry or impatient or unnerved by my pointed questions. Same went for their equally irritated and upset staff. More than one suggested strongly that I leave, but it wasn't until a white jacket-clad Amanda herself exited one of the examination rooms that I was given a direct order.

"You're supposed to be helping me," she hissed, "not putting my job in jeopardy. Get out of here."

"Sure thing," I said. "I'm just doing my best to absolve you of Leon's murder."

The whites of her gray eyes were shot with red, and I noticed wrinkles at the edges of her eyelids and mouth that had appeared overnight. The woman was aging before my eyes.

Which, nasty person that I was, seemed

just fine with me.

"Well, until you do, I don't have to stay away from Jeff," she said with a snotty smile.

Incredible! I drew in my breath. Talk about things growing old. I was getting damned tired of my disagreements with this irritating ex-wife. And, by extension, with her ex-husband. "Fine. Knock yourself out," I said. "Better yet, knock *him* out." I stomped out of there.

Only . . . well, I didn't expect her to take me literally.

But late that night, when I'd finished my pet-sitting and picked up Lexie, and she and I sat on my small living room sofa staring at some silly TV sitcom, my cell phone sang. It was Jeff, not much of a surprise at that hour.

But what he said nearly knocked my socks off.

"Kendra?" His voice sounded weak. "Can you come over to my place and take me to the emergency room? Amanda just ran me over with her car."

CHAPTER SEVENTEEN

"She may not have killed Leon Lucero, but she sure as hell tried to kill you!" I exclaimed to Jeff a couple of hours later, after he'd gone through the emergency room and been poked, prodded, x-rayed, and bandaged.

He looked truly awful, but he was going to live. I helped him climb into my Beamer in the parking lot of St. Joe's — the Providence St. Joseph Medical Center in Burbank.

I always adored how Jeff's blue eyes twinkled, but just then they looked more like black holes than lively stars. "She didn't try to kill me," he protested. "The woman's just at her wit's end. Like I told you, I made the mistake of explaining to her I'd continue helping you find suspects in Leon's murder, but reminding her yet again that she wasn't welcome to drop in on me at home. I made the even bigger mistake of walking her out to her car. I walked behind the car to get back on the sidewalk, and she backed into me. She claimed she lost control."

"Not of the car, but her emotions," I said. "Even if she didn't intend vehicular homicide, it could have been the result. And she didn't even stick around to see if you survived."

"No," he said sadly. He stayed quiet for the rest of the ride to his home.

We'd gone through most of this before. He'd no intention of reporting anything to the cops, and he'd prevaricated plenty at the hospital when asked what had happened.

He was protecting his ex-wife, who'd bopped him with her bright red car.

He'd claimed over and over that he was over the woman, but this said otherwise.

Tonight wasn't a good time for me to make up my mind where my relationship with Jeff was heading. But I was afraid I had a pretty good idea.

Under Amanda Hubbard's wheels.

Back at Jeff's, Lexie and Odin acted delighted to see us. Yes, I'd brought my pup when I'd dashed to Jeff's. I figured poor Odin would need company while I rushed his master to medical care. I was especially glad about the dogs as a diversion while I helped an aching Jeff sponge-bathe and change into nightwear — no nudity or canoodling this night, that was for sure.

Lexie and I slept — or at least I tried to — not in Jeff's spacious bedroom, but back in the semistoreroom where I'd spent nights when I'd first started pet-sitting for the P.I. and his Akita. I didn't snooze much. I spent too much time checking on Jeff, standing in his bedroom door and listening for his breathing. Yes, he stayed alive for that night. And my feelings for him?

Well, let's just say they'd started hovering somewhere in purgatory.

I definitely drifted off, since I was awakened in the morning by barking dogs and chiming doorbells. I hurried to the front door. Unsurprisingly, Amanda stood there.

"Let me in," she insisted. Her beautiful blond hair was in absolute disarray, and her eyes were red enough to assert that she'd cried all night.

I opened the door but stayed in her way. "Jeff's okay, more or less, no thanks to you," I said.

"I can't believe what I did," she said, ending on a sob. "Okay, I promise I won't see him anymore. I wanted everything — your help, and him, too. But he told me off, and I couldn't take it. He's yours, Kendra. But, please, let me apologize to him."

Since I sensed his presence behind me, I couldn't forcefully say no. When I turned, I saw that the expression on his bruise-blued face was hard. "Apology accepted," he grumbled inamicably. "But don't come in, not now or anytime." Obviously he was as ambivalent about what was between them as I was about what was between him and me. Last night he'd sorta defended her. Today, he'd kicked her out.

Could I continue to attempt to clear this wild and miserable woman from a possible murder charge? Besides the challenge, all that was in it for me was her commitment to clear out of my lover's — former lover's? — life.

Did I care if he didn't see her again?

"What should I do, Darryl?" I asked out loud about an hour after the scene with Amanda. I'd taken Lexie and headed to Doggie Indulgence, needing the sage advice of my dearest human friend.

We sat in his office overlooking the rest of his resort, which he now kept open most weekends to accommodate his many customers in the entertainment industry. Fortunately. Although I'd have sought him out at home if I'd had to. Lexie was loose in the playroom, and last I'd seen her, she'd headed for the human furnishings area — probably needed a nap on the people sofa after our disquieting night.

I pushed some of the papers stacked on Darryl's desk out of my way and folded my head in my arms on top of it.

"What would you like to do, honey?" Darryl asked me. "Do you want to dump the whole defend-Amanda idea?"

"I don't know," I said miserably.

"Do you think she killed Leon?"

"That's the thing." I lifted my head and looked beyond Darryl's wire-rims into his sympathetic and omniscient brown eyes. "Whatever else she's done, I think she's being framed for Leon's murder."

"And how do you feel about that?"

"Who turned you into a shrink?" I demanded irascibly. Then I sighed and said, "Sorry. How do I feel, Doc Nestler? Shitty. I mean, I know what pressure the woman's under, and she obviously can't take it. And I'd feel a hell of a lot worse if I didn't help to clear her and she was tried and found guilty."

His smile was sympathetic. "Well then," he said, "what's your game plan for today?"

I'd already intended to seek out some of

241

Leon's alternate stalking victims today. He'd selected several in Southern California besides Betty Faust, but all had resided in different areas.

One was in Redondo Beach, and after Lexie and I enjoyed our pet-sitting rounds, I decided to head that way, with a stop en route in Santa Monica.

At Kennedy McCaffrey's office.

He was the patient of Dr. Henry Grant's to whom Amanda had introduced me. The contractor who appeared athletically gorgeous but actually evinced some symptoms of heart disease.

The painter who'd had his palette piqued when Leon copied from him.

Did I know he'd be in? Sure did! I called first, using one of those cards with long distance minutes on it, in case he had caller ID. Not that I knew of any reason for him to avoid me, but I hated to drive all that distance and find that *he* knew of a reason.

His tiny office was many blocks from the beach, in a small complex of three-story buildings connected by a central courtyard. I skipped up the steps to the second floor, found "McCaffrey Contracting" on a door and walked in.

The first room I entered was small and empty but had a couple of doors leading out of it. I knew I'd found the right place since every wall had several seascapes on it, most resembling those I'd seen at Amanda's.

Only — were hers Kennedy's or Leon's? They mostly looked alike to me.

I chose the door on the left, since I thought I heard a muffled voice from that direction. Sure enough, there he was, sitting behind a desk large enough to unroll blueprints on, chatting on a cell phone. He still looked well built, tanned, and handsome, but I remembered how he'd coughed and grown ashen at our last encounter. I'd try not to upset him — too much — today.

When he looked up at me, recognition dawned in his eyes, chased by a frown on his mouth. He said goodbye to whomever he conversed with and demanded, "What are you doing here?"

"Looking for you," I replied. "I happened to be passing by and hoped to see some of your artwork, since you said Leon Lucero had stolen from you."

"Copied me," Kennedy grumbled. "Same thing, to an artist."

"Right. I saw some of your work on the walls in the other room. They're really nice! Did you give some of your paintings to Amanda? Or sell them to her?"

"Gave her a couple," he said. "If she's got

more, then they're his."

"Oh." Would that be motive enough for Kennedy to kill Leon? We'd gone over this once before, and I hadn't thought so then. But now I was more eager to lay the blame on someone besides Amanda. Had I slipped this guy off the hook too easily?

"Like I told you before," Kennedy continued, "yes, I hated the guy and his thievery. But no, I didn't kill him. Is that what you're here about today? I've got a potential customer coming in, so let's talk and get it over with."

"I'm that potential customer," I admitted, sagging against his doorframe. "I just called to see if you'd be here."

"Well, I am." His scowl grew darker. "So what is it you really want?"

"Help," I said. "I'm stuck. I'm still tracking down people Leon harassed, but some live outside this area. I'm not sure I can track everyone's schedules to see which non-locals happened to be visiting when Leon was killed. There were simply too many people with motive to kill him — did you know the guy was a serial stalker?"

He leaned back in his chair and shook his head. "Why am I not surprised? He didn't stalk me, though. And if I knew who had more than a motive to kill him — like, who really did it — I'd be glad to tell the cops."

"Did he ever confront you?" I persisted. "Or did you ever confront him?"

"Yes to the latter," Kennedy admitted. "But the guy was essentially a coward. I looked him up when I was seeing Amanda to tell him to lay off her. He did for a while, maybe because he figured I knew where he lived and I'd have no hesitation about beating him up. What he didn't know, then, was that, appearances notwithstanding, I have to limit my exercise." His sudden smile was sad. "He took up against Amanda again with a vengeance after he first saw me at her doctors' offices as a patient."

"Interesting," I mused, eyeing a chair across Kennedy's office. Did I want to sit there?

Not really. I'd left Lexie in the Beamer in the parking lot next door. And, despite Kennedy's questionable health, I preferred being near enough to the door to escape, if necessary.

"So, did I tell you anything helpful?" Kennedy asked, obviously ready to dismiss me — a good thing, I thought.

"Maybe," I said. "I admit I'm floundering. I'm just hoping something someone says will turn on a light and let me see Leon's killer."

"I specialize in foundations and walls," Kennedy said. "But I'd be glad to refer you to an electrician."

"Very funny," I said. After handing him another of my cards and getting his concurrence to call if he thought of anything enlightening, I left.

Lexie listened sympathetically as I told her what a waste of time that had been. "But he was sort of on the way to our next stop," I assured her.

Which was another beach community not many miles down the coast, still in Los Angeles County. There, at an address on Pacific Coast Highway, I'd be able to locate Nellie Zahn — or so Althea's superb info said. The data indicated that Nellie had been stalked by Leon about four years ago, which was when she'd obtained a TRO.

I pulled into a parking space on the block containing Nellie's address. When I regarded the single-story building, I blinked in surprise. The sign over the big front window read, "Nellie's Super Self-Defense." Which didn't suggest a stalking victim to me. Especially a victim of Leon's, whom Kennedy had suggested was a sort of wimp.

I tucked Lexie under my arm and headed inside.

There, a whole flock of women were dressed in a variety of gear, from sweats to white martial-arts wear. Shouts mixed with grunts as they kicked and punched in unison.

Facing them, at the front, was a lady whose fighting skills seemed excellent. I watched for a while, until the class ended, keeping a wriggling Lexie under control.

The crowd soon disbursed, and I headed toward the instructor as she likewise headed toward me. We met in the middle of the polished hardwood floor.

"Hi, are you interested in self-defense lessons?" she said. "Unfortunately, we don't have any available for dogs."

"Oh, Lexie's pretty good at knowing when to growl and when to run," I said. "I'm looking for Nellie Zahn."

"Look no longer," she said. "That's me."

Somewhat shorter than my five-five, she wore a white canvas toga over loose white pants, and a black belt tied about her waist. Her blond hair was short and curly, and there was a pugnacious and proud set to her thick jaw.

Some of my puzzlement must have been written on my face, since she said, "You were expecting someone else?"

"It's just that I came here to speak with

one of Leon Lucero's stalking victims," I said, "and, frankly, you look less like a victim than nearly anyone I could imagine."

Her face suddenly seemed cast in stone. "Come with me," she insisted. I followed her from the workout area into a small office. "Sit." She pointed to a green upholstered metal chair. As if I were Lexie, I obeyed. She took her place behind a small wooden table stacked with promotional brochures for this place. "Now, who the hell are you?" she demanded.

I handed her one of my law office cards. "I'm not here representing a client, exactly," I admitted. "The police are investigating a . . ." What was Amanda to me? A friend? An acquaintance? A highly hated bitch I was attempting to boot out of lives including my own? "Er, let's just say I'm looking into Leon Lucero's murder for motives of my own."

"The bastard got exactly what he deserved," Nellie spat, contorting her face belligerently. "Whoever killed him did the world a humongous favor."

"I can't disagree," I said, "but the reality is that he was unlawfully killed, and whoever did it will be tried for murder. I'm just hoping to ensure the wrong person isn't railroaded."

"I see your point." She settled back in her seat. "I'd be glad to help with the legal expenses of the *right* person, though. What do you want to bet it was done in self-defense?"

"Maybe, but if so, why not come forward and admit it? And it was done in someone else's house."

"I've seen stuff about it on the news," she admitted. "In fact, since hearing that Leon finally got his, I've been addicted to seeing what the media say about it. I recognize you now from some of the reports — the nosy lawyer who solves murders."

I tried to swallow my irritated reaction and managed a weak smile instead. "That's me."

"So you think the main suspect, Amanda whatever, didn't do it? She was one of his stalking victims, or so the reports say."

"I know firsthand that she was a stalking victim," I said, "but even though his body was found in her house, I doubt that she did it."

"Maybe not," Nellie said. "And I assume that, since you're here, you wanted to find out if it was me. Well, Leon's been out of my life for a long time, thank heavens. And in a way I have him to thank for all this." She waved blunt-nailed fingers in an arc that seemed intended to encompass the whole gym. "I was an actress before. Got a lot of character roles — you know, the ingenue's best friend. Then Leon decided he loved me, the bastard. I got damned tired of running away from him, hollering at the cops to stop him before he hurt me, and not just arrest him after. I realized real soon that no one was really going to help me but *me*. That's when I started taking self-defense lessons. And did it ever feel fine to kick Leon's butt the first time. And the second. There never was a third. I didn't see him again after that."

"How long ago was that?" I asked.

"A couple of years," Nellie said. "I might have murdered him before then, given an opportunity. Now, I'd take great pleasure in squashing his balls with my best karate kicks. But kill him? No, Kendra, it wasn't me."

CHAPTER EIGHTEEN

"I believed her," I said to Lexie while we navigated the San Diego Freeway north on the way home. "How about you?"

As always, my cheerful Cavalier seemed to agree with me as she looked over and smiled — well, panted. She then stuck her nose back toward where the passenger window was cracked open a bit to let her enjoy all the scents we passed.

It was early evening, but the sky was darkening. We fast approached Saturday night with no social plans. Oh, well.

Worse, I realized, was that tomorrow was Valentine's Day. We'd spend it together, but, undoubtedly, alone.

Except . . . well, there'd been a little scheme I'd been mulling. The answer to two people's problems. And maybe I could fix things for them both with a smidgen of my specialty: ADR.

As I exited the freeway awhile later, I

made a couple of cell phone calls. Amazingly, both people were available. I scheduled a Valentine's Day dinner for more than two.

Little did I know then how Cupid had decided to deal with us that day.

I took a generously long time with my pet-sitting rounds that evening, reveling in my visits with Stromboli, Piglet, and my other cute charges. With these guys, at least, Lexie got along famously, so I walked her right along with them.

I realized I'd soon have a passel more clients without a whole lot more time to tend to them if I didn't corral some backup during Rachel's unavailability. I'd call my new pet-sitting cronies tomorrow. And subtly query them about any penchant for customer-pinching.

I called Jeff that evening after Lexie and I returned home. He claimed to be recuperating well from his confrontation with Amanda's fender. And, no, he still had no intention of reporting her to the authorities, or even his insurance company — which slew most of the sympathy I felt for his sore body.

"Sorry," I said to his repeated dinner invitation, delighted that my response would ring of truth. "I already have plans for a

Valentine's Day dinner." I cringed at his sudden silence. Did I honestly want him to exit my life?

Hell if I knew.

The next morning, after a surprisingly sound sleep, I engaged in déjà vu, seeing most of the same animals again, all except for a couple of cats whose visits were confined to one a day. I even waved to Maribelle Openheim, who surprisingly was in her yard with Meph that morning.

"See you tonight," she called.

"Right," I returned.

Then, speaking of cats, I called Amanda. "Can I come talk to you about what I've been learning lately?"

"Sure," she said. "But I gather you haven't solved Leon's murder yet."

"I need a lot more clues," I admitted, shifting irritably in the Beamer. Lexie glanced at me in apparent alarm, and I reached over to pat her pretty head. "I'm hoping you can give me a few."

"I've told you all I know," she stormed.

"Have a fun time on trial," I countered sweetly.

"Okay, come on over."

There was a car in Amanda's driveway in addition to her red Camry — one of those hybrid Toyotas that were supposed to provide better mileage than the majority on the road did by gobbling gasoline like chocolate and belching smog.

Definitely not Jeff's gourmet Escalade.

I pulled my Beamer behind Amanda's car. The day was overcast enough that I didn't have to find a shady spot for Lexie. I went up the walk and stopped on the porch of the plain stucco cottage as I'd done days before, when Amanda wound up conning me into caring for her cats. It felt like a distant memory — long before Leon had leapt out at me, then got screwed with a lethal screwdriver, and I'd wound up entering into a devil's bargain with Amanda, with Jeff as our possible pawn.

I looked around toward the pittosporum, but no Cherise or Carnie appeared. I rang the bell.

Amanda answered, dressed in a green gauzy thing over slacks. She appeared exhausted. "Come in," she said. I followed her down that hall lined with seascapes, wondering which were Kennedy McCaffrey's and which were Leon's likenesses. There were several different signatures on the pictures' respective corners. Walking as fast as I was, I couldn't make out the names or count how many of each. In any event, their styles still seemed similar to me. Cheap style-copying? Amanda's art preference? Both?

I couldn't see how this related to Leon's demise, but without any suspect taking precedence, my mind stayed open.

As I'd surmised, Amanda had company. A man I hadn't met sat smack in the middle of her red-pillowed Scandinavian sofa. Obviously overweight, he had little hair and lots of flesh pudging out his round cheeks. He stood as we entered the room.

"You're Kendra?" he asked. "You're younger than I thought you'd be, with that mouth on you."

He absolutely had me at a disadvantage, but solely for a moment. "You must be Bentley." Amanda's brother, the booze-drinking bailiff I'd spoken to on the phone.

"Yes, I must."

As I recalled our conversation, *he'd* been the one with the annoying mouth. I'd simply suggested some directions for him to wander in. Like, had he happened to have driven up from San Diego the night Leon was murdered in his sister's home? He'd said no, but who knew? Only Leon and him.

Sitting in one of the matching white loveseats at the sides of the sofa, Amanda appeared confused. "How do you two know each other?" she asked.

"Your ears weren't burning the other night when we talked about you?" her brother inquired. "I'd tried calling you here, and Kendra picked up."

"The night you were being interrogated," I explained, seating myself on a wooden chair atop the striped, shaggy rya area rug adorning the hardwood floor. Interesting, I thought, that Bentley Barnett would look so different from his annoyingly beautiful sister. What genes did they share? None that I could see. "I'd come to take care of Cherise and Carnie. Where are those cute cats, by the way?"

"Around," Amanda said distractedly. "How come I didn't hear about this call?"

Why did she seem so concerned about it? Could she be worried that her brother'd been the one to off her stalker?

"Never came up in conversation," Bentley replied.

Amanda looked nonplussed. "So what did you want to talk about?" she grumped, aiming her annoyance at me.

"I'm still trying to fulfill my end of our bargain," I said. "I wanted to run my progress, or lack thereof, by you for your edification and any information it brings to mind." I described my discussion with Kennedy McCaffrey, followed by stalking-victim-turned-self-help paradigm Nellie Zahn.

"She sounds perfect!" Amanda gushed when I'd finished. "I mean, there she is, all buffed up and strong enough to stab someone right where it hurts. She's got to be our murderer."

"Did you listen to what I said?" I asked incredulously. "Sure, she won't mourn Leon, but she wisely put that part of her life far behind her. Even used it to better herself. What would her motive be now?"

"What if she planned it all this time?" Bentley interjected. "She could have started her martial-arts stuff intending to get into top condition, then get back at the jerk who'd stalked her."

Amanda clapped her hands. "Good thinking, baby brother."

I leaned back on the stark wooden chair and pondered this proposition. They could be right. Not that I bought it, but I couldn't necessarily eliminate Nellie from the suspect list.

Any more than I could dump Bentley Barnett. I mean, the guy obviously cared about his sister. And San Diego wasn't so far from the San Fernando Valley. But Leon had had the strength of possible insanity. Bentley appeared too soft to get very far in any physical altercation.

On the other hand, he was a bailiff. He was therefore a sworn peace officer with the San Diego County Sheriff's Department, so he'd had law-enforcement training. He probably knew moves to put a suspect — or in this instance, victim — off guard.

"You could be right," I said. "I'll look a little deeper into Nellie's background and location on the night in question."

"Have you talked to Mitch lately?" Amanda asked. "He called late Friday to ask how well your investigation was going and didn't sound pleased with your progress."

"He called *you* to criticize *me?*" I found that a whole lot irritating. I mean, Amanda's lawyer could have discussed things further with me. Besides, he was supposed to be setting up a lunch so I could meet Quentin Rush — and talk about the case then.

"That's not exactly how it went," Amanda admitted. She sighed. "He mostly asked if I'd heard any more from the cops. Which I had. That Detective Noralles of yours certainly likes to ask questions. I've had to tell him more than once that I'll want my attorney involved if I answer any more."

"Good call. And for your information, he's

absolutely not *my* detective. Although the way he keeps showing up in my life, I sometimes wonder if he has it in for me personally."

"Do you think?" Amanda asked anxiously. "If so — well, is it possible to ask for a different detective to head the investigation about Leon?"

"No way," Bentley broke in. "Don't you watch all those detective shows on TV?"

I considered contradicting Bentley for assuming that what he watched was true. He should have known better. Most other people in the know, like Jeff and even my nemesis Noralles, were quick to say that the spate of TV crime-scene analysts, although absolutely enthralling at times, didn't exactly do things the way reality required.

"Anyway," Amanda went on, "I informed Mitch you were doing a great job, and that the only thing I'd told the cops was that you were coming up with lots of better suspects than me."

"I bet Noralles loved that," I said, shaking my head. "He gets particularly peeved when he thinks I'm butting into one of his investigations and showing up his detective skills." Something I intended to accomplish this time, too. I hoped.

That was when the two little felines stalked proudly into the room. The one in front — Cherise, since she was larger — had a small and definitely dead rodent hanging from her mouth.

"Eeew," Amanda groaned. "What are you doing, Cherise?"

Both continued their approach until they'd walked onto the area rug and Cherise deposited her prize in front of Barnett. Interesting. Once again I wondered: The cats either gave presents to people they liked, or they considered Amanda's brother an interloper.

Giving weight to the latter possibility, the kitties both raised their hackles when Bentley stood and kicked at them. Or at least at the mouse. Either way, I started liking Amanda's brother even less than I had a few moments earlier — which hadn't been much.

"Don't do that!" Amanda ordered, even as the two Bengal cats backed off a bit and regarded Bentley as if he were scum beneath the feet of the deceased rodent.

"They're disgusting!" Bentley exclaimed. "Why are they carrying dead mice?"

"According to Amanda, they give mice as warnings to people they consider intruders in their home. And that might basically be true, since one was found by Leon's bloody body."

"Ugh. Get rid of them, Amanda."

"I'd sooner get rid of you, baby brother." She stooped and picking up Carnie, who went limp with apparent ecstasy as Amanda stroked her furry back.

"Time for me to go." I stood. Because I felt sorry for poor Cherise, who still stood on the floor staring haughtily toward the humans, I went over and picked her up. Damned if the little snooty little feline didn't start purring at me. I grinned. "I think we're finally friends," I told Amanda.

"Don't count on it." She didn't exactly sound thrilled. "So, do Jeff and you have something romantic planned to celebrate Valentine's Day tonight?"

The nasty way she smiled over those words suggested she knew I'd brushed Jeff off. But at least I now knew the two of them hadn't made hot plans, either.

Maybe.

"Nothing for certain yet," I said, speaking the truth. "Anyway, I'll be in touch when I have something else to report. And keep me informed about any other people you think of who could be suspects."

"Sure thing."

I put Cherise down, and said a brief and

insincere goodbye to Bentley. Amanda saw me to the door.

"Have fun tonight," she called as I strode down the walkway toward my Beamer.

As always, I yearned for a shower after leaving Amanda's company. Maybe more so, having met her dork of a brother.

Instead, I said to Lexie, "I need chocolate. Mind if I stop at Ralphs?" The supermarket wasn't far away, and Lexie seemed amenable — most likely because I had a hard time shopping anyplace there were doggy supplies without buying her some treat or other.

I found a spot in the crowded parking lot, once again glad that the day remained overcast since I didn't have to be choosy about seeking shade. "I won't be long," I told her.

Which I wasn't. Though we'd only recently started spending all our nights at home alone, I had adequate supplies to feed us, but, heck, you can never have enough salad or fruit . . . or chocolate. Or dog biscuits.

I didn't spend long in the store. But when I pushed the cart up to the trunk of the car, I didn't see Lexie.

I did, however, see a piece of paper stuck in the windshield wiper.

My heart racing, I first rushed up to stare

in the driver's side window.

Lexie was there, thank heavens. That was the good thing.

The bad thing was that she was cowering on the floor.

I pushed the button to unlock the door and dashed inside. Seeing me, she leapt up onto the passenger seat and into my arms. She was trembling as she laid her head on my neck and cuddled close.

"What's wrong?" I asked her. Sometimes, I've known what my pup was trying to tell me as if she could speak English. This time, I didn't. And it was one of those occasions when I ached to understand Barklish.

As I sat there holding her, my eyes lit on that piece of paper lodged beneath the windshield wiper. I felt certain it would give at least some explanation.

I snugged Lexie under my arm as I slid back out of the car and reached for the page. It appeared to be a common sheet of paper, and its contents had probably been printed on an ordinary computer.

Its contents, though, were anything but ordinary:

No more prying, or your dog will pay.

CHAPTER NINETEEN

Lexie still beneath my arm, I rushed around frantically, attempting to find anyone who'd seen what happened. I mean, Lexie wasn't exactly the most timid pup, yet she'd seemed awfully intimidated. Whoever left the note must have menaced her in some manner. At least the car windows were intact, so hopefully the threat hadn't been too traumatic.

But if someone had viewed whoever had approached my car, left the note, and possibly yelled at my poor puppy, no one still scrambling about in the busy parking lot admitted to seeing anything.

"If only you could tell me who it was," I said wishfully to Lexie once we were both ensconced back in the Beamer. "You might even be able to tell me who killed Leon. But who even knew we'd be here?"

The disquieting answer was that someone had followed me from Amanda's. Amanda herself? Bentley? Another person who was Leon's killer, still casing the place to see what progress was being made in his or her identification? Had someone pursued me to Amanda's in the first place?

Did this mean I was getting close to identifying the murderer without even knowing it?

If only I had a clue!

As I got ready for my Valentine's Day "date" much later in the day, I was still pondering who the menacing party might be.

Standing in the shower, I considered . . .

Had I shook Kennedy McCaffrey enough to cause him to stalk me for the rest of the day? Had Nellie Zahn's recently acquired self-defense skills allowed her to kill Leon, as Bentley had alleged, then threaten my beloved pup as a result of my even suggesting her as a suspect?

What about onetime stalking victim Betty Faust, or her lover and protector, the muscular Coprik? Were one or both hanging around this area in an attempt to see if anyone suspected them in Leon's death? If they'd killed him, they'd know where Amanda lived, of course, since the stalker was eliminated right in her home. Perhaps they'd followed Leon around a bit before he died to see where he hung out, and who his current victim was.

Amanda's employer, Dr. Henry Grant, would know where she resided. Could he be watching over Amanda, to protect her — or to ensure all police fingers pointed toward her?

Someone else at Amanda's office?

Someone else altogether, whom I hadn't considered, yet had worried with my continued questions?

Well, hell. Whoever it was had done one of the worst things I could imagine: threaten my little Lexie. I had to ensure her safety at all times.

I toweled myself dry and put on my big, fluffy robe. I turbaned my deep brown hair, now stringy and wet, beneath another towel as I chose the top and slacks to don for my matchmaking shindig.

Like tonight, I thought. I wouldn't bring Lexie along on pet-sitting rounds, since that would mean leaving her alone in the car at some stops. Instead, she'd stay here, locked in our upstairs apartment behind our enhanced security system.

Poor pup would spend Valentine's evening alone. At least I'd make up for it later with an extra biscuit before bedtime.

"I'm really sorry, Lexie," I said, wishing I

could explain better in a language she'd understand. She wagged her long white-and-black tail, obviously comprehending the loving spirit of what I said, if not the exact sense of my words.

She'd also spend a lot more time, on weekdays while I worked, with Darryl and his Doggy Indulgence Day Resort, where I'd warn him to watch over her carefully. Which he would. And he'd ensure the same of his staff.

Still, I'd worry.

I selected a pale pink sweater from my closet, along with snazzy magenta slacks. I dried my essentially unstyled hair, then donned a light amount of makeup.

I studied my face. Not too bad, even if it had never approached Amanda's unquestionable beauty. Ordinary nose. Observant blue eyes. All a-okay . . . except, were there some wrinkles at the corners of those eyes that hadn't been there before because of concern about Lexie?

Well, hell. I'd already thought the same about Amanda's suddenly aging face, and I hated the idea — regarding me, not her. If I didn't fix the situation, I might stay worried indefinitely — and who knew how many new lines that might etch into my face?

"Know what?" I told my ever-present pup,

who sidled up against me as I sat at my makeup mirror on the desk in my den. "Whoever threatened you may never know it, but he or she has caused the exact opposite result from what they likely wanted. Instead of backing off, I have to figure this out all the faster. No way will I let whoever it is hurt you."

She stood on her hind legs, front paws on my legs as she stared searchingly into my face with her cute, huge brown eyes.

"See those wrinkles?" I asked her, still obsessing. "No, don't tell me. But I'll insist they go away when this is behind us."

My cell phone started to sing before Lexie could react. I reached for it across my desk, and didn't recognize the number as I answered.

"Hi, Kendra? This is Tracy Owens. We met at the Pet-Sitters Club of SoCal meeting."

"Sure. Good to hear from you. In fact, I've been meaning to give you a call."

"Did you mention at the meeting that you've had a snake as a client?"

I looked down at the deep pink shade of my slacks, nearly one of the colors of the pretty blue-and-magenta Py. "Yes, a ball python."

"Great! I've just been asked to care for a

California king snake while its owner's out of town, and instead of totally cringing and saying no, I've said okay. But I need pointers. Maybe a pep talk. I never thought about caring for a snake before."

"I don't know about king snakes, but ball pythons aren't bad. In fact, Py and I are good buddies. He did me a big favor."

"How about if we get together for lunch one day this week so you can tell me about it?"

"Great! And I need to talk to you about backup pet-sitting assistance." We set a time, date, and place. "See you then," I said, then hung up. I looked down at Lexie, who lay with her head on her paws regarding me solemnly from the floor. "Time for your dinner," I said, which brought her fast to her feet. "Then I'll need to leave."

I left my visit to Stromboli's for last. Of course. My Valentine's Day dinner would be next door.

I met Baird Roehmann on the street, right after I'd finished walking and feeding Stromboli.

"Then this is the right place," said His Honor, the silver-haired judge with the roamin' hands. "I wasn't sure." He paused. "You say the lady who lives there" — he pointed toward the house next door — "is the one with a really nice dog she can't keep?"

"That's right," I said. "Did you bring dinner?"

"The best from Georgio's." Which was a really good but underrated Italian place in a shopping center along Ventura Boulevard.

"Great. I'll help you carry it in."

Baird had dressed nicely for the night, although not in the usual black robes or business suits I was used to seeing him in. He wore a black sweater from which a white shirt collar peeked at the top. Below were black trousers and dressy top-stitched loafers with thick, shock-absorbing soles.

Black, to meet a fuzzy, possibly shedding dog? At least Meph was more gray than white. Even so . . .

Yes, my intended matchmaking that night was to introduce a judge who'd recently lost his beloved dog, to a dog whose owner couldn't keep the one she had. Couldn't . . . or wouldn't. No matter. The result would be the same.

I noticed, as I carried a plastic food bag and led Baird up the front walk, that Maribelle Openheim must have finally hired a gardener. Or mowed and trimmed the front yard herself. Even in the faint twilight, it appeared a whole lot better kept than it had before.

As I reached the front door, I pivoted back toward Baird, who also toted a bag. "Now, remember, just say so if you don't like Meph enough to adopt him. It won't do the poor dog any good if you take him home and change your mind."

"I wouldn't do that." The usual judicial boom was back in his voice, which almost made me smile . . . as long as I wasn't arguing a matter before him.

I rang the bell, and from inside we heard a dog bark. "He sounds good and spunky," Baird said.

Before I could comment, the door was pulled open. Maribelle with the wiry, wriggling terrier Meph beneath her arm, had also dressed for the occasion. Her yellow cotton shirt was belted into dark brown slacks. As always, her short hair looked meticulously styled, and she'd put on enough makeup to make her appear attractive, instead of baggy eyed and washed out.

"Hi. Come in, please."

Once we'd complied, I introduced her to Baird. We followed her into the truly compact kitchen and set our bags on the butcher-block style table. She put Meph down on the mock-brick linoleum floor.

Speaking to Baird, she said, "Kendra said that you recently lost your dog. I'm sorry."

"She told me that you lost your husband. My condolences on that."

Maribelle shook her head. "I didn't mean to, but I'm afraid I took my loneliness out on his poor dog, Meph. Meph, come here and meet Judge Roehmann."

"Please call me Baird."

"Baird." She drew out the name as if she took pleasure in its sound. "You have the most lovely silver hair. Only —"

"Only what?" I'd expected Baird to get upset at any slight to his appearance. Instead, he sounded interested.

"I don't know if Kendra told you I'm a hairstylist. I've got a shampoo-conditioner that would make your hair shine even more. And if you wore it just a little longer at the top, tapered slightly more at the sides . . ."

"Really? Where do you work? Maybe I could make an appointment."

"Sure." I'd never before seen Maribelle smile so broadly.

Baird dropped to his knees and let Meph sniff his hand. And then he started gently roughhousing with the game, friendly terrier.

"He's quite a bruiser, isn't he?"

"He does love to play," Maribelle acknowledged. Taking a rubber dog toy from the counter, she, too, stooped.

And smiled into Baird's eyes when he took the toy and started playing terrier tug-of-war.

This was going a whole lot better than I'd ever imagined.

The judge sure seemed attracted to widowed Maribelle Openheim, and vice versa.

Did they need me here to get better acquainted?

Not likely, although I was reluctant to depart without ensuring my initial impressions weren't false.

And so, I joined them in a delightful dinner of antipasto, lasagna, and Chianti. At least the food was good. Me? I felt like the proverbial crowd, as in "two's company."

Especially since Meph, the fourth in this cozy party, formed a common bond between them.

Still, I waited for a while after dinner as the two humans talked. Seemed like they had more in common than a love of Meph and Baird's silver hair.

"I was a court reporter many years ago," Maribelle said. "Before my kids were born. I got out of practice, though, and went into hairstyling instead of taking it up again." She sighed. "Now that I'm alone, I was thinking of trying again, only I'm awfully old to start competing with all the young people who know all the new recording systems so much better."

"I could help you get started," Baird said.

"Oh, I couldn't impose . . . only, I really did find the judicial process so fascinating. Maybe someday you could tell me about some of the most interesting trials you presided over. It must be so wonderful to be a judge."

"Most of the time." Baird sounded a whole bunch more modest than I was used to. Meantime, he'd taken Meph onto his lap, and the pup looked absolutely ecstatic — though that could be because of all the delicious odors of food remains on the kitchen table.

Time for me to talk, then exit. "Well, it looks as if Meph and you are getting along fine. Maribelle, are you willing to let Baird adopt him?"

"Oh, yes. I'm sure he'll take good care of him." But Maribelle's tone sounded sad.

"Of course I would, but you don't sound ready to give him up," Baird said.

"He did belong to my husband, and as Kendra convinced me, I've not taken the best care of him . . . because it hurt too much to see him. Before. But now that I realize I was hurting Meph, I've kept him with me more."

"Well, I really like him," Baird said. "But I understand what you're saying. Tell you what. You hang on to him for now, and I'll visit you both. Then we'll see."

"That sounds wonderful," Maribelle said.

I suspected he'd be visiting not solely to see the happy Meph.

When I left a few minutes later, Baird stayed there. How very odd, I thought. He was the judge who'd gone after every female who ever appeared in his courtroom — mostly those young enough to be his daughters. He'd not seemed at all interested in the many women nearer his own age.

But there'd clearly been chemistry between Baird and Maribelle. Who could have guessed?

I had a feeling that from now on, one way or another, Meph would be subject to all the human attention he could ever want.

CHAPTER TWENTY

So Valentine's Day was Valentine's Day after all, although not for me.

Even so, I held out hope I'd hear something from Jeff before the day was over. Maybe a phone call containing an immense apology for Amanda's intrusion into our lives and an attestation of undying love?

"Hah!" I said as I hugged Lexie upon my return to our comfy garage-top home. At least my puppy was safe. Under the circumstances of a threat hanging over our heads, I determined to let her romp in our fenced in yard, absolutely supervised, rather than taking a walk outside our grounds.

No incidents overtook us, and although I heard Beggar barking within the big house, I didn't see Rachel. Nineteen years old, she probably had a hot Valentine's date of her own.

Her dad, Russ, remained out of town, or I'd have invited him inside for a nightcap —

in the unlikely event he was spending this evening alone. He was a redheaded hunk, and although he was a little old for me, I'd considered him for a fleeting flirtation.

Which would have been especially nice on Valentine's night.

Okay, I was lonesome. "I admit it," I told Lexie. Canine company, especially of the Cavalier kind, was delightful, but it didn't make up for my lack of a real, human female-male relationship.

Especially when I'd assumed, not long ago, that I had one.

Although it wasn't especially late, I considered heading to bed early with a good book, preferably a thriller that contained a lot more killings than kisses.

That was my kind of mood.

Only, just as I started stripping for the shower, my cell phone rang.

Oh joy, I thought, sardonically scanning at the caller ID. I didn't need a gloating good night from Amanda.

And if she just happened to be with Jeff . . .

Oh, hell. I answered anyway.

"Kendra? Kendra, please call Mitch and come to the North Hollywood Police Station with him. I'm under arrest for murdering Leon!"

I hadn't a chance to speak before she hung up. Why had she called me? She should have phoned her attorney first.

Despite feeling irritable, I couldn't help a sense of sympathy. I'd nearly been in her situation, too. Fortunately, I'd figured out what happened while the multiple cases involving me were still under investigation, so I'd never been arrested.

But I'd expected it at any moment.

Consequently, I did as Amanda asked and called Mitch. He didn't answer his phone at first, and as I was tossed into voice mail I shouted, "Mitch, if you can hear this, pick up. It's an emergency."

He sounded miffed when he responded, and I thought I heard a female murmur in the background. Maybe he had a hot Valentine's date. Well, good for him. But if I had to suffer by hearing from Amanda, so should he. He was, after all, her actual attorney. I was merely her surrogate investigator who also happened to have a law license.

"I just heard from Amanda," I told Mitch, then repeated what she'd said. "I'd rather not go to the police station, but —"

"Me, too, but I'd appreciate it if you'd come. Obviously Amanda wants you there."

It wasn't as if I had anything else exciting to do that night. "All right," I said. "But I won't stay long."

"Fine."

"There's some stuff you should know." I quickly ran down the extent of my recent investigation, including my visits to Kennedy McCaffrey and Nellie Zahn, plus meeting Amanda's brother, Bentley, in person, and finishing with the threats to Lexie. "Nothing conclusive," I admitted as I ended.

"Well, something there might be helpful." He sounded as doubtful as I felt.

"Should you discuss it with Quentin Rush?"

"I will as soon as I can," Mitch agreed. "For now — well, I'll see you in a bit."

Okay. I finally had my good excuse, although there were others I'd have latched on to, given a chance.

I called Jeff.

"Kendra," he said, picking up immediately. Was that pleasure from hearing from me that I heard in his voice?

Or was I engaging in some serious wishful thinking?

Hell, I was the one who'd made it clear I didn't want to see him tonight, that I had other plans.

Yeah, like playing Cupid for Baird Roehmann, of all people. When all I'd intended was to throw the not-so-poor man a bone. Or, rather, introduce him to a possible pet.

Anyway, I hesitated barely a moment before explaining to Jeff why I'd called. "I just heard from Amanda. She's under arrest."

"What?" Any pleasure I might have previously imagined was now absolutely absent from his voice. "Where is she? Is Mitch there?"

"North Hollywood station, and he's on his way. Me, too."

"Me, three," Jeff said.

Hey. I was going to see my erstwhile lover on Valentine's night after all.

At the same time he attempted to play knight racing to his ex-wife's aid on the steed of his Cadillac Escalade.

As I'd anticipated, there wasn't much I could do at the station. I got to say hi, lucky me, to Ned Noralles and his sidekicks Howard Wherlon and new-guy Detective Elliot Tidus. But not being Amanda's attorney, I couldn't see her.

Mitch dashed in only minutes after I did. He was the one allowed to see to Amanda and get the details of her detainment.

I got to sit in the neighborhood-friendly

yet nevertheless chill-provoking reception area of the North Hollywood station, watching the uniformed officer behind the desk answering phone calls and greeting the scant additional visitors that night.

Then Jeff arrived.

"Where is she?" he demanded when he spotted me. He was dressed in jeans and a black leather jacket. His light brown hair was mussy and begged to have fingers run through it to tame it. Damn him! Why was he looking so sexy tonight, when I wanted so badly to get over him?

I'd not seen much of him since Amanda ran into him with her car. Yet here he was, dashing figuratively to her side to defend her.

"Somewhere inside." I gestured toward the door to the inner law-enforcement sanctum. "Mitch is with her."

He pulled me to the side of the room, shifting his head down so his mouth neared my ear. Time for a sexy nibble? No way.

"I know what you're thinking, Kendra," he said softly. "And you're wrong. I'm still mad as hell at Amanda for everything, including hurting me with her car. But she didn't try to kill me. Whatever she is, she's not a cold-blooded murderer."

"Then you're a hundred percent sure she

didn't kill Leon?" I was stuck at about ninety-eight percent, but not absolutely positive.

"Maybe in self-defense. That I could believe. But if that was what had happened, by now she'd have said so."

"I can't disagree," I said. "But —"

I stopped speaking as Mitch came through the door. "I figured you both were here."

As he should have at least with me, since he'd insisted that I come.

"Not much can be done tonight, but I've insisted on a speedy arraignment, and we'll ask for bail then. Probably tomorrow."

"She can make bail?" Jeff asked.

"Depends on the amount. We'll ask for O.R. — own recognizance — but the chances of that aren't high since this could be a capital case. Failing that, we'll try for as low as we can convince the judge."

"Well, let me know," Jeff said. "I know some good bail bondsmen."

I wasn't extremely familiar with the criminal world, but in my limited experience I suspected that was an oxymoron.

"I could kick in something," Jeff said. To get the ex-wife he purportedly disliked out of jail.

Jeff and I walked out together to the small parking lot for the public in front of the station, and he invited me to join him for a drink.

No time to answer before Ned Noralles strolled up to us. "Hubbard, how are you?" Obviously not caring a whit, he continued to me, "And Kendra. You haven't handed me a better suspect than the one I've got. You must be slipping. Or, gee, could it be that I'm right this time?"

"Sarcasm doesn't become you, Ned," I said, "especially when you're wrong once more. And this time it's personal . . . again. The killer threatened my little Lexie."

"Your dog?"

"Yep. You've met her. Anyway, I'll be sure to let you know when I determine who the real murderer is."

"Don't bet on it," he said with a scowl. "We've all the evidence we need. Amanda *Hubbard* is definitely it." He stressed the last name, stealing a nasty grin toward Jeff.

"Oh, you bet I'll bet on it. As if you didn't know, I love a challenge." With that, I slipped into my Beamer.

What an interesting end to Valentine's night.

I couldn't let Ned win that way. With Amanda under arrest, I obviously had to pick up my investigating pace.

I called her home the next morning, just in case she'd gotten out of jail earlier than anticipated. Not reaching her, I added her home to my list of pet-sitting places for the day.

Cherise and Carnie shouldn't have to suffer due to their mistress's untimely incarceration.

First thing, though, after dressing in a relatively casual skirt and blouse for an off-court day, I took care of my own pup — as well as my unsteady frame of mind. Lexie and I headed for Darryl's.

"Kendra!" He sounded pleased to see me as we entered. Clad in his usual green Henley-style knit shirt with the Doggy Indulgence logo on the pocket, he was busy checking in the day's clientele at the big front desk by the door.

Lexie beneath my arm, I watched in amusement as a large-sized shepherd mix played with a shih tzu, both tearing around the doggy resort, from the peoplelike sitting area to the canine toy-filled side and back again. Some of Darryl's employees appeared a little less enthused, especially as other guests whose leashes or collars they held started woofing and acting eager to join the fun.

My own pup started to wriggle in earnest,

but I held on.

"They just got here," Darryl said with a little-boy grin. "They're good buddies and like to wear off excess energy together first thing in the morning."

"Cute," I said. Then, "Could I see you in your office?"

"Sure."

I kept Lexie in my arms, of course. For her protection, in the unlikely — I hoped — event that the boogeyman that threatened her still followed us.

Of course, Darryl didn't know about that yet. "Is something wrong with Lexie?" he asked anxiously as he closed the door behind us.

"Not if I can help it." I filled him in on all that had happened. "Ned Noralles notwithstanding, I must have worried someone. I don't want to take Lexie with me, since that could mean leaving her alone in the car. But if I leave her here —"

"No worries," he assured me, holding out his arms till I shifted Lexie into them. He gave her a big Darryl hug and held on. "You know I'm always around. I'll tell everyone that she gets special attention, but the most special of all will be that she and I will be joined at the hip. Okay with you, girl?"

Lexie wagged her approval.

I headed out to see to Cherise and Carnie and my other charges.

The cats seemed surprisingly happy to see me — or at least to get some human company. They padded immediately into the seascaped hallway from the vicinity of the kitchen.

As if they'd anticipated my arrival, Carnie carried a poor, slain rodent that she dropped proudly on the pumps I'd put on for a day at the law office.

"Love you, too," I told them both, then impulsively did lift the closest — Cherise — and give her a hug.

Damned if she didn't give me a pleased purr. At least until I gingerly, and with a grimace, disposed of the day's dead present.

"With luck, your mom will be home by tonight," I told them, hoping it was so for all our sakes.

I kept my ears open all day for my cell phone to sing. And when it did, I felt a huge sigh of relief each time when it wasn't Darryl telling me that disaster had struck.

And late afternoon, I did hear from Amanda. "I'm finally home," she said in relief. "Did you look in on Cherise and Carnie this morning?"

"I sure did. Did they tell you otherwise? They even brought me a mouse."

"Thanks, Kendra." She sounded exhausted, and I knew she wasn't her usual difficult self — not when she actually sounded appreciative. "I want to tell you what the cops said, what evidence they claim they have against me. We'll get together soon. But when the hell will you figure out who's doing this to me?"

CHAPTER
TWENTY-ONE

To my amazement and irritation, three days passed with no additional information.

At least there also were no miserable contacts with Amanda to elevate my blood pressure — just a few quick phone calls now and then to put off our strategy session.

Which was fine with me.

There were no further threats to my Lexie, whom I ensured was always well watched and as protected as possible. Which was more than fine with me.

A phone call from Jeff, but not to verbally slap me down or seduce me. He merely hired me to come care for Odin while he traveled once more.

"We'll really talk about us when I get back, Kendra," he told me. "I promise."

I could wait.

But I got too busy at the office on Borden's burgeoning cases to do much more about Amanda's arrest — Ned's challenge notwithstanding. I was arguing motions that week for some of Borden Yurick's senior-citizen clients — one claim against a car insurance company and another defending the client against an overzealous overcharging and under-installing swimming pool outfit. Nothing was happening yet regarding the Shermans' claim against the schlocky Santa Barbara resort, but a response to the complaint we'd file would ultimately be due.

I attempted to relax by performing my usual enjoyable pet-sitting rounds, visiting pups and pussycats all over the east Valley. Each time I saw Stromboli, I looked outside for Meph but didn't see the little wire-haired guy. I did hear from Baird, though, nearly every day.

"I can't thank you enough, Kendra," was his general conversation. "Meph is just the greatest dog. And Maribelle . . . did you know what a whiz she is at hairstyling? She's given me a whole new look. I'll show you someday. She's sure I'd be a great new owner for Meph but doesn't want to give him up now. She told me how depressed she was before, and that she'd unintentionally wound up ignoring Meph, but no more. I'm seeing enough of both of them, though, that I feel like I have a whole new family. I owe you a drink. Dinner. Both. Whatever you want."

I felt certain, with that kind of enthusiasm in Baird's tone, that Maribelle was most likely messing up his hair each night and restyling every morning.

Although, if so, they trysted with some kind of discretion, since I never ran into Baird while strolling with Stromboli.

Judge "Roamin' Hands" may have met his match — both human and canine. Hey, maybe I could increase my pet-sitting and attorney-related ADR into a matchmaking service involving pets, too!

Sure thing.

In any event, I was relieved that Rachel's latest trip to film her new movie role was postponed by a few weeks. Which should work out well, now that I'd scheduled a lunch with Tracy Owens of the Pet-Sitters Club of SoCal for Thursday to discuss snake-sitting. It was important enough to fit in among Borden's cases. I intended to get advice from Tracy about obtaining assistance without ceding clients to other sitters. I hadn't yet phoned my other best contact from that enjoyable evening — Cavalier owner Wanda Villareal. Between both of them, I hoped to gain a lot of good guidance.

Later that day, there would be another attempt at settling the Mae Sward Pom-spaying situation: a conference including attorney Gina Udovich and her seemingly caring client, veterinarian Tom Venson. Althea had searched her many sources and had found no other complaints filed against the guy.

Meantime, I took on another pet-sitting client. Well, not exactly a new one. I was back to watching one of my longest-term pup charges, a pit bull named Alexander.

I was busy, yes, and loving every second of it. But at the same time, I was irritated that I'd eked out no time to excavate in Amanda's quagmire.

Thursday soon slapped me in the face, and I stole off to the area around Beverly Center where I was meeting Tracy for lunch in a trendy yet not too expensive restaurant. The moderate-weight pet-sitter with the chubby face was puggle-less, just as I hadn't brought my sweet Cavalier along. Waiting for me near the entrance, Tracy was clad in a nice blouse over a sparkle-designed shell, loose slacks, and athletic shoes. I felt a little overdressed in my lawyerly purple pantsuit.

"Hi, Kendra. Good to see you." She gave instructions to the hostess that she wanted a seat near a window so she could observe the parking lot. "I've got Phoebe in my car today along with one of my clients. We're off to a dog park after lunch."

"I know how that goes," I said.

"How do you handle your law career along with pet-sitting?" she asked as we took our seats.

"I juggle a lot," I replied with a wry smile.

Her close-set light brown eyes seemed to sparkle with admiration as I described a typical day: a conversation, when possible, with my sometime-assistant, Rachel; then off to Darryl's; early and protracted pet-sitting rounds; then a full day at the office — usually sans a lunch break — followed by more pet-sitting; back to Darryl's for Lexie; then slipping into exhausted vegging out by the TV at home.

No need to tell her that, as a murder magnet, I also slipped in inquiries and investigations when I could.

"Then you don't do daily exercise romps for owners who stay in town?"

Since the smiling female server, clad in the place's black-shirted uniform, suddenly hovered above us, I held my answer until we'd placed our orders — mine a Cobb salad and Tracy's a tostada.

"Not anymore," I eventually answered Tracy. "Not myself, at least. My assistant takes care of midday stuff. Only, her services are a lot less predictable right now." Tracy nodded her sympathy as I told about Rachel's intent to become a film star. "That's one reason I thought that Pet-Sitters of So-Cal could be so helpful. I'd love to have a set of someones to back me up so I don't have to drop good clients when Rachel's not available."

"A bunch of us work in the Valley," Tracy said. "You should absolutely stay in contact with Wanda Villareal. She's the one who had her Cavalier King Charles spaniel at the meeting."

"I know. I've wanted to get together with her but I've been too busy. I'll absolutely give her a call."

"Do that."

"Er . . . one thing, though. If sitters in your organization are asked by other members to help as backup in a crunch, do many try to keep the clients they've assisted with?"

"Only the awful ones," Tracy snarled indignantly.

"But I overheard someone say something at the meeting —"

"About a former member whose butt we'd just kicked out of the club," Tracy said. "We have our standards."

"Great." Relief rushed through me. Not that I'd begrudge a dissatisfied client's finding someone more suitable to care for a beloved pet — as long as that someone wasn't backbiting me.

"Anyway, be sure to come to our next meeting," Tracy said. "I'll bring up our anti-client-stealing policy. We'll also have someone talking about animal first aid. And we'd adore having you speak someday on combining careers, or legal aspects of pet-sitting. And . . . well, a vice president who'd intended to stay on next year just found out her husband's being transferred out of town. I'd love to say you've agreed to replace her."

I felt myself blanch. "I know you asked, but I didn't expect to be considered for something so soon. I doubt I'd have time to do justice to a club office."

Tracy's grin widened her already pudgy cheeks, revealing her perfectly straight, white teeth. "Someone as busy as you can slip in a dozen new responsibilities without a second thought."

"Well . . . Send me an e-mail about what I'd have to do, and I'll think about it." And take the time to come up with a suitable excuse to say no.

We soon segued into the real reason she'd wanted to get together. At her request, I told her my experiences sitting for Pythagoras, the ball python. "He wasn't a whole lot of trouble," I said, "although there were times he was so sedentary I was concerned he'd died." I explained his habitat with multiple temperatures to suit the cold-blooded reptile's moods, plus feeding him defrosted mice. "His owner said that live ones weren't a great idea since they could attack him."

"Right," Tracy said, starting to look as green as her salad.

"It's not as bad as it sounds," I assured her. "Obviously you'll have to get instructions from the king snake's owner, though, since things could be quite different from a python."

"Yeah, like maybe I'll need to feed it live mice so it can have a good fight first."

I laughed, and so did she. I said, "There's a lot more contact with rodents in our business than I ever anticipated." I told her about Cherise and Carnie and their pride at their presents — whether warnings to their perceived enemies or gifts for their human friends I couldn't yet tell.

Which started something percolating back at the edges of my brain. Not that I extracted it quite then.

Our lunch was soon over. I exited with Tracy after we'd paid and got to say hi to

Phoebe the puggle as well as her companion for the day, a black, fuzzy mixed breed twice her size.

"This was fun," Tracy said.

"I agree." We vowed to do it again soon.

"I'll send you that e-mail right away about the vice presidency. We're fairly informal and could hold a vote at the next meeting to get you in."

"I'll definitely think about it," I said, holding my sigh inside.

I had to scurry the Beamer back over the hill toward the Valley fairly fast to get to the settlement meeting for Mae Sward.

But scurrying over boulevards like Beverly Glen wasn't always as fast as one intended. Still, I made reasonable time, hopped on the Ventura Freeway west, and was soon in Tarzana, outside the bland, short building housing Dr. Thomas Venson's veterinary clinic.

Mae was already pacing up and down the sidewalk, appearing thunderous. "You're late," my largely built client berated me. She looked ready to do battle in a bright red tunic over dark slacks, her feet slipped into surprisingly high heels.

"By" — I looked at the serviceable round-faced watch on my wrist — "five minutes.

They'll still be there." I nodded toward the building.

"I almost wasn't," she fumed, and somehow I forbore from rolling my eyes. "Do you know what that horrible vet wants? I can't imagine he'll say anything that'll make me change my mind about suing him."

"A lawsuit is intended to seek payment for damages you've suffered," I reminded her as we headed toward the front entrance. "If he's offering to pay you something, we should listen."

"Nothing will be enough," was her parting shot as we stepped into the vet's den. I didn't bother asking if she'd considered a compromise to suggest, as I'd requested. I'd no doubt what her answer would be.

We sat in the waiting room for a minute before we were ushered into the same examination room where we'd met before. The metal table in its middle seemed newly polished, as did the gleaming linoleum floor.

"Have a seat," I told Mae, gesturing toward a vinyl chair.

She complied, her ample form hanging a bit on either side. I took a seat, too.

Soon, Gina Udovich and her client, Dr. Tom Venson, slipped into the room. "Hello, Kendra," Gina said. Her designer black dress, simple but elegant and definitely not formal enough for a soiree, suggested that this had been a court day for her. Or maybe she merely wanted to impress me. I was glad for my nicely styled purple suit.

"Hi, Gina. Dr. Venson."

The vet was clad, of course, in his usual white lab jacket. Which, of course, set off the blackness of his hair. He appeared un-harried, and unfazed by this meeting in the middle of his busy pet-healing day. His brown eyes held mine as he shook my hand hello.

Damn, but there was something appealing about this guy despite his position on the opposite side of my litigation table!

Once again, he took his spot near the door as the rest of us, all women, sat in the room's three chairs.

"Why are we here?" demanded Mae. "What are you offering?"

Gina's plain but well-made-up face ap-peared shocked. This wasn't how settlement conferences were played.

But heck, I hardly ever stood on ceremony. Even so, I said mildly, "Your client asked for this meeting, Gina. You have the floor."

"I'll turn it right over to Tom." She glanced toward her standing client.

"I have an idea that might get us past this disagreement, Ms. Sward." His eyes were on Mae. "You're unhappy because I spayed Sugar."

"I most certainly —" Mae began, but I held my hand up in a shushing gesture.

To my great amazement, she actually shushed.

"My opinion was that it was medically necessary, and —"

My hand went up again as Mae's mouth opened. Again she sat back, although the expression on her red, round face suggested she choked on her words.

"And I know you don't agree. In any event, I understand that you want to have more Pomeranian puppies." This time he seemed to want a response, so I allowed Mae to give one.

"I certainly do," she said.

"Now, I know you have other bitches at home who can have puppies, but that doesn't fix things about Sugar. And I have concerns about how often they should be bred. So what I'm suggesting is that I provide you with a new Pom puppy from champion stock. One of my colleagues is the vet for one of this country's best-known kennels, and he's put me in touch with its breeders. I will buy you one of their pups that you select, at my expense . . . but there are conditions attached."

Mae's features had started to soften as he spoke, but they steeled up again. "What conditions?"

"That you will stay in close contact with those breeders and follow their guidance about when and how often to breed, and at what age to stop breeding, not only for this new puppy but also your other dogs."

What a wonderful solution, I thought. I started to smile at Tom Venson before I caught myself.

It had to be Mae's decision.

"Would you like to think about it?" I asked her.

"I already have." She was smiling, which was a good sign. "As long as I can choose the puppy, and the breeder is one of the top ones like you said, we have a deal."

I caught Gina's eye. She appeared as if she'd suddenly been struck in the stomach. I suspected she'd wanted to continue collecting lucrative fees from her veterinary client for many more months.

"We'll still have to document the settlement," I said softly to appease her.

"Of course," she said.

Things seemed almost amenable as we said our farewells that afternoon. I hung back just a little to speak with Dr. Venson. Sure, he was still represented by counsel, but Gina hadn't gone far, and I wasn't about to say anything to negatively impact the case.

"That was a fantastic idea," I told him. "I ought to hire you."

"As your vet?"

"Well, maybe that, too. But I meant mostly as an advisor for my 'animal dispute resolution.' You obviously excel at ideas!"

His warm grin set me to tingling everywhere. Damn, but I really liked this guy.

"Are you interested in having dinner with me sometime, after we get this all resolved?" he asked.

Was I ever! I stayed suitably sedate, though, as I told him yes.

I wondered, on my way east again toward Darryl's, how I'd ultimately square the possibility of having both Dr. Thomas Venson and Jeff in my life.

CHAPTER
TWENTY-TWO

I nearly whistled while I worked out with my pet charges that afternoon. Alexander the pit bull was in rare form, ready to romp right along with me around his owner's hilly residential street. Stromboli was a shade less energetic, and I stared at his next door neighbor's house as we strolled first up his street, then down again. No sign of Maribelle Openheim and her sweet, wiry Meph. No sign either of my one-time least favorite, yet most often seen, jurist Judge Baird Roehmann.

I had a couple of other dogs to see to, plus a once-a-day visit to a cat's home to take care of, and then I was done — thanks to Rachel's availability for now. But after my lunch with Tracy, I felt a whole lot surer I'd be able to find help to handle my thriving part-time pet-sitting business notwithstanding my current helper's cinema career.

Lexie looked a bit bedraggled when I

picked her up at Darryl's — literally, since I lifted her into my arms. "Is something wrong?" I immediately demanded, concerned that someone had attempted to hurt her. I glanced around the almost empty main room of the doggy resort. Nearly everyone was gone for the evening, including most of Darryl's staff.

"Just a typical doggy fight over a tug-of-war toy." Darryl slipped a finger behind one of his spectacle lenses to rub one of his brown, puppylike eyes. "Lexie was on one end, Lester the basset hound was on the other, and a bad-tempered beagle decided he wanted a turn."

"But we know Lester bit someone while under duress," I said, Lexie wriggling as if she wanted down. "A person, of course, but does he chomp other dogs that torment him?"

"Not that I've seen," Darryl said. "And tug-of-war is different from an intrusion onto his turf. Lexie and he were playing just fine till the beagle broke in — and he's now canine-non-grata around here until his owner can show he's passed an obedience course."

"But you're okay?" I asked my Cavalier. She'd given up attempting to leave my arms and instead licked my chin.

"Her feelings were hurt when the beagle and Lester started playing without her," Darryl said, "and she tried to show them whose game it was. Lots of growls and nips, but more barks than bites."

"I hope so."

"You okay?" he asked.

"Sure," I said.

"Anything new on the Amanda front?"

"No time again today. But I've promised myself to do better tomorrow."

"Yeah, you can't let that Detective Noralles win."

"You bet."

"Sure do. And I'm always here with my big mouth at the ready if you want to brainstorm about slimy suspects."

With Lexie squished between us, I stood on tiptoe and kissed Darryl briefly on that same big mouth — a sisterly buss, of course, for my very best friend.

"I appreciate it," I said.

On my way home, my mind circulated around all the stuff I'd do the next day to reinsert myself into Amanda's investigation — until it was interrupted by my cell phone's sound. I didn't recognize the number on caller ID but should have, since it had shown up there, uninvited, before.

"Hi, Kendra? This is Corina Carey.

How've you been?"

"Fine until now," I said grumpily. Since I had slowed down for a red light, it would have been somewhat safe to give the reporter the finger, invisible to her. Only, other drivers around might see it and assume I aimed it at them — not a good idea, given L.A.'s penchant for road-rage retaliations.

"I just wanted to check in with you," she said, ignoring my cantankerous comment. "Have you solved that latest murder you were involved in — that Leon Lucero thing?"

"Number one, I'm not involved." I lied. "Number two, I've no intention of telling you anything, and —"

"Number three," she broke in, "you obviously haven't figured out who the killer is yet, or your friend Amanda wouldn't have been arrested. Right?"

I could have engaged in an explanation of exactly why Amanda wasn't my friend, but I was certain Corina knew it already. She just wanted to pull my chain. And I wanted to unhook that very same figurative chain from around me. Maybe its symbolic metal links were polarized — making me a murder magnet.

"You're right, more or less, Corina," I said

with an exhausted sigh.

"But you'll call me when you have something exciting to tell the world, right?"

"Sure thing." I fibbed again to get her off my phone, since the light had turned green again. *Hold your breath till you turn blue, why don't you?* "Bye, Corina," I said and flipped the phone shut — once again without figuratively flipping anything in the reporter's direction.

Later on, I prepared for bed at Jeff's, with Lexie and Odin already curled into one mass of merged fur on the floor.

I'd stopped at home on the way here to grab a change of clothes and to check in with Rachel, who remained rarin' to go with our pet-sitting plans for another week or so. I told her about my lunch with Tracy Owens, and she was enthused about my potential involvement and officer status with the SoCal Pet-sitters.

To my surprise, so was I.

And now, I'd showered and changed into a loose T-shirt for bed.

Then my cell phone rang . . . as I'd expected it to.

"Hi, Kendra," Jeff said. "How are the dogs and you? And not necessarily in that order?"

"Odin's adorable, as usual. Lexie's fine,

and I'm glad to have her here, behind your even spiffier security system than mine — although there've been no further threats, thank heavens."

"And you? Are you naked? I am."

It was a conversation we'd held lots of times before, and even now, when I was ambivalent about the hunk on the other end, it still sent shivers of excitement through my sexiest body parts.

"Not tonight," I said with a hint of admonishment in my tone. Didn't he know I was still upset with him?

Didn't *I* know?

"I'm wearing a really unsexy shirt," I finished.

"Well, I'll still imagine that you've taken it off for me. Good night, Kendra." And then he was gone.

But not, darn it all, forgotten.

I'd intended to devote a lot of the next day to Amanda's plight, but she beat me to it.

She called early and begged me to come to her home.

Call me stupid, or a sadist, or all the ugliest epithets imaginable, but I did it. I mean, I could have continued to work behind the scenes without subjecting myself to Amanda's irritating presence anymore. But I'd promised her my assistance, and she might even have something helpful to say.

Sure, she could actually have killed Leon, as alleged. In her position, with that god-awful, scary creep stalking her, I might have done the same thing. But the weapon, a screwdriver, still seemed all wrong. I'd have assumed someone as snide and attention-seeking as Amanda would have used something with more pizzazz to go after her tormenter — her car, for example, as she'd done with Jeff. Besides, she'd been advised that, if she'd done it, pleading self-defense could get her off the hook.

"I really didn't do it, Kendra," she whined later that morning, as I sat on her Scandinavian sofa facing her.

Lord, how I'd learned to loathe that whine.

She looked pale and fragile and, yes, pitiable after all, wearing a loose white T-shirt with the expression, *Cardiologists have hearts,* on it, tight blue jeans, and blond and bedraggled hair.

"If I say in court that I did, but it was self-defense," she continued, "it would be perjury if I lied, right?"

"Sure, but if it's the truth, then you've a good shot at getting off scot-free." Even wearing the skirt and periwinkle rough-knit sweater I'd chosen for today, I felt gauche compared with the pretty-even-while-suffering princess across from me on the couch.

"It's not the truth," she protested, pouting. And then, more angrily, "I want whoever did it to be caught. To pay for taking a human life, even one as miserable as Leon's."

Well, heck. When she spouted dramatic and politically correct statements like that, I considered sending her along with Rachel to whoever was producing her movie. Maybe Amanda should be writing trite but theatrical scripts.

As if cued by their mistress's outburst, Cherise and Carnie strolled in. And, yes, one carried a mouse corpse, which she deposited proudly upon my pump-clad right foot. Yech! Carefully, I pulled my toes out from under and said sweetly to the kitties, "Hi, ladies. Thanks for the present. Are you mad at me today?"

And just like that, the thought that had been hovering somewhere beneath consciousness within my percolating brain poked through.

I felt my grin uplifting every inch of my face. "Amanda, I have an idea."

She aimed suspicious silver eyes in my

direction. "You want me to confess to everything without claiming self-defense. Right? I know you'll stop at nothing to get rid of me."

"Oh, but I want to do it in a way to rub your nose in how wonderful I am — and how you've promised on paper to stay away from Jeff."

She brightened considerably, straightening from her partial slouch on the sofa. "You *do* have an idea," she said with more animation than I'd seen from her all day. "What is it?"

I told her.

I felt even better about the idea when I discovered a screwdriver on the pavement beside my Beamer outside Amanda's. Could have been an innocent misplacement of someone's prized tool, but I doubted it.

There was a long, ugly scratch in my driver's door.

Well, better a threat against me than Lexie, 'cause I could take care of myself. I hoped.

I was at Amanda's for the first time after her arrest, which had likely provided some measure of relief. The killer didn't want me messing with the status quo. "You wish," I whispered. I enclosed the screwdriver in a plastic bag from my trunk, careful to avoid handling it much and marring any fingerprints. Not that I anticipated any. The killer would be too careful for that.

I left the bag at the North Hollywood Police Station for Ned Noralles to check out, just in case.

As I drove away, I thought even harder about my trap.

CHAPTER
TWENTY-THREE

"I really appreciate you coming here, Corina," Amanda said the next afternoon as she sat back in the same sofa spot where we'd last connived together, here in her home. Today she wore a lime turtleneck over deep green corduroy slacks, and looked absolutely Amanda perfect with her blond hair styled flawlessly and her makeup immaculate.

Reporter Corina Carey had dressed to rival her, though. Completely business casual, she looked like the zingy reporter she was, in a violet striped shirt tucked into cuffed slacks, with a purple blazer finishing off the outfit. Her dark hair was short and wispily combed to look casually unstyled. Good thing her mouth was so wide, with all the nasty words it spouted so often. Her teeth were bright, white, and undoubtedly bleached often. Her cunning brown eyes tilted slightly, suggesting some possible

Asian ancestry somewhere.

Okay, I'd seen the woman a lot on TV, spoken with her on the phone much more than I'd wanted to, but this was our first encounter in person.

If I sound a little catty — as I am wont to do sometimes — well, so much the better, considering my scheme.

"No problem at all, Amanda," Corina was saying, rummaging in a big black leather shoulder bag — undoubtedly for a recording device. She sat on one of the simply styled Scandinavian loveseats across the coffee table from us.

"It's just that, with all that's happened, I'm feeling a lot more comfortable staying at home with my cats whenever possible." Amanda shot a subtle glance at me before turning her attention back on the reporter. Good thing Corina was still fussing with her bag, or she might have seen that little look.

"I understand. And I'm really pleased that you decided to tell me your side of the whole, sad story. Kendra, I want to thank you for setting this up."

"You're welcome." I carefully corralled any reaction to the utter truth in the words she'd inadvertently used. But this was absolutely a contrived setup, and I hoped

I'd stay proud of it.

Speaking of cats . . .

Well, I also hoped Cherise and Carnie would come in on cue . . . soon.

Meantime, I sat and simply listened as Corina interviewed Amanda about how the awful Leon Lucero had entered her life.

"You mean he painted some of those gorgeous seascapes I passed in your hallway?" Corina asked.

"Well, yes," Amanda said. "Although their composition wasn't entirely original, but the actual paintings were." She went on to tell about how "her" Dr. Henry Grant enticed cardiac patients with artistic ability to use his medical services. And that had included Leon — who'd *way* overstayed his welcome.

Soon, they segued into the whole bit about how Leon had manufactured cardiac symptoms to book appointments at the office . . . to see Amanda. And how, after she'd only gone out with him once or twice, he'd insisted on more. And showed up wherever she was — a lot.

Until, eventually, she'd had to get her ex-husband to help her stop the stalking. That had involved hiring a lawyer and getting a temporary restraining order.

Which was when Carnie and Cherise

strutted in, in all their feline glory.

Sans mouse this time, thankfully.

"Hi, ladies." I reached down to stroke them, pleased to hear them purr.

I allowed Amanda to perform the introductions to Corina.

"They're beautiful," the reporter said. "I love cats. These are so unusual. They look like little leopards."

"They're Bengal cats." Amanda explained the breed.

"They're really smart, too," I added when she was done. "They're watch cats, kinda like watchdogs. Not that they bark, but they're not only opinionated, they warn people they dislike to leave."

"How?" Corina turned her incisive reporter's gaze to me.

"Well, a lot of cats give presents of their prey to people they like. Not Cherise and Carnie. In fact, when I first pet-sat for them, that's what I thought, until Amanda set me straight. The dead mice they deposited at my feet were a warning that I didn't belong here, that I should leave or suffer the consequences — whatever they might be. Fortunately, the kitties never let me know. Now they're used to me, so I'm not on the receiving end of their threatening presents."

"Sounds far-fetched," Corina said, a

skeptical scowl creasing her high forehead.

"I'm sure Leon Lucero would have though so, too," I replied, snuggling my smug smile deep inside my head instead of pasting it on my face. This was going as well as I'd wished.

"What do you mean?" Corina said.

"A dead mouse was found with his body," Amanda explained. "Right there in my bedroom, where he was killed."

"That's right," Corina said pensively. "I remember reading about that."

Amanda shuddered. "Poor Cherise and Carnie must have seen the whole thing. They undoubtedly brought the dead mouse and deposited it by Leon when he broke in. And I've no doubt they'd now do the same thing with whoever else was here that night."

"You mean Leon's killer?" Corina asked.

"Exactly," Amanda replied.

"You think she bought it?" Amanda asked awhile later, after Corina had packed up recorder, pad, and pen, and taken off.

"Doesn't matter," I said, "as long as she includes the possibility in her story."

Which she did, in the Sunday paper the next day, as well as in her on-air report, including shots of Amanda and her home that she'd taken with a video camera — also

extracted from her big black totebag —
before she left.

Amanda called me first thing on my cell phone, but I was already communing with pet clients despite the early hour. "She did it!"

"I saw — I checked the paper before I left Jeff's this morning." Lexie remained there with Odin, behind Jeff's superior security system . . . just in case.

"Left? You're already out, at this ungodly hour on a Sunday morning?"

"The trials and travails of a professional pet-sitter," I reminded her.

"Sounds as bad as being a lawyer. Anyway, tell me when I should start making calls."

"Right away," I said. "Although . . . you're right about the ungodly hour, at least to some folks. Give 'em time to wake up and go to church, if that's what they do. If all goes well, someone may need to make his peace with his — or her — maker before we're finished."

"Amen," Amanda responded, right on cue.

"Amanda said you told her to grant an interview to Corina Carey," Mitch Severin said when he called me a half hour later. I was in the middle of walking Alexander the playful pit bull along his hilly home stretch.

That usually took two hands if he spotted another pup. Not that he'd attack — I didn't think — other than to nuzzle the other canine till it rolled over.

And, of course, I saw someone else out for a morning constitutional — fortunately before Alexander did.

"I'll have to call you back, Mitch," I said, and was treated to a substantial roar from the other end before it was cut off as my phone's flap fell.

Oh, well. I couldn't have my concentration severed by two kinds of distractions, so I chose the one that was my current responsibility: Alexander and his amazing antics.

I encouraged my charge to concede to the bullying standard schnauzer he'd charged, then herded him back down the steep hill to his home. Only once I'd returned to the still-scratched Beamer did I call Mitch back.

"Sorry," I said. "Duty called." I realized right away what normal bodily functions he might assume I was talking about. In a way that was true, since that was the main reason besides exercise for walking dogs. *Their* functions, though, not mine. "Anyway, what's on your mind?"

"That damned news article in today's *Times,*" he exploded. "Plus, that reporter is also talking about the case against Amanda on her TV shows. Amanda said you talked her into giving an interview. That could hurt her case, Kendra."

"Actually," I said, sitting back in my car seat, "the point was to help it." But I'd discussed with Amanda the importance of not letting anyone in on our little plan, not even Mitch. For one thing, it could be totally unsuccessful, so why embarrass ourselves . . . mainly me?

For another, part depended on absolute secrecy. Sure, Mitch was on our side, but what if he let something drop to someone whose knowledge ruined the entire endeavor?

"Well, I don't like it," Mitch said. "For one thing, putting things out on the news sounds like a last-ditch effort to save her, an attempt to sway public opinion since the evidence is against her."

"The evidence *is* against her," I reminded Mitch, as if I needed to. "Leon was a threat to her and he was found dead in her house." Recalling my pet-sitting requirements, I reached into the glove compartment and pulled out the small notebook I used to keep track of my client visits. Sticking the cell phone under my chin, I noted my latest Alexander call.

"But not beyond a reasonable doubt. Plus

we can always use self-defense. And — well, hell, even though you're an attorney, I can't discuss my strategy with you. You're not helping with her legal defense, only as an outside investigator, and you're not even licensed for that."

"We've already discussed that, Mitch. I'm working within the aegis of Jeff Hubbard's license, as his investigator trainee."

Maybe. Jeff and I had decided several murders ago I could claim that when I dug in to find out who really did it. And right now, Jeff had to back me up, especially if he aspired to resolving this situation with our relationship still possible.

"And Amanda and I have an agreement that requires my assistance," I continued. I returned the notebook to the glove compartment. "Besides . . . have you discussed this with your cocounsel, Quentin Rush? With all the media attention he engenders in all his high-profile cases, I'll bet he'd applaud your ingenuity" — why not let the guy get the credit, as long as we got the results we wanted? — "for swaying public opinion to Amanda's side. Or, if you'd rather, you could let *me* talk to him about it. You've said you'd set up a lunch for all of us to talk." Hey, why not follow up on an opportunity to meet someone as savvy and celebrated as Quentin? "Anyway, I need to get going now. And Corina Carey's news is already out there. Maybe someone knows something about who was sneaking around her property the day Leon died but hasn't come forward yet. Sympathy might make that silent witness speak up."

"I'll talk to Quentin, but I still don't like it," Mitch grumped.

What, no lunch? No meeting? What a bummer. But I wasn't entirely discouraged. I'd insist on an intro some other time.

"I've told Amanda," he continued, "and I'll tell you, too, that before you pull anything else like this, you check with me. No more contacting the media. No contacting anyone else involved with the case, not even discussions with possible witnesses, unless you clear it with me. I didn't insist on it before, but this changes things. I'll make myself available as much as I can so you can get my okay, but no more talking to anyone, *anyone,*" he stressed, "without my prior, preferably written, approval. Are we in agreement on this, Kendra?"

"Sure, Mitch," I said, even as I stared straight at my lie-hiding, crossed fingers resting on my steering wheel.

CHAPTER
TWENTY-FOUR

First things first. I couldn't count on cats Cherise and Carnie to come through with what we needed, at least not every time, so I had to be prepared.

Which called for a call to my longtime pet-sitting client Milt Abadim, owner of Pythagorus, the ball python.

I used the phone in my apartment when my morning pet-sitting cycle was complete. It seemed odd and lonesome being there sans Lexie, but she remained at Jeff's with Odin, so *she* wouldn't feel odd and lonesome that day — with a nice, protective Akita by her side.

"Hi, Milt," I said into my portable phone receiver as I sat on my living room's comfy beige sofa.

"Kendra! How wonderful to hear from you. Must be ESP. I was going to call to ask you to watch Py starting later this week."

"Really? It'll be great to see him." Whoever

imagined I'd ever say that about a snake? Not I, until a bunch of months ago when the python had won my heart . . . and helped me solve some murders. "You, too, of course."

Milt laughed. "I need to go out of town again because of — who else? — my mom. She's reconciled with her new husband, so they're renewing their vows."

"Really?" I didn't even try to remove the surprise from my voice.

"Yeah, I know. It's only been a few months since they took their vows in the first place, and they came so close to getting it annulled right away . . . Anyhow, what's your schedule like? Can you come over this afternoon?"

Could I ever! That worked perfectly into my plans. "How's two o'clock?" I asked.

"See you then."

Milt's modest one-story home in North Hollywood served as a showplace for Py's habitat, which sat squarely in the middle of his small living room. Or at least it had when I'd been there last to care for the colorful snake.

"Great to see you, Milt," I said when he answered the door, then gave the sweet and pudgy man a big hug. He still looked somewhat nerdy with his handlebar mustache emphasizing the lack of hair on his head. Today he wore a white T-shirt with red letters that read, *Get squeezed by a python today.* Appropriate.

I couldn't help recalling how, the first time I'd seen him, I'd immediately noticed the brilliant-colored tie around his neck . . . that just happened to be his pet python.

"Likewise, Kendra. Come on in. Py's waiting for you. I told him you'd be visiting again, and he seemed really excited to hear it."

Most pet owners were guilty of anthropomorphism, so why should Milt be any different? Of course, pets like dogs and cats had traits that could, without straining one's imagination, appear somewhat human. But a snake?

Sure enough, the large glass enclosure still took up most of Milt's living room. It consisted of two connected chambers kept at different temperatures, so the cold-blooded Py could choose his environment.

And there he was, curled in the corner of one of his rooms. Darned if he didn't lift his head when I looked in and said, "Hi, Py!" Maybe there *was* something to what Milt said about Py's recognizing and reacting to my name.

Or maybe I'd been pet-sitting too long.

No, never. I loved animal tending. So . . .

"You remember the routine, don't you?" Milt asked. He waved me to an easy chair facing Py's home and took a seat on a metal folding chair.

"Sure do. That's one of the reasons I called you in the first place. I need to know where you get Py's food."

I'd never asked before where the abundant carcasses of deceased mice that Milt kept in the freezer for Py came from. But now the information was absolutely necessary.

"I order it online." His smile pudged out his poochy cheeks even further and revealed his slightly uneven teeth.

"Oh."

My dismay must have been obvious in my tone, since he said, "Why do you ask? Kendra, are you getting a pet python?" He sounded absolutely ecstatic.

"Well, no. But I do need some frozen mice . . . for a friend." I didn't want to explain, even to someone as easygoing as Milt, exactly why I needed a supply of deceased rodents. "Could I buy some from you? Do you have enough in stock to do that?"

"Sure. I'll order more in any event, and they'll arrive when I get back in a week — although you can keep an eye out for them in case they come early. The shippers sometimes act fast since they don't want to be responsible for what happens if the dry ice evaporates. Meantime, help yourself. Okay?"

"Okay." I was delighted when Milt picked Py up and draped him around my neck.

I went over my new paperwork with Milt, had him fill in the info I needed and sign the agreement, and put a set of his keys in the appropriate corner of my large purse.

And left, a little while later, with a plastic bag filled with regular, refrigerator-generated ice . . . and frozen mice carcasses.

I went straight to Amanda's, where she reported to me right away, really excited. She'd gotten a better response to her invitations than I'd ever imagined.

"The first person will be here in about an hour," she said with a cat-that-ate-the-canary grin, shooing me quickly into her kitchen, and from there into her living room.

I only hoped her cats were as accommodating. Or at least didn't mess things up.

She wore a snug red ski sweater over leg-hugging stretch slacks. As if Los Angeles was cold enough for such a form-enhancing outfit.

Me? Well, it was Sunday afternoon, after all. I'd chosen a bright blue turtleneck over relatively new jeans — becoming enough for this less-than-gorgeous attorney's off time.

Dr. Henry Grant arrived ten minutes early. I went with Amanda to open the door — starting the routine we'd ultimately decided on. No sense in her facing her guests first thing all by herself. The one we were seeking might do something nasty, if there was even a hint of suspicion about what we were up to. Maybe even if there wasn't.

The cardiologist with the Welsh terrier whiskers seemed somewhat startled to see me standing in the doorway, but he regained his aplomb instantly. "Are you all right, Amanda?" he asked at once.

"More or less," she responded. "Come in, Henry."

"Well, if you're okay, why did you want to talk to me here on a Sunday, rather than at the office tomorrow? Oh, by the way, hello, Ms. Ballantyne."

"Kendra," I corrected. "Hello to you, too."

We led the doctor down the seascape-laden hallway and into the living room.

"Nice house," he said, his short neck still craning as he took a seat. "I like the way you've showcased our patients' artwork."

"To answer your question, Henry," Amanda said, "I wanted to see you here because I'm a little nervous. I mean, the police arrested me for murdering Leon right here in my house, but, of course, I know I didn't do it." Her tone went up in a wail, which I could understand, even if she was acting. Maybe she wasn't. "What if they don't find out who really killed him? What'll happen to me?" Her eyes misted up as if on cue, and the doctor, sitting at the far side of the Scandinavian sofa from her, also took his cue and slid closer.

"I'm sure you'll be fine." He took her hands in his. "Leon was my patient, and I'll be glad to testify in court how he was stalking you. How miserable he was around our office. How he even threatened some of the staff."

Interesting. And kind of what I'd suspected. "Were any of them" — *You included,* I kept to myself — "upset enough with him to harm him, and let someone else take the blame?"

Henry turned his affronted gaze toward me. "I certainly don't think so," he huffed.

Not that I'd take that as gospel, even about him.

Now came the tricky part. We'd talked ad nauseum about how best to stage this — especially considering how unpredictable two of our players were.

I gave a teensy nod that I hoped was nearly imperceptible to Amanda, who acknowledged it by looking away.

"Henry, I have some coffee and scones in the kitchen." She all but fluttered her eyelashes.

I'd already assumed that "her" doctor and boss was sweet on her . . . like a certain P.I. I knew, who always denied it. Not that I was worried, at this moment, about him. "Will you please help me bring them in?" she finished.

"Of course."

Their departure allowed me to do as we'd intended. Quickly, I slipped to my knees, opened a wooden door in the side of the coffee table, and extracted a plastic bag we'd stuck there just before Henry's anticipated arrival. Keeping my eye on the door and my ear on the conversation from the kitchen, I reached into the bag, happy that my hand first encountered a paper towel. I used it to remove the bag's other, more important contents, which I positioned on the floor near the couch.

Then I started talking despite remaining alone in the living room. "Well, hello, girls. Good to see you. What's that?" Followed by a shout, "Amanda!"

She entered seconds afterward, carrying a

couple of mugs of coffee. Henry was behind her, and he also held coffee plus a plate of scones.

"It was the strangest thing," I said to Amanda. "Cherise and Carnie came in, put that there, then ran right out again."

I half anticipated those intelligent cats to come in and set the story straight — that everything I said was a lie. But, fortunately, they didn't.

So the dead mouse, defrosted from the stash I'd obtained from Milt, lay on the hardwood floor near the side of the sofa where Dr. Henry Grant had previously been parked.

"Do you suppose," I said, "that they were trying to tell us something?"

"Like what?" Henry's face constricted into a clueless expression.

"Didn't you see the articles in the paper about how my cats leave presents as threats for people they don't like — like Leon?" Amanda said. "Right there, where he died? I've been wondering whether they'd give a mouse present to his killer, if they happened to see him."

"Who has time to read the paper?" Henry asked, stepping gingerly over the mouse and placing his mug and plates down on the coffee table. "Ugh. A dead mouse. Well, I don't buy into cats giving meaningful presents." Amazingly, the man appeared to have an appetite, since he lifted one of the pastries to his lips. "Great scones, Amanda."

Cherise and Carnie took that moment to make their grand entrance. "Hi, girls," Amanda crooned. "Did you leave Dr. Grant a present? Is he the one you saw kill big, bad Leon?"

"Now, wait a minute," Henry said, standing so suddenly that his scone dripped crumbs near the mouse corpse. "I didn't even know where you lived before today."

"It's in your office records," I reminded him, also standing. Amanda's eyes switched anxiously from Henry's face to mine, then back again. Only Cherise and Carnie seemed calm, continuing to pad closer to us.

"I've never been here before. And I most certainly did not kill Leon Lucero here or anywhere else. Is that why you wanted me to come here — to accuse me? Amanda, I'm disappointed in you."

At least he didn't fire her. And, not that I'm an expert, but his tone suggested sincerity. This wasn't evidence I'd ever consider bringing to court — assuming I ever started arguing criminal cases — but I felt somewhat convinced that Dr. Henry Grant could be crossed off our suspect list.

And so, I was quite ready to see him leave when he departed indignantly a few minutes later.

Visitors number two and three that day: former Leon stalking victim Betty Faust and her dear defensive friend, Coprik.

Since they lived an hour away in Channel Islands Harbor, it made sense to see if they could come on a Sunday, rather than during the week. Whatever Amanda had said to them had made them curious enough to show up on her doorstep late that afternoon.

Unlike Dr. Grant, these two arrived late. Due to the distance? Traffic? Unwillingness to step into a possible trap? Well, they were unlikely to know about the latter, but I supposed they could have considered it.

In any event, it was nearly five o'clock when the doorbell chimed. Meantime, I'd had to pass tedious hours in Amanda's irritating presence. I felt ready to accuse them, then absent myself, fast.

But this scheme of mine required a whole lot more subtlety.

Once again, I was with Amanda when she answered the door. Due to the time of year, it was nearly dark outside.

There stood short, squat Betty, with her

beautiful black hair swept up on top of her head in a strange, unkempt kind of do. Beside her was the hulk called Coprik, clad, like last time, in a partially unbuttoned workshirt over jeans that were a whole lot more scruffy than mine.

"Please come in," Amanda said. "You remember Kendra Ballantyne, don't you?"

"I remember her, not you," grumped Coprik while obeying her and entering. He glanced with only minor interest toward all the artwork along her hallway.

Betty, on the other hand, stared at it in awe. "These are beautiful," she said in a hushed voice. "Who painted them?"

"Several different people," Amanda said. "Mostly patients at the doctors' office where I work. And these two" — she pointed toward a couple across from each other — "were Leon's work."

"Really? That awful man had a talent like this? Why didn't he concentrate on that instead of scaring people?" As Betty shook her head, some of her hair escaped its mooring and formed curlicues at the sides of her broad, arresting face.

" 'Who knows what evil lurks in the hearts of men?' " Coprik quoted from *The Shadow* comic strip, radio, and TV shows. "Or what good stuff, either." He seemed pleased enough to plop his substantial bod down on Amanda's couch that, with its thin wooden legs, appeared too rickety to accommodate him. Fortunately, it didn't fly into pieces, even when Betty sat down by his side.

Amanda's excuse for inviting these two over was that she said she was considering forming a support group for stalking victims, especially Leon's. "Assuming I'm not convicted of killing him," she said with a sorrowful sigh.

"Did you?" Coprik asked. Which didn't mean *he* didn't do it, or Betty, either. He could have been affecting ingenuousness.

"I admit I wanted him out of my life, in whatever manner it happened," Amanda affirmed. "And I also admit it looks suspicious that he died here, in my home. But I didn't do it."

"Not even in self-defense?" Betty inquired. "You'd surely not get sent to prison then."

"Maybe that's why he was killed here," Coprik added. "Someone who hated him as much as you did but didn't want to fry for it — or make you fry, either. Whoever it was could have assumed you'd get off."

"Convoluted," I chimed in, "but possible. Since you came up with the idea, do you want to confess, just to us?"

Betty laughed, albeit a little nervously. "It

wasn't either of us," she said sans any hesitation.

"I'll bet Coprik knows his way around a screwdriver," I persisted. "Since he owns a boat sales and repair shop. Leon was slain with a screwdriver," I added, most likely unnecessarily.

"If he'd still been nosing around Betty, I might have done it," Coprik belted out belligerently. "But I'd already scared him off."

Maybe. Still — "Weren't there times you preferred not telling Coprik when Leon was around, Betty? I mean, to keep him from murdering the bastard — like what happened — so Coprik wouldn't get into trouble? Maybe, to protect Coprik, you'd even kill Leon yourself."

Betty shrugged a thick shoulder beneath the bright green sweatshirt she was wearing. "If I'd been the violent type, I'd have gone after that horrible man even before Coprik came into my life." She leaned sideways onto that very man's substantial bulk, and he put an arm protectively about her.

My assumption so far was in favor of their innocence, but we still had our scenario to play out.

Amanda obviously thought it was time, too, since she rose. "I've got some refreshments in the kitchen. How about you two helping me carry them? We can talk about my support group idea on the way."

I did my part while they were gone, depositing cat prey on the floor near where they'd sat.

This time, to my amazement, Carnie and Cherise padded into the living room as I finished positioning their purported prey. They sat down on the floor and simply stared — a good thing, since I'd had concerns they'd start playing with the dead mouse.

"Amanda!" I called, keeping an eye on them.

In mere moments, the threesome returned to the room. I started into my spiel about what Corina Carey had reported on TV and in the papers as being true . . . as Coprik came closer, and the kitties did, too, waving their long leopardlike tails in the air.

"Ugh," Coprik snorted. "Cats." He looked away quickly until his eyes lit on another spot on the floor . . . then screamed in a shrill, unmasculine tone, "A mouse!"

And passed out.

Betty rushed to his side, hanging on as best she could to lower him to the floor without him suffering damage, or foisting any on Amanda's furniture.

"Coprik!" she cried. "Honey, it's okay."

She looked up at Amanda. "Do you have any smelling salts?"

"I thought that stuff went the way of corsets and feathered hats," our hostess grumped. "Vinegar, maybe?"

"Maybe," Betty replied dubiously.

In a moment, Amanda returned with a rag that reeked through the entire room. With it held beneath his broad nose, Coprik started to stir.

"Poor guy," Betty said sotto voce. "You'd never know it to look at him, but he's afraid of all sorts of things."

"Like?" I encouraged.

"Little animals, for one thing. And you wouldn't believe how sensitive he is when he sees blood."

They left a little later, once Coprik was awake enough to walk out, leaning on Betty's shoulder. Meantime, we'd stashed the mouse and shooed the cats.

"What do you think?" Amanda asked when we were alone.

"I don't think Betty would have killed Leon on her own," I said.

"And Coprik?"

"You'd have found his body on the floor along with Leon's, if he's that sensitive to blood," I said. "I think we'd better scratch these two off our suspect list, too."

Three down, and an infinite number to go.

But we arranged to try our little act again tomorrow.

No screwdriver by the Beamer that night, and no new scratches, either. Maybe that was because I'd backed into Amanda's driveway and ensured my car was under a whole lot of light.

Plus, Ned Noralles had informed me, after the last screwdriver incident, that he was stepping up patrol car pass-bys in Amanda's neighborhood — to catch her in the act, since he was certain she'd left it there to scare me. No prints on the threatening tool, of course. But I felt reasonably certain Amanda was innocent of this act, too. And I was glad for the cruising cops.

I sighed as I locked the Beamer's doors. Assuring myself I'd get the scratch fixed soon, I drove off.

CHAPTER
TWENTY-FIVE

"You're what?" Jeff shouted after he'd called his home that night to check on the dogs and me, and I'd explained how his ex-wife and I had spent the day. "How stupid can you get?"

I hissed at him, "It's under control." I hoped. "By the time you get home, we'll have figured out who really offed Leon."

"Kendra, at least wait till I'm back. I can protect you two if —"

"What a nice thought," I replied, more with irritation than appreciation. I'd just come in from walking Lexie and Odin, keeping my eyes wide open for any intruders on Jeff's street. No extra police patrols here, so I was on full alert, notwithstanding Jeff's asinine suggestion that I was less than intelligent. "We'll be fine. See you when you get back, Jeff."

The next day passed like normal — scooting around pet-sitting, followed by a fine day practicing law, and then yet another battery of fun pup and kitty care.

I dropped in at Jeff's to feed Lexie and Odin and assure myself they were doing well without me. While there, I changed from my dressy attorney-wear into comfy jeans and sweatshirt. Once I'd told the dogs I'd return soon, I aimed my Beamer toward Amanda's for our next anticipated visit.

This time, Amanda's quarry — er, houseguest — was Kennedy McCaffrey, the great-looking cardiac patient who hated Leon for stealing artwork ideas from him.

He looked askance as Amanda led him down the hall where some of his pictures — and Leon's — hung in places of honor.

"That dirty S.O.B.," Kennedy grumbled. He pointed to one of the paintings. "That's a nearly exact replica of one of mine — a scene right off Dana Point, I'm sure of it."

"But it's Leon's?" I asked.

"Yeah, it's Leon's." Kennedy strolled down the hall staring, then said, "You got anything to drink, Amanda?" I doubted he was talking about tea. He headed straight for the kitchen, which told me he'd been here before.

Ah, a good clue that this suspect belonged on our little list. Had he found a way in before, when I was pet-sitting? Left the refrigerator door open after pouring himself a libation?

Returned days later to kill Leon?

But their heading to the kitchen first re-arranged our routine a bit. I scrambled for a reason to head to the living room first. "I need to get my notebook," I dissembled.

Amanda had gotten Kennedy here on the pretext of discussing other possible Leon-slayers. She'd said she wanted his input.

Long story short? We sat in the kitchen for a while and talked stalkers. And Leon. And Corina Carey's articles about Amanda and her cats and the accusations against her. And in the meantime, Kennedy kept look-ing deeply into Amanda's eyes . . . and below.

Which wasn't much of a surprise, since she'd worn a skimpy top that revealed her midriff when she turned certain ways — which she did a lot with him around.

I had the impression the guy would have slain dragons for her.

Had that included Leon?

After a while, I attempted to lead them into the living room — but found I didn't have to. To my surprise, the mouse I'd left on the floor — somewhat reluctantly, since I hadn't seen Amanda's cats and feared

they'd stalk off with our evening's prop —
did in fact appear in the kitchen, in Carnie's mouth. The clever, smaller kitty deposited the prey right at Kennedy's feet.

I wanted to ask Amanda if she'd trained
her felines that afternoon, but kept silent on
that subject. Instead, I suggested, "Gee,
Kennedy, the cats apparently don't like you.
They're warning you . . . just the way we
figure they did with whoever killed Leon.
Did you do it?"

He looked absolutely affronted. "I'd never
have done such a thing . . . here. I would
never have wanted to implicate Amanda."
He turned toward her and smiled moonily.

I didn't bother going into what we'd
discussed with Betty Faust and Coprik
yesterday, about how whoever did it could
have intended that it happen right here,
since Amanda could assert self-defense.

Instead, I said, "Well, I'd better go take
care of my dog — and Jeff's."

Amanda shot a glare at me for even mentioning her ex. Apparently, Kennedy's interest in her could be mutual.

I didn't get to talk to Amanda about
Kennedy's presence on our suspect list until
she called while I was at the office the next
day.

"He didn't do it, Kendra," she insisted.

342

I wasn't so sure.

Even so, I cooperated as she set forth her next list of guests for our interrogation and accusation-by-mouse.

The next of Amanda's invitations to be accepted was by Nellie Zahn, the self-made self-defense guru formerly stalked by Leon who'd used that lemon of a situation to make lemonade of her life. Since I'd admired her, I didn't desire that the muscular yet feminine, self-assured diva act guilty . . . and she didn't. She arrived at seven o'clock on Wednesday evening in — what else? — a workout suit, one in multiple and becoming shades of blue.

Sitting in Amanda's living room, Nellie said in response to one of our canned comments, "I don't need a support group myself to deal with what Leon did to me, but I'd be glad to join to help others. Especially you, Amanda."

Thus, Nellie had driven the distance from Redondo Beach to show support to Amanda whether or not she'd killed Leon — and she indicated applause, in the event Amanda had been the slayer.

And when the dead mouse magically appeared at the foot of where she'd been sitting?

"What great cats you have!" she gushed. "I'd love to meet them. Maybe next time, they won't leave me their sweet little threat against people they think are trespassers."

So, as I'd hoped, Nellie slid way low on my little list.

Next to visit Amanda's was Bentley Barnett, who popped in on Friday night. Amanda had objected strenuously to putting her own brother through our test, but I'd prevailed.

"You want him cleared once and for all, don't you?" I demanded.

She did, and so she got him to drive all the way up from San Diego.

Of course our little scenario didn't play well with someone who knew the cats as well as if they were his nieces. Bentley saw through our scheme nearly immediately.

"You're trying to get the killer to confess by having the cats menace him into it?"

"Or her," I said in agreement.

"Cool," he said. "Let me know if it works. Oh, and by the way, as much as I hated that little shit Leon, even if the cats bring me a hundred mice, it still wasn't me who killed him."

No more takers for a few more days. Meantime, Rachel gave me the actual date she'd be exiting town for a while: next Tuesday.

I called Tracy Owens, but she said she was swamped. "Try Wanda Villareal. I talked to her the other day and she said she had a couple of clients who'd be coming home this weekend."

I called, and she sounded delighted to take on my overflow.

Plus we made a dinner date, one where we planned to meet at a restaurant with outdoor dining. That way, we could bring our respective Cavaliers.

"Basil will be so excited," she said.

"Lexie, too."

Saturday afternoon finally rolled around, and I again rolled my Beamer to Amanda's — once more leaving Lexie behind Jeff's protective security system with her buddy Odin.

Today's guest was to be Piper Erlinger, another of Leon's former stalking victims. I had previously tried to interview Piper at the time I'd visited Betty Faust and Nellie Zahn, but she'd not responded to my calls.

But Amanda had reached her, and apparently had convinced her to come, one former stalkee to another.

As had become our habit, we both answered the door, at eleven o'clock Saturday a.m., when Piper was scheduled to arrive.

Only . . . the person who stood there wasn't a female stalking victim, but a guy, maybe five-ten, mid-forties, moderate length dark hair with a hint of gray starting to appear, and a reserved smile revealing stained teeth in the midst of the merest shadow of a beard. He wore a trendy leather bomber jacket.

Another Coprik, who'd come instead of his lady friend to warn us away? And hadn't he heard of tooth whitening?

"Hello, Piper," Amanda said. "Come in."

"But —" I began.

"Piper Erlinger, meet Kendra Ballantyne. She's a friend who's helping me get over this whole Leon thing."

Which was our canned spiel, designed for anyone who hadn't been privy to Corina Carey's news reports and wouldn't therefore necessarily know my background and association with Amanda's situation. Only —

"But —" I said again, then blurted, "I thought you were one of Leon's stalking victims."

"Come on in, Piper," Amanda said. "We'll sit down and talk about this. Okay?"

"Sure."

I brought up the rear as Amanda led him down the hallway of seascape dreams.

Slowly. Piper picked on each individual picture, assessing and critiquing it.

"Nice job," he said of one. "Obviously not Leon's. The tone it sets is mellow and lovely, definitely Southern California coastal." The next? "Childish brushstrokes, and uneven, so they weren't intended that way. Not horrible overall, but not something I'd want hanging in my hallway. Leon's?"

Amanda acknowledged it was. "I kind of liked its naïveté," she admitted. "But if I were to sell it, I know it wouldn't bring as much as, say, one of Kennedy McCaffrey's." She pointed out the next one down, and Piper nodded.

"Very good work. I'd like to meet this artist."

"I'll introduce you," Amanda said. And then she ensconced us in the living room, once again at the opposite side of the stark sofa from her guest.

Who, finally, looked at me. "I gather, Kendra, that you didn't know that Leon was a stalker of opportunity, not sex. And, before you ask, I'm not gay. The guy just latched on to people he liked, for whatever reason, and most were female. With me, he liked the fact that I teach art at the community college he attended, and he became my constant companion, whether I wanted him there or not."

"Interesting," I asserted. His sex elevated Piper a few notches on my list. The screwdriver stab wounds had been deep, indicating someone strong. Like workout queen Nellie Zahn, sure, but I'd already decided I didn't like her as a suspect. But this guy, artist or not, seemed to have muscles. He'd doffed his bomber jacket and lain it beside him on the back of the sofa. Beneath was a white knit shirt, short sleeves, that didn't quite cover his biceps.

Only, he'd done such a minute assessment of the hallway paintings that I had to surmise he hadn't seen them before. Sure, Leon could have left Amanda's refrigerator door open as a warning, which meant the killer didn't need to have entered this home before doing the dastardly deed. But someone like this art critic would surely have noticed the seascapes on his stroll down the hall to stab Leon, right?

"I've done some research into stalkers," I said, "and most of the time they seem to be domestic situations, not near-strangers. Where the stalker does it in a serial manner, they usually choose a type of victim to prey on. I guess Leon was unique."

"I'll say," Piper agreed. "He kept insisting that he'd leave me alone only when he was sure I couldn't teach him any more. Then he latched on to one of my female students, which initially was a relief to me, but when I changed my mind and began to help her, he started stalking both of us."

Amanda was clearly listening, one of her miniature snide smiles marring her face. She'd obviously known Piper's sex, having spoken with him, but she hadn't let me in on this little tidbit. She let me rattle on, during our premeeting meeting, about how we'd handle our little drama with this latest suspect. And how we'd deal with several possible scenarios, depending upon how *she* reacted.

Even though we were working so closely together, Amanda still enjoyed humiliating me whenever she could get her digs in. I'd be so glad when all this was over and her claws were no longer embedded beneath my skin.

"Was this going on recently?" I asked. "Was he stalking you and your student at the same time he was harassing Amanda?"

"No. He stopped suddenly. I didn't dare ask why — but he did show up for one of my classes a few months ago. I tried to be kind, yet not too friendly. I nearly lost it when he stayed after class, since I thought he would start it all over again. But instead he just thanked me for teaching him so much and said he had some new friends, art lovers, that he was seeing a lot of. I breathed a sigh of relief for myself and my student, even though I figured he was after new game."

"Me," Amanda said angrily.

"That's what I gather," Piper acknowledged.

Which was when Cherise and Carnie entered the room. This wasn't exactly the optimum time, but Amanda quickly requested Piper's assistance in the kitchen after he'd greeted the cats.

Fortunately, the felines remained in the room with me, so I was able to stage our usual scenario.

Piper clearly wasn't pleased to be allegedly threatened by some nasty cats, but he didn't act especially suspicious, or nervous, either.

I reserved him mentally where I'd stuck him earlier, near the top of my list.

But as I left Amanda's after Piper's departure, I realized that my head spun with the new information that this male victim had imparted.

And I thought I finally knew what had actually happened to Leon.

Now, all I had to do was prove it.

CHAPTER
TWENTY-SIX

Okay, despite the way the rya rug added some pizzazz, I was getting decidedly bored with the stark Nordic décor in Amanda's living room. And the slight scent of the herbal tea she seemed to favor over coffee. And the even slighter smell of kitty-in-the-house, although the litter box was in a corner of the kitchen.

But I soon wouldn't have to hang out there to catch a killer.

I knew who it was . . . or at least, I believed I did.

Now I had to do something about it, to save Amanda's neck. And maybe my relationship with Jeff.

At this moment, on this Tuesday evening, I had a case to lay out and some convincing to do.

"We could have come to your office to explain it all, Mitch," I mentioned to Amanda's attorney, who sat at the opposite end of the red-upholstered sofa from his fidgety client. I'd not given Mitch many of the particulars but said that we'd been inviting suspects over and using a super-special technique to give them a grilling, and that we now had a really great theory now about whodunit.

"Sure, but you said you set your trap here," Mitch said. He'd casualed down before coming here from his law digs, still wearing shiny slacks that I assumed came from a suit but no tie, and the neck of his white cotton shirt was undone. His hair, or lack thereof, appeared casual, too, but I suspected he had a heck of a time attempting to tame the few frizzies that were left. "I wanted a demonstration of what you did, and how it showed what really happened to Leon. If there's enough evidence, I'll try to get the charges against Amanda dropped right away."

I sat in my now-usual chair, a loveseat across from Amanda's coffee table. Since this meeting was scheduled for evening, I'd had a chance to change clothes into something more casual, too, and chose a loose, flaw-hiding large white sweater over comfy, snug and warm workout leggings. "I wouldn't count on any evidence that could be admitted in court," I cautioned him.

"Oh, but I'd love for those charges to be dropped," Amanda asserted, stretching out long legs encased in gray sweatpants over fluffy blue-striped socks. On top, her matching gray jacket hung open to reveal a similarly coordinated blue-striped knit shirt to complete her ensemble. Not exactly what I'd have suggested she don to discuss case resolution with her lawyer, but this was, after all, her home.

"That's what we're working on," I agreed. "And even if nothing's actually admissible, it could be enough to at least interest the cops to do more digging into our suspect's background and whereabouts on the night Leon was killed."

"Then you haven't turned anything over to the authorities yet?" Mitch asked. Although he'd mastered the art of near-expressionlessness, his sparse brows lifted enough to suggest he was incensed.

"Not yet," I admitted.

"But this time I was the one to call that awful Detective Noralles," Amanda added. "I told him we needed to see him. Which was when I called you."

"You should have spoken to me first." All aplomb evaporated, Mitch Severin stood and seemed to steam right before our eyes. "If you want me to continue to represent you, Amanda, you need to confer with me at all stages. I've told you that before, and you've ignored it. You shouldn't have started doing whatever you're doing to trap the killer without my input. You most certainly knew better, Kendra. Are you trying to get yourself in another ethics mess?"

"Not hardly," I said stonily. I'd never directly discussed said ethics mess with Mitch, but knew the entire community of California attorneys could have read about it in various legal publications when it was going on — since all punishments of ethical problems were made public by the State Bar.

"You know that I have to consider my client's best interests above all," Mitch intoned. "If you've done something stupid, I have to ensure it doesn't reflect badly on her."

A scathing retort rushed to my lips, but I swallowed it before I *really* did something stupid. "I understand," I said in a sham of meekness.

"Tell me about this trap you laid." He resumed his seat almost haughtily, as if deigning to remain as a result of my abject — but absolutely imaginary — plea.

"It was pretty amazing," Amanda gushed. "It involved Cherise and Carnie. Sort of."

Mitch's face contorted even more, and he leaned forward in his chair. "You tried to trap a killer with house cats?"

"They're Bengal cats," Amanda corrected. "They look just like little leopards."

"Does that matter?" Mitch shook his head as if he couldn't believe the idiocy piled onto stupidity around this place. Which again nearly got me going.

"Not really," I said. "What does matter is what Corina Carey put in her *Times* article and on her TV show."

"Yes, I saw them," he said. "As you know." And sounded damned irritated about it, even now.

"Here's what we did," I said. Standing to show the room's significant locations, I gave the rundown of how we'd gotten suspects off guard by convincing many to come here and consider joining a stalker victim support group. And then get menaced by a mouse allegedly left by a resident cat.

"Fascinating," Mitch finally said, his tone sounding a whole lot less than enthralled. "And did someone actually get so rattled by a defrosted mouse that he — or she — confessed?"

"Well, no," I admitted, sitting once more. "But I started to put two and two together after I found out that one of Leon's stalking

355

victims had a name I assumed was female, but he happened to be extremely male. That got me to thinking about how Leon must have been an indiscriminate stalker. And in that instance, he'd given up on the guy victim in favor of another girl — until that very same guy stepped in and tried to protect the new female target. Leon resumed stalking the guy again in retaliation."

Something seemed to twitch in the corner of Mitch's stony eyes. Was he stifling a bored yawn at all my tale-telling and speculation? But what he said was, "And this is significant because . . . ?"

"I'm going to state a hypothetical." I turned to Amanda and said, "It's an attorney thing. We like to talk in suppositions and scenarios and pretend they're our imagination — only it's no huge surprise that we really believe in them." Then I said to Mitch, "Suppose one of Leon's lady victims went after a temporary restraining order."

"You've told me they all did." Mitch's tone sounded even more indifferent.

"Right. Well, let's take just one of them. Leon was probably damned tired of having courts tell him whom he could and couldn't stalk. And who got the courts to order him around? His victim's attorney. That made him mad. Mad enough to retaliate by stalking the lady's legal counsel."

Mitch didn't sport a California tan, but what little color there was in his cheeks seemed to drain immediately away, like water and whatever down a toilet. "Why didn't he stalk all the lawyers involved?"

"Ask him," I suggested flippantly and futilely, considering Leon's demise. "Maybe he only just thought of it. Maybe he had a particular hatred for a single victim's lawyer. That's something we'll never know. But in this hypothetical scenario, the lawyer freaked. Didn't try to obtain his own TRO, since he knew Leon ignored them. He'd done his homework and knew lots about all the other TROs and the stalking victims who'd obtained them — not that he let his client or anyone else in on what he'd learned. He'd found out that reasoning with the maybe-insane Leon didn't do anyone much good. So, this lawyer did something Leon would understand — he threatened the stalker right back."

I paused to pray for a reaction, but Mitch had his courtroom stone-face chiseled back on. "Go on," he said apathetically.

"Well, first this lawyer told Leon he'd do something bad to him if he ever got near either the lawyer or his client again. Leon thumbed his nose by sneaking past the security system at his client's home — who, by the way, was out of town and had a sitter minding her pet cats — and making sure everyone knew he'd been there. Left the refrigerator door open. And that only made the attorney angrier."

Again I paused. This time, Mitch stood and rolled his shoulders as if he'd stayed in one spot too long. "I ought to go," he said. "I really thought you'd found the killer, Kendra, but you just have some wild speculation that not only wouldn't be admissible in court, but I doubt any cop would do more than kick you out on your butt. I'm disappointed."

"The screwdriver murder weapon is a clue, Mitch." I inserted myself in front of him so he couldn't take a step without walking into me. "Run of the mill, the kind you can buy at any hardware store, but this particular one happened to be yours, didn't it? Which suggests premeditation. Not a good thing in a murder case — at least not for the defense — as any lawyer knows. There was a second one, too, left as a warning for me. A while back, you considered asking contractor Kennedy McCaffrey for help on a do-it-yourself project you'd started, which suggests you own basic tools, even if you couldn't finish your project."

Mitch wasn't a whole lot taller than me, but he drew himself up to his full height and stared down his haughty nose. "You know, Kendra, you're becoming too much of a nuisance. Even though you'll never be able to prove this drivel, I can't allow you to ruin my reputation by even suggesting it. I, for one, don't want to be reproved and ridiculed the way you were, in every legal publication in the state."

He pulled a small pistol from his pants pocket.

Amanda gasped, right on cue.

Actually, so did I, though I'd anticipated this Leon-driven lunatic would pull *something . . .*

"I can come up with hypothetical scenarios, too," he snarled, aiming his weapon at my left breast, of which I was particularly fond, not that I disliked the matching right one. "Like, what would happen if a lady lawyer with an axe to grind against her lover's ex-wife cooks up an elaborate scheme to get rid of the ex by murdering someone and setting it up to appear that the ex did it? She dreams up an even more twisted scenario, pretending to look for the real killer. Only the ex figures out what's really going on and accuses the crazy lawyer of setting her up. The ex schedules a meeting with the cops, and the lady lawyer freaks. She's been accused of murder before, but convinced the cops of her innocence then. But she's not so sure of herself this time. She leaves threats against herself and her dog. Then she gets herself an unregistered gun from an untraceable source, and shoots the ex — right in the same home where she committed the murder in the first place. But in an agony of remorse, she turns the same gun on herself."

I saw from the corner of my eye that Amanda had used the opportunity of Mitch's squirrelly speech to start sidling toward the door.

Unfortunately, Mitch saw it, too, and turned only slightly sideways — enough to get the gun to menace us both equally.

I wished I knew how skilled he was with it. Could he shoot us both before the one not hit at first could leap onto him? Would Amanda even try, if I happened to be unlucky number one?

"Get back here, Amanda," he ordered, "or I'll start making my little story come true."

Fortunately, that was enough of a diversion for me to put into motion the next step in my own scenario of this evening. I yanked a gun of my own from the shoulder holster hidden beneath my loose sweater. Well, not my own, exactly. It, and the bulletproof vest beneath, were on loan from the LAPD. Detective Ned Noralles, to be precise.

Noralles suddenly stood cockily in the doorway to Amanda's living room. So did his cohorts, Detective Howard Wherlon and the new guy, Detective Elliot Tidus. All three had their weapons drawn and aimed right at attorney Mitch Severin.

That was my cue to step gingerly back.

"You okay, Kendra?" Ned inquired politely as he and the others started their familiar procedure to take Mitch into custody. Heck, we now had a course of conduct started for this, too, along with initial murder interrogations.

"Kendra? Are you all right?"

Was there an echo in this room? No, this time it was Jeff Hubbard's inquiry as he rushed in and took me tightly into his arms. I hugged back, letting my beleaguered body begin to shake, now that the worst was over.

Only then did I hazard a glance at Amanda, who watched us with an expression on her beautiful face that suggested she had spent the evening sucking lemons, not solving a murder.

I enjoyed rubbing it in, of course. But there was more to be done just then. Like,

"Did you get it all recorded, Ned?" I asked.

"*I* sure did," said Detective Tidus, once again in a garish plaid sports jacket. He obviously enjoyed being noticed. And being given credit for whatever he did while on duty.

When Ned Noralles scowled at him, I basked in this young guy's ballsiness even more.

Then there were Ned's cranky over-his-shoulder congratulations for having solved yet another of his cases. I'd met his challenge. I'd won!

I loved it.

I listened for the ever-popular refrain, "You have the right to remain silent," and the rest of the inevitable Miranda warnings as Mitch was cuffed and taken into custody. He'd seemed at first like a reasonable attorney who championed his clients rights — but he'd put his own interests ahead of Amanda's.

Too bad. He was another of those attorneys the media would love to shriek about, who gave the profession its less-than-stellar reputation.

Which reminded me. I owed Corina Carey.

I'd call her in awhile.

But before any of us could exit this very

eventful living room, two small forms stalked in.

I hadn't seen Cherise and Carnie earlier this evening, and I kind of assumed that, for our purposes tonight, Amanda hadn't wanted them around and had locked them in somewhere.

Instead, I had to assume they'd been out casing the neighborhood.

The one in front — Cherise — had a dead mouse in her mouth. There was a gash in its side and its tail hung limp.

The felines came to a full stop right in front of the person both cats undoubtedly recognized as an intruder on at least one fateful night — the one where Leon had been eliminated.

Damned if they didn't deposit the ruptured rodent right at Mitch Severin's soon-to-be-permanently-shackled feet.

CHAPTER
TWENTY-SEVEN

"Isn't that a real, live ethics violation?" Darryl inquired early the next morning.

I'd brought Lexie into the Doggy Indulgence Day Resort before my pet-sitting rounds. After all, she needed a little more indulgence than I'd been able to engage in lately. I'd been busy a lot — including well into late last night, while I graciously allowed Detective Elliot Tidus to interview me about how I'd happened upon Mitch Severin as a more likely suspect in Leon Lucero's murder than Amanda Hubbard.

Now, we were in Darryl's untidy office, standing side by side at the picture window looking out over his doggy domain. Canines cavorted everywhere, egged on by the energetic staff.

Lexie, playing tug of war with a good-natured gold miniature poodle, was obviously having a blast.

"I'd say Mitch was guilty of an ethics

violation about as big as they come," I replied to Darryl, whose lanky length stood right beside me. Of course, he was in one of his normal green knit shirts with the Doggy Indulgence logo on the pocket. "Talk about having a conflict of interests. It'd be a whole lot better for him if his client were tried, convicted, and fried for the little felony that he'd actually committed. But that's just my opinion, of course. Never mind all the evidence the cops are collecting, now that they have a different suspect to go after. Like everyone else, Mitch is innocent until found guilty."

Darryl peered down at me over his wire-rims. "Never mind his confession to you and all his guilty behavior, like threatening to kill you and frame your client for another murder?"

"A good criminal attorney will bring up how this so-called confession was his attempt to get his own client to 'fess up, all the better for him to figure how to defend her ass. Or he was trying to get me to admit *my* guilt. Or it was coerced without Mitch's being read his Miranda rights, so every bit of evidence collected afterward is tainted and inadmissible, the 'fruit of the poisonous tree,' so to speak. Don't you just love legalese?"

"Obviously you do," Darryl said dryly.

"How can you tell?"

"Was Mitch the one who threatened Lexie and you?"

"He sure was. He got a bit nervous that his prime patsy, Amanda, had another attorney championing her defense. He was hoping to scare me so far out of the picture that I'd sail into one of Amanda's seascapes, taking my poor, threatened pup along, too. He'd apparently been following me closely enough to scare Lexie in the supermarket parking lot and leave me a note. I'll never forgive him for that. He also kept an eye on Amanda's house and scratched my car with a screwdriver as an added warning."

"Do you suppose he'll hire Quentin Rush to represent him now?" Darryl inquired. I, of course, had informed him about Mitch's claimed cocounsel.

"Assuming he even knows him," I said with a sigh. "Quentin's involvement could have been as fictional as Mitch's ethics, a ploy to ensure he could control Amanda's case. Too bad, though. I was hoping to meet the guy."

"In any event, you done good, kid," Darryl said and gave me a great big bear hug.

I left there soon afterward, leaving Lexie still playing gleefully, and went first to Alexander the pit bull's place, where I cavorted with him before walking and feeding him.

Sitting in my Beamer on Alexander's hilly street, I called Rachel's cell phone to see if she, too, was on schedule. "Sure am, Kendra," she said. "But next week . . ."

"Don't worry," I said. "I'm getting together over the weekend with Wanda Villareal and her Cavalier, Basil. We're going to exchange Cavalier stories and make plans for her to provide backup sitting when you're unavailable."

"Good deal," Rachel said. But I heard something sorrowful in her tone.

"Something wrong?" I asked.

"I'd just hate for you to get so much help that you won't need me anymore when I *am* available."

"I'll always have need of your services," I told her. "Someone as enthusiastic as you should be great at selling pet-sitting services for Critter TLC, not just performing them."

"Hey. Yeah! That's great!"

And even though I'd been irritated before when I'd heard of Rachel's bet, I heard myself pridefully putting in, "By the way, that bet you made on me, that I'd solve the murder that Amanda was accused of —"

"You did it?" she shouted in my ear. "I knew it! Wait till I tell the others."

"They'll hear about it soon enough, I'll bet."

But she'd already hung up.

So, I'd set her back to her rounds with a story to lay on her friends later. Or now, while on the road, I suspected, since she had her cell phone in her hand.

Speaking of learning what happened, my next call was to return several messages that Corina Carey had left. "You promised me an exclusive," she said.

"Sure thing," I agreed. For speed's sake, she interviewed me over the phone.

"And I'll want to do an in-depth interview in person," she persisted. "Later today."

"Tomorrow," I said. "I promise."

Grumbling, she agreed.

Then I headed to Stromboli's — not to tend him, but to see his owner, Dana Moroni, who'd gotten back into town late last night. She wanted her keys back, and I wanted her check, a pretty fair exchange.

"Thanks so much, Kendra." She looked as if she'd already been up romping with her dog this morning, since her short brunette hair was mussed and she still wore a sweatshirt despite having the heat on in her house. Stromboli, panting slightly, came over and insisted that I pet him before I slid out the door.

Then I saw Maribelle Openheim walking down the street with the little wiry fellow Meph on a leash.

"Hi, Kendra," she called.

I joined her in front of her house, where I stooped to stroke a tail-wagging Meph. "How are Baird and you getting along?"

"We're not," Maribelle said, a surprising smile crinkling the wrinkles at the edges of her eyes. Despite the slight breeze, her highlighted hair wasn't a smidgen wind-blown, nor did it appear over-sprayed and stiff. Well, hey, a hairdresser surely had her secrets.

I hoped one of them wasn't the reason for her unexpected comment.

"Dare I ask what happened?" I dared to ask.

Her expression turned wry. "That Judge Baird Roehmann's really a charmer, isn't he? I was taken with him. Started thinking future and everything . . . until I called him one evening when I needed an answer about some plans we were making for over the weekend. There was a whole lot of background noise. He'd said he was going to a bar function, and I assumed it was the lawyers' kind of bar, not a saloon. Even so . . . well, when he came back to my place later to say good night, there was alcohol on his breath. Not that it particularly mattered, except I wound up walking Meph alone while Baird spent some time in the bathroom. I happened to glance into his car when we passed it, and that's when I saw — well, you'll never guess."

I *could* guess, but I didn't tell her that. "What was it?"

"A piece of ladies' underwear. Well, not really a *lady's,* in the real sense of the word. It was *so* skimpy — well, probably someone a whole lot younger and skinnier than me wore it," she finished.

So, Judge Roamin' Hands had done it again.

"Naturally, I told him to leave. Would you believe he had the nerve to ask if I'd let him adopt Meph?" Her eyes rolled but, amazingly, she was smiling again.

"I'd believe you told him no," I replied.

"Exactly. But you know what? I really thank you for introducing us, Kendra. Before, I was still terribly depressed over losing my husband. Now, though, I'm convinced I have a life left — without someone as fickle as Baird. And I still have Meph to share it with." She knelt and hugged her sweet terrier, who wriggled in happy response.

So, I was smiling when I finally headed

for my law office. There, I decided it was time for some self-back patting, so I asked Mignon to assemble everyone present, including Borden, associates, partners, and paralegals into our bar-boardroom.

"Hey, gang," I told the assembled throng, most of whom were of the senior lawyer variety. "This murder magnet has done it again!"

"You solved another case?" Borden graced me with one of his adorable lopsided smiles. Today his aloha shirt was mostly pale pink.

"Sure did." I proceeded to regale those assembled with my story of cat collusion and suspect entrapment.

"Let's hear it for Kendra!" said Geraldine Glass when I'd finished. The senior attorney, her reading glasses once more holding back her curly brown hair, raised her large white coffee mug.

"Yay, Kendra," echoed the others, and I was toasted by the whole fine and friendly firm.

Which made me feel warm and fuzzy all over.

Borden took me aside. "The Shermans' case? Turns out that there've been dozens of similar suits filed against the resort. The actions are likely to be consolidated."

"Figures," I said. "Maybe we can get it

settled ultimately with some real ADR. Would your clients like to wind up owning part of a resort?"

"Maybe." But Borden sounded doubtful.

"I'd still like to handle it, if I can. I'd also love to see Charley training some of his studio animals, too."

"I'll keep that in mind."

The day's smiling wasn't over, either. That afternoon, I'd a post-settlement conference to attend, at the Tarzana veterinary clinic of Dr. Thomas Venson.

This time, one of the blue lab-jacket clad assistants showed Mae Sward and me into a different room from the one where we'd held our earlier meetings with the vet and his lawyer, Gina Udovich. They awaited us in a compact but absolutely clean office not unlike an organized lawyer's — except that the books on the shelves along one wall weren't legal tomes but animal anatomy volumes.

As always during any meeting, I turned my cell phone off. I didn't even want to know someone was calling by feeling a subtle vibration.

Today, Mae wore a satin tunic over dark slacks. The tunic's orange shade clashed garishly with the not-really redness of her dyed hair. But unlike with my other meetings with this client, a huge smile lit her round face.

Like me, Gina had selected a pantsuit that day — hers a chic designer style in a muted plaid wool, and mine a sky-blue knit. She, too, smiled, enough to display her bright, white teeth.

Well, what wasn't there to smile about? Tom Venson stood behind his immaculate desk — and there was an absolutely adorable Pomeranian puppy in his arms. The white of his lab jacket set off the pup's rusty shade, and he was smiling, too.

Had I thought him kind of plain for a guy? Maybe, but right then he looked really good.

Maybe that was because the pup he held symbolized yet another success for my ADR.

"Here are the settlement papers," Gina said, stooping to pick up her leather briefcase from the floor. She extracted a folder, then passed me its contents.

They consisted of four copies of the same agreement form that she and I had negotiated since our last meeting in this office. I scanned them to ensure myself nothing had changed from our last e-mailed and approved version.

"These appear in order," I said. "Mae, we've talked before about their contents. You understand what you're giving up by signing. This settles all your claims against Dr. Venson for his care of Sugar, including that she is now spayed."

"I get it," Mae said. "And I've already scheduled some visits to this puppy's breeder so we can talk over when and how often to let her and my other Pomeranians have babies."

"Good," I said. "You can go ahead and sign and date the agreements."

She did, and so did Tom Venson — after handing me the little Pom pup to hold. It was incredibly sweet as it attempted to clamber inside my suit jacket, and I laughed.

Then, once all the agreements were signed, I handed the pup over to my client.

"Her registered name is something long and Polish," Mae said as she held the puppy close. "Did you know that most of what was once known as Pomerania is now part of Poland? That's where this breed originated, of course, although it was part of Germany then, and its ancestors came from Iceland . . . Well, anyhow, I've decided to call her Kendra."

Talk about a wide grin — What else could I do?

Mae soon left with Kendra the Pomeranian in her hands and her original of the settlement agreement in her purse. Gina accompanied her out.

That left me with Dr. Tom Venson.

"This was such a lovely way to settle the dispute," I told him once again. "Thanks so much for coming up with the idea."

"I had an ulterior motive," he said, still smiling. I enjoyed the sincerity in his brown eyes as they settled on mine, and how his dark hair formed that widow's peak in the middle of his high forehead.

"What motive was that?" I asked.

"Well, now that Mae's claims against me are settled, I figured it wouldn't be forbidden to ask her lawyer to join me for dinner tonight."

I put a finger on my chin and raised my gaze to his ceiling. "Let's see." I pulled my hand back down to my side and smiled at him again. "Nope," I said. "I still can't reveal anything that's attorney-client privileged, and Mae's still my client. But I don't think it'd be forbidden for a lawyer to dine with the opposition after a case is resolved."

"Good," he said. "Then let's go."

I couldn't right then, of course. I had pet-sitting to perform. But I promised I'd be back in a couple of hours.

He promised to still be there.

I picked up Lexie from Darryl's and took her home to our garage apartment.

Then I aimed my Beamer back to Tarzana.

There was a perfectly charming Italian restaurant only a block down the street from Tom's veterinary clinic, so we walked there. The ambiance was awesome — lit largely by candles in empty Chianti bottles, the place was small and intimate and had strolling musicians singing Italian songs. Well, I assumed "O Sole Mio," which they repeated often, was genuinely Italian. And the fact that they weren't always on key? Well, who cared? Tom and I enjoyed a delightful dinner of antipasto, seafood linguini and chicken Marsala — all of which we shared. Along with long, lascivious glances.

Hey, the guy was really one hot dude, once he wasn't my client's opposition.

We discussed why he'd become a vet, and why I'd become a lawyer. Why we hated L.A. Why we loved L.A.

Afterward, when we walked back to his office, he held my hand.

When we reached my Beamer in his clinic's parking lot, Tom pulled me so close that I could feel his elevated heartbeat hard against my chest. Hey, if I noticed things like heartbeats, maybe I could become a veterinary assistant in my off time.

As if I had any off time.

"If I promise not to neuter any of your other clients' dogs without their permission," Tom whispered, "can we do this again sometime. Like, soon. This weekend, maybe?"

"Maybe," I said, only the word got lost somewhere in one very sexy kiss that left my insides lavalike and my legs limp.

He promised to call me the next day.

I didn't turn my cell phone back on until I was at home and had walked Lexie. It beeped at me immediately. I checked.

Five phone messages. "They're all from Jeff," I told Lexie, who'd leapt up onto my lap on the living room sofa. "Do you think I should respond?" I asked her. She cocked her head as she listened and pondered.

Sure, she soon said by wagging her tail.

I agreed absolutely.

After all, I owed him my thanks for being there last night.

Plus, I'd mailed to Amanda my exorbitant cat-sitting bill with a reminder that the terms of our other written contract were fulfilled. She was now absolutely out of Jeff's life.

Did I want to be in it?

I hugged Lexie, then touched my lips where they'd previously been locked with Tom's . . .

And smiled at how interesting my social
life had suddenly become.

ABOUT THE AUTHOR

Linda O. Johnston is a lawyer and a writer of mysteries and romantic suspense. She lives in the hills overlooking the San Fernando Valley with her husband, Fred, and two Cavalier King Charles spaniels, Sparquie and Lexie. Her two young adult sons visit often.

You can visit Linda and *her* Lexie at Linda's website: www.LindaOJohnston.com.

We hope you have enjoyed this Large Print book. Other Thorndike, Wheeler, and Chivers Press Large Print books are available at your library or directly from the publishers.

For information about current and upcoming titles, please call or write, without obligation, to:

Publisher
Thorndike Press
295 Kennedy Memorial Drive
Waterville, ME 04901
Tel. (800) 223-1244

or visit our Web site at:

www.gale.com/thorndike
www.gale.com/wheeler

OR

Chivers Large Print
published by BBC Audiobooks Ltd
St James House, The Square
Lower Bristol Road
Bath BA2 3SB
England
Tel. +44(0) 800 136919
email: bbcaudiobooks@bbc.co.uk
www.bbcaudiobooks.co.uk

All our Large Print titles are designed for easy reading, and all our books are made to last.